A Shadowed Charade

THE LOCKWOOD FAMILY

LAURA BEERS

Text copyright © 2025 by Laura Beers
Cover art copyright © 2025 by Laura Beers
Cover art by Blue Water Books

All rights reserved. No part of this publication may be reproduced, stored, copied or transmitted without the prior written permission of the copyright owner. This is a work of fiction. Names, characters, places and incidents either are the product of the author's imagination or are used fictitiously. Any resemblance to actual persons, living or dead, business establishments, events or locales is entirely coincidental.

Chapter One

England, 1813

Lady Melody Lockwood tapped the end of the quill against her lips as she studied the coded message before her. It was one that she had not seen before. It was frustrating and time-consuming work, but she loved nothing more than when she could crack a difficult code.

No one, not even her family, knew about her covert activities. It had to be this way, since she had been recruited as a spy at her boarding school. She didn't want to put them in danger. Although there was little chance of that. She received coded messages from Lord Emberly—under the guise of Josephine. As far as her family was concerned, her friend was the most proficient letter writer.

However, Lord Emberly was not truly her friend. When they crossed paths at social events, their interactions were nothing more than formal pleasantries, the type of exchanges designed to maintain the appearance of civility. He was certainly handsome enough but far too solemn for her taste.

This coded message was different. It hadn't come from

Lord Emberly, as all the others had. Instead, it had arrived by post, sealed with an unfamiliar wax stamp and bearing no return address. The handwriting on the front was neat but unfamiliar. The absence of any clue to the sender's identity only added to the mystery.

A knock came at the door before it was pushed open, revealing her lady's maid. "Good morning, my lady," Lydia greeted.

Melody placed the quill next to the ink pot. "Good morning," she responded.

Lydia walked over to the wardrobe and retrieved a pale pink gown. "Shall we dress you for the day?"

Folding the paper, Melody slipped it into the top drawer of her desk. "I suppose it is that time of day."

"You must hurry if you wish to join your family for breakfast," Lydia encouraged.

"I am not sure what the point is, since Bennett is in Scotland with his wife, and Winston is on his wedding tour," Melody said. "I should just have a tray sent up to my room."

Lydia placed the gown on the bed. "I do believe your mother enjoys eating breakfast with you and Lady Elodie."

Melody rose from her seat. "You are right," she said. "I should not deprive my mother of my company."

Her lady's maid smiled. "You are most kind and gracious."

The door suddenly opened and her twin sister, Elodie, entered the room. "I just heard the most distressing news."

Melody knew her sister was prone to exaggeration, so she wasn't overly worried. "And what is that?" she asked, feigning interest.

Elodie dropped down onto the bed in an unladylike fashion. "The dancing master has arrived, no doubt to torture us," she declared. "I don't know why Mother sent for him."

"That is an easy enough answer, considering you are a terrible dancer," Melody teased.

"It is hardly my fault," Elodie contended. "I was born with the inability to dance."

Melody laughed. "You would have been much more proficient if you hadn't skipped dancing lessons at our boarding school."

"Those were so boring," Elodie remarked.

"My point exactly," Melody said. "Besides, you know how Mother is. She is ensuring we are prepared for the upcoming Season."

Elodie let out an exaggerated sigh. "Do not remind me. I feel like a cow being put on display for the highest buyer." She paused, a frown marring her features. "Life was much simpler when Father wasn't a marquess. Mother is undoubtedly trying to marry me off to a prince."

Melody rose from her seat and walked over to the dressing table. She removed her cap, and Lydia began to arrange her hair.

"You would make a terrible princess," Melody remarked, watching her sister's reflection in the mirror.

"Precisely, but what else am I supposed to do?" Elodie asked as she adjusted the sleeves of her blue gown.

"You could do precisely what Mother expects you to do and learn from the dancing master," Melody suggested.

"Where is the fun in that?" Elodie asked with a twinkle in her eyes.

Lydia spoke up as she stepped back. "Do you like your hair, my lady?"

Turning to the side, Melody admired the elegant chignon. "It is lovely," she said. "You outdid yourself."

"Shall we dress you?" Lydia asked as she moved to retrieve the gown.

As Melody dressed, Elodie glanced at the corner writing desk. "Were you writing to Josephine again?"

"I was," Melody confirmed.

Elodie frowned. "Why can't I remember Josephine from our boarding school?"

Melody felt a twinge of guilt for lying to her sister, but it had to be done. She didn't dare reveal the truth. It would put her sister—and her entire family—at risk.

"She was only there for a few months our first year," Melody said. "She was rather reserved. It doesn't surprise me that you don't remember her."

"I should remember her, considering how close you two are."

"We didn't get close until we started writing back and forth," Melody responded as she smoothed her gown.

Lydia held Melody's discarded clothing in her hand and asked, "Will there be anything else, my lady?"

Melody shook her head. "Not at this time."

Elodie jumped up from the bed. "Shall we go to breakfast?" she asked, a grin spreading across her face. "I find that I am famished."

"You are always famished," Melody joked.

"Luckily, with Bennett and Winston gone, no one can steal the food off my plate."

Melody walked over to the door. "Yes, but I know you miss them terribly."

"I do," Elodie admitted.

Stepping out into the corridor, they headed towards the main level of Brockhall Manor. Once they arrived at the entry hall, Melody acknowledged the butler with a tip of her head. "Good morning, White."

The tall, lanky butler responded in kind. "Good morning, my lady," he greeted with his usual stoic expression.

"Has my mother come down for breakfast yet?" Melody asked.

"Indeed, she has," White responded, his posture as straight and formal as ever.

Melody offered him a brief smile before she walked

towards the dining room. Once she arrived, she saw her mother sitting at one end of the long, rectangular table, engrossed in the newssheets. Her once vibrant blonde hair had faded, and the lines around her face had deepened.

Her mother looked up when she saw them enter. "Girls," she said, a warm smile lighting her face. "I was wondering when you two were going to come down."

A footman stepped forward to pull out a chair, and Melody sat down, reaching for a white linen napkin. "Is there anything interesting in the newssheets?"

Her mother folded the newssheets and placed them next to her. "You know your father doesn't like you to read the newssheets."

"Well, Father isn't here, is he?" Elodie asked, reaching for the newssheets with a mischievous glint in her eyes.

With an unconcerned look, her mother picked up her fork and knife. "Well, do try not to be overinformed on any specific topic."

Melody ate as White entered the room with a letter on a silver tray. He approached her and announced, "A messenger just arrived with a letter for you, my lady."

"Truly?" Melody asked as she placed down her fork and knife with deliberate care. She reached for the letter and saw it was from Josephine, or rather, Lord Emberly.

"Who is it from, Dear?" her mother asked as she dabbed at the corners of her mouth with her napkin.

Melody placed the letter on the table. "It is from Josephine, but I can read it later."

Her mother waved her hand in front of her. "Why not read it now?" she suggested. "After all, Josephine went through all the trouble of having it sent by a messenger."

"Very well," Melody responded. She unfolded the paper and read.

. . .

A problem arose. En route to speak to you. —J

Melody stared at the letter, her mind racing with possibilities. What kind of problem could have arisen that would cause Lord Emberly to seek her out? He was the last man she wanted to call upon her.

Her mother's voice broke through her musings. "What did she say?"

Bringing a smile to her face, Melody replied, "Nothing of note." She slipped the paper into the folds of her gown. "I shall write to her later."

Melody was worried that her mother would press her for details, but fortunately, she changed topics with an air of excitement. "I have the most wonderful news," her mother declared. "I have invited guests to our estate."

Elodie groaned. "Guests? Whatever for?"

"I thought it would be good practice for the upcoming Season," her mother responded, unperturbed by Elodie's lackluster response. "They should be arriving soon."

"Who did you invite?" Melody inquired, trying to mask her apprehension with polite interest.

Her mother's hands grew animated as she spoke. "Just a few people," she said. "Lord and Lady Kinwick, their son, Anthony…"

Elodie picked up her knife and held it up. "I guess I will need this," she remarked, speaking over their mother.

"Whatever for, Dear?" her mother asked with a furrowed brow.

With a slight shrug, Elodie responded, "So I can protect myself from Anthony's tomfoolery."

"By stabbing him?" Melody questioned, her tone incredulous.

"It would be much easier than speaking to him," Elodie stated.

Her mother did not look pleased by Elodie's antics. "No one is going to stab anyone," she insisted. "Anthony, or rather, Lord Belview, is a viscount and is heir to an earldom."

"Yes, but he is also very cocky, annoyingly so," Elodie said. "Stabbing him will bring him down a peg or two."

"Regardless, they will be our guests, alongside Mr. and Mrs. Nelson," her mother shared. "And lucky for us, their son, Artemis, will be accompanying them."

Melody saw this for what it was. Her mother was trying to play matchmaker, but she had no intention of falling for Lord Belview or Mr. Artemis Nelson. She was well enough acquainted with them to know they would not suit.

Her mother continued. "The dancing master has arrived and is getting settled. Mr. Durand came highly recommended, so please do not scare him off," she said, giving Elodie a pointed look.

Elodie, adopting an innocent expression, widened her eyes. "Why are you looking at me?"

"I think that is fairly obvious, especially since your dancing needs work," her mother responded.

"That doesn't mean I will scare him off," Elodie muttered.

Her mother didn't look convinced. "Just try your best," she encouraged. "You must remember that you are a reflection of this family."

White stepped back into the room and met Melody's gaze. "Lord Emberly has arrived and has requested a moment of your time, my lady."

Melody stared back at the butler with disbelief. "He is here? Now?"

Her mother interjected, "Were you expecting him?"

"No, of course not," Melody rushed out, trying to keep her composure. "I am just surprised that Lord Emberly is here—at this early hour. That is all."

Pushing back her chair with a graceful movement, her mother suggested, "We should go greet him."

"Yes, we should," Melody agreed, albeit reluctantly.

Why was she reacting so strongly to seeing Lord Emberly? They would speak briefly, and he would return to his country estate in the next county over, which was good. The more distance between them, the better. But as they neared the drawing room, Melody couldn't help but wonder what urgent matter had brought him here.

Wesley Ainsworth, Earl of Emberly, stood in the drawing room of Brockhall Manor. He was not one to waste a moment, but he needed to speak to Lady Melody at once.

He had been informed that there had been a leak at headquarters, and Lady Melody's cover might have been blown. It was not known for certain, but it was a risk he wasn't willing to take. He needed to ensure that Lady Melody was safe at all costs. She was his responsibility, and he took that rather seriously.

When his older sister, Rosella, had informed him that she had a student at her boarding school who excelled in linguistics, Wesley knew he had to meet this young woman, eventually recruiting Lady Melody to work for the Crown. He had promised her that no one would ever know the truth of what she did. He wasn't about to go back on his promise now.

Lady Dallington stepped into the room and Lady Melody followed her. His eyes lingered on Lady Melody's enchanting face. She was extraordinarily beautiful, with blonde hair, blue eyes and an oval face. Yet it wasn't her striking features that captivated him the most. It was her eyes. They held a keen intellect and wit.

A smile came to Lady Dallington's face. "Good morning, Lord Emberly," she greeted. "What a pleasant surprise." She turned towards her daughter. "Isn't it, Melody?"

Melody smiled, but she wasn't exactly welcoming. "It is, Mother," she agreed, her tone cordial.

Wesley bowed. "Thank you for agreeing to meet with me at such an early hour."

"It is our pleasure," Lady Dallington responded, gesturing to the tea service on the table. "Would you care for a cup of tea?"

"Tea would be nice," he lied. He had no desire to have tea but needed to bide his time. His mother would chide him if he were rude to Lady Dallington, but he wondered how to get Melody alone to speak privately with her.

Lady Dallington walked over to one of the settees and sat down. "How is your mother?"

"She is well," Wesley replied.

"I haven't seen her since…" Lady Dallington's voice trailed off.

Wesley knew precisely what Lady Dallington would say, so he nodded. "The funeral," he said, finishing her sentence. He appreciated what she was attempting to do, but he saw no reason not to speak about his father's death. He died. That was the truth. Everyone needed to stop tiptoeing around that fact.

Lady Dallington offered him an apologetic look. "I do apologize for bringing it up. That was terribly unfair of me to do so."

"It is all right," Wesley assured her.

Melody sat down next to her mother. "How is your sister?"

As he went to sit across from them, he replied, "Rosella is still a teacher at the boarding school despite being an heiress in her own right. She insists that she is doing what she loves."

Melody reached for the teapot and poured three cups of tea. "Then I am happy for her. It is a rare thing indeed to find your calling in life."

Wesley should have known that Melody would have approved of what Rosella was doing. But that didn't mean he had to. His sister should be married by now. Instead, she was adamant to remain a spinster and a spy. He didn't know which one bothered him more.

As Melody handed him a cup of tea, he said, "I do apologize for missing Winston's wedding, but I had some urgent business that came up."

That was the right thing to say because a bright smile came to Melody's face. "You missed the most wonderful wedding. Winston and Mattie were so happy that it was nearly impossible not to be happy for them."

"I am glad to hear that," Wesley said. And he meant it. He was happy for his friend, but he had no desire to fall for the parson's mousetrap at this time. His life was complicated, and he rather quite liked being alone. It was simple. Predictable.

Lady Dallington sipped her tea before saying, "It is a shame that you are in the next county over, since we hardly see you."

"I do apologize, but I have been rather busy running my estate," Wesley responded, which was somewhat true. He was running the estate and working as a spy. He had no time for anything else, much less socializing.

Melody met his gaze and asked, "Would you enjoy a tour of our gardens? They are most exquisite this time of year."

Yes.

But he didn't want to appear too eager. "I would enjoy that." There. That was a safe answer.

Turning towards her mother, Melody asked, "Would it be permissible to show Lord Emberly the gardens?"

Lady Dallington granted her permission with a nod of her head. "Yes, but do not dally for too long. The dancing master will no doubt be waiting to start his lessons."

"Perhaps Elodie can start the lessons and I will join when I can," Melody suggested.

"You make a good point, considering she needs the most help," Lady Dallington said.

Wesley stepped forward and offered his arm. "May I escort you to the gardens, Lady Melody?"

Melody placed her hand on his sleeve and allowed him to lead her through the manor. Once they arrived at the back door, a footman opened it, and they stepped outside.

They started down a path and Melody slipped her hand off his. "What has happened?" she asked directly.

Wesley should have known Melody wouldn't have been interested in exchanging pleasantries. That was one of the many reasons why he thought so highly of her. He decided to say what needed to be said and be done with it. "There was a leak at headquarters and the spymaster is worried your cover might have been blown." He wasn't sure what kind of reaction Melody would have at that news, but he didn't expect the silence that followed.

"Did you hear me?" he asked.

Melody tipped her head. "I heard you, but there is no reason to be alarmed, considering my cover *might* have been blown. I tend to deal in facts."

"All right. Let's deal in facts, then," Wesley said. "You had a coded message delivered directly to you, bypassing every precaution we have set in place. That, in and of itself, is suspicious. To me, that is a glaring sign that your cover might have been compromised."

"That is quite an assumption. Shouldn't we reserve judgment until I have had the chance to decipher the message? Jumping to conclusions won't help us."

Wesley stopped on the path and turned to face her. "Regardless, I am taking this threat most seriously and will stay close to ensure you are safe."

"For what purpose?" Melody asked. "I am safe here at Brockhall Manor. I assure you that no harm will befall me here since servants surround me."

He wasn't sure that Melody understood the gravity of the situation, so he decided to explain it to her. "You are one of the agency's top code breakers. Your safety is paramount," he said. "And I assure you that if someone was sent to kill you, I can't promise that it would be swift and merciful."

Rather than cower or appear afraid, Melody held his gaze. "I will be just fine. You can return home."

His brow shot up. "Did you not hear what I said?"

"I heard you, but I respectfully decline your assistance."

"You decline my assistance?"

Melody bobbed her head. "I can take care of myself."

Wesley frowned. "Can you, now?"

"Yes," she replied, tilting her chin. "I am quite proficient at shooting, and I can ward off any threats that come my way. Besides, I carry a pistol in the folds of my gown."

He didn't know what was more ludicrous—that Melody had said such an utterly ridiculous remark or that she actually seemed to believe her words.

Taking a step closer to her, Wesley asked, "What do you think would happen if a sharpshooter was in the birch tree behind you?"

Melody glanced behind her, unconcerned. "But there isn't one, is there?"

"No, but that was one of the first things I noted when we stepped into the gardens," Wesley said. "You must take proper caution, at least for now. The agency can't risk losing you, which is why I am here to protect you. And that is the end of the discussion."

She pressed her lips together. "No," she stated. "You do not get to come to my home and order me about."

"Are you always this infuriating?"

A smile played on Melody's lips. "I am," she replied unabashedly.

Looking heavenward, Wesley knew that he needed to try a different tactic. Melody was undoubtedly stubborn, but surely she could see reason. This could be a matter of life or death for her.

He brought his gaze down to meet Melody's and noticed the determination in her eyes. There was no fear or hesitancy. How could she remain so calm, not knowing if her cover was blown? He hadn't anticipated Melody becoming a simpering miss, but he had expected some apprehension.

Melody took a step back and glanced at the manor. "If that will be all…" she said, her voice trailing off.

"I am not going anywhere, my lady," he responded firmly.

"Then we are at a standstill, my lord," she stated dryly. "Because I have no intention of changing my mind."

Wesley narrowed his eyes at Melody, feeling frustration welling up inside of him. He had never met a more obstinate young woman before. But he couldn't just back down and return home. No matter what happened, Melody was his responsibility.

As they stood there, Lady Dallington approached them. "Lord Emberly, I just had the most wonderful idea," she started. "Why don't you stay for a few days? We are having a few guests over, and you would make a brilliant addition."

Melody's eyes darted towards his. "Lord Emberly was just leaving," she protested.

Wesley considered Melody for a moment. He hated social events, mainly due to scheming matchmaking mothers, but it would give him the perfect opportunity to keep an eye on Lady Melody. And by the look on Melody's face, she did not want him to stay, which made staying all the more appealing.

He shifted his gaze towards Lady Dallington. "Thank you. That sounds delightful."

"Wonderful. I will have one of the guest bedrooms made up at once," Lady Dallington responded.

Wesley resisted the urge to smile when Melody rolled her eyes. He didn't know why he found her reaction to be so amusing.

Lady Dallington turned towards her daughter, and

Melody quickly schooled her features. "Isn't it wonderful that Lord Emberly will be joining us?"

Melody smiled, but it was hardly convincing. "It is, Mother," she replied.

"Well, if you will excuse me, I need to speak to the housekeeper," Lady Dallington said before walking back towards the manor.

"Are you truly trying to make yourself a nuisance?" Melody muttered.

Wesley grinned. "Some women would appreciate my company. I am an earl, after all."

"I am not one of those women, and your title does not impress me," Melody said. "Your staying here is a waste of your time and mine."

He brought a hand up to his chest, feeling an immense desire to tease her. "Every moment I am with you is a moment I cherish."

Melody arched an eyebrow. "Are you quite done?"

"I am, but only because I need to settle into my bedchamber," he replied. "It appears that I will be here at Brockhall Manor for a few days. I must admit it will be much better than the coaching inn in the village."

With a shake of her head, Melody walked away, and he remained rooted in his spot. He understood her reluctance, but he wasn't about to walk away. Not when so much was at stake. He refused to lose another agent for whom he was responsible.

Chapter Two

Melody was infuriated. She didn't understand why Lord Emberly thought he had a right to tell her what to do. He had gotten his way again, which only added to her exasperation. From the moment she had met him, she found him to be the most vexing of men. The only reason why she had agreed to work with him was because she wanted to do more than what was expected of her.

As she walked away from Lord Emberly, she was entirely displeased by the situation. Lord Emberly was staying, and she would be forced to endure his presence for the foreseeable future. He didn't seem to believe she could care for herself despite her insistence. How she hated to be underestimated. It had been that way her entire life.

A footman opened the door to the manor and Melody stepped inside, where Elodie met her.

Her sister had a bemused look on her face. "Why were you speaking to the boring Lord Emberly in the gardens?"

"I thought he might like a tour of the gardens," Melody lied.

Elodie didn't look convinced. "While our gardens are

expansive, they are nothing special," she said. "You aren't going to marry him, are you?"

Rearing back, Melody repeated, "Marry him? I would never marry Lord Emberly. Not even if he were the last man on earth."

"Then why did he call on you?"

Melody should have known that Elodie wouldn't let the matter drop, so she decided to change topics. "Why are you not with the dancing master?"

That was the right thing to say because Elodie let out a loud, decisive huff. "I am hiding," she revealed.

"Hiding?" Melody repeated. "Whatever for?"

"Mr. Durand hates me," Elodie declared. "He thinks I am hopeless."

Melody laughed. "How could he determine that in such a short time?"

"I am not quite sure, but I slipped out when he turned his attention to the window," Elodie revealed. "Now, I am hiding in the shadows."

"Mother will find you," Melody said.

"Perhaps, but it might take some time before I must return to performing like a monkey," Elodie remarked, a hint of annoyance in her voice.

Melody gave her sister a knowing look. "Mother is only doing what is best for you."

An undeniable sadness came to Elodie's eyes. "I doubt that," she said. "Do you ever wish you could leave this life behind?"

"What is wrong with this life?"

"Nothing, but I want to do more than what is expected of me," Elodie replied. "I want to go on an adventure."

Melody knew precisely what her sister felt, considering she had felt the same way before being recruited by the agency. She wanted to help Elodie but wasn't sure how to do such a thing. It wasn't as if she could ask her to be a spy alongside her. Not that Elodie wasn't capable of being a spy. But the dangers of espionage were too great to risk involving her sister.

Elodie continued. "I should be grateful for what I have, but I want more. Is that wrong of me?"

"No, it isn't," Melody replied. "And I think it is perfectly normal."

"Mother doesn't think so," Elodie muttered.

Melody placed a hand on her sister's sleeve. "Just be patient with yourself and Mother. She only wants what is best for you."

Elodie offered her a weak smile. "I know. You are wise, Sister."

Melody dropped her hand to her side. "Offering brilliant advice is the job of any older sister," she remarked.

Elodie's smile grew genuine. "You are only a few minutes older than me."

Glancing down the corridor, Melody asked, "Shall we go to the music room now?"

Her sister's smile vanished. "Do we have to?" she asked. "I think it would be far better to go on a ride."

"Mother would be furious."

"Do you intend to always follow the rules?" Elodie asked.

Melody bobbed her head. "I do," she replied. "Besides, you don't want to risk Mother's ire. Do you?"

"I hate it when you are right."

"I am surprised you aren't used to it by now," Melody quipped.

As they started walking down the corridor, Melody saw her mother approaching them with a stern look on her face. "Girls!" she shouted. "Do not dilly-dally. Mr. Durand is waiting for you."

Elodie grew visibly tense. "What if we forgo the dancing master today?"

"For what purpose?" her mother asked.

"I just don't feel like dancing today," Elodie responded.

Her mother was not swayed by Elodie's remark. "You need to practice before the upcoming Season. I have never met someone that has such an aversion to dancing."

"I just feel like when I am dancing, I am on display, almost like a prized stallion going to auction," Elodie said.

Melody's lips twitched. "Are you truly comparing yourself to a stallion?"

"I am trying to make a point," Elodie argued.

Her mother interjected, "A poor one, at that. Stop arguing and go to the music room."

"Yes, Mother," Elodie said with a mock salute.

Turning her attention to Melody, her mother asked, "Will you ensure Elodie arrives at the music room? I am having tea with Mrs. Walker."

Melody locked her arm with Elodie's. "I accept the challenge."

Her mother didn't look amused. "What am I going to do with you two?" she asked, almost to herself.

Melody started leading Elodie towards the music room and she could sense the dread coming from her sister. "It will be all right," she encouraged.

Elodie shook her head. "I doubt that. The dancing master truly does hate me."

"How could he hate you?" she asked. "He doesn't even know you."

"He knows enough."

Melody knew what she needed to do to help her sister. She glanced over her shoulder to ensure they were alone before saying, "Go on your ride. I will pretend to be you."

Elodie came to an abrupt halt. "Pardon?"

"There are some advantages to being identical twins," Melody said. "I doubt the dancing master would even notice."

A bright smile came to Elodie's lips. "Are you in earnest?"

"I am. Now, go, before I change my mind," Melody

replied. "And do not let Mother see you. She would not be amused."

"No, considering she does not like when we trade places," Elodie said, excitedly dancing on her two feet.

"Enjoy your ride," Melody encouraged, returning her smile

Melody headed towards the music room with a determined stride as her sister hurried off. She knew her sister well and did not doubt that she could accomplish this simple enough task.

Once she stepped into the music room, she saw a short, stout man with slicked-back black hair dressed in fine, tailored clothing. He held a violin in one hand, and as he turned to meet her gaze, she could see the flicker of irritation in his eyes. "Lady Elodie," he snapped in a thick French accent. "It is about time you showed back up, and I see you have changed gowns."

Melody smiled, hoping to disarm him. "I do apologize for running off earlier."

The dancing master approached her, and his gaze swept the length of her. "You are a pretty enough thing, and I do not doubt you will attract many suitors."

"Thank you—" Melody began.

He put his hand up. "I am not finished," he snapped. "But they will lose interest the moment you step on their boots. Now, dance!"

Melody's eyes went wide. "I'm sorry. What exactly do you want me to do?"

"Dance!"

"Now?" Melody asked, glancing around the room.

Without another word, the dancing master brought the violin up, tucking it snugly beneath his chin, and began to play a lively tune. "Yes, now."

Melody stared at him, utterly confused. "What dance would you like me to execute? The quadrille? The waltz?"

The dancing master spun on his heel, gliding across the floor with effortless grace. "Let your feet do the talking, my lady. Feel the music inside of you."

"What if I don't have the music inside of me?"

Ignoring her question, the dancing master closed his eyes and continued playing as he danced around the room.

Melody wasn't quite sure what she should do. She was quite sure that this dancing master was rather mad, but she didn't dare contradict him. Tentatively, she took a few uncertain steps, trying to follow his lead as best she could. With awkward movements, she began to dance, mirroring his motions while feeling completely ridiculous.

Time seemed to stretch on as she danced, though it couldn't have been more than a few moments. Finally, the dancing master abruptly stopped, lowering the violin. He studied her with an unreadable expression before giving a curt nod. "Well done, my lady," he praised. "You are not quite as useless as I believed."

"Thank you—"

He cut her off once more. "Enough talk. We must express ourselves through music." He raised the violin again, the bow poised to strike the strings. "Dance!"

Melody sighed inwardly, but she knew what was expected. As he began to play again, she resumed dancing, her feet moving across the polished floor, feeling more absurd with every step. She resisted the urge to question his methods, especially since she was impersonating her sister, and any misstep on her part could get Elodie in trouble. But this aimless twirling around the room, with no direction or purpose, seemed utterly pointless.

Just as she was beginning to wonder how long this charade would last, a flicker of movement outside the window caught her eye. Peeking through the glass, she saw Elodie riding freely through the open fields. Melody couldn't help but smile.

Perhaps this ridiculous dance was worth it, after all.

A Shadowed Charade

Wesley's sole responsibility was to protect Melody—at all costs. Despite her resistance to his protection, she would receive it, nonetheless. The haunting image of Dinah flashed through his mind, but he swiftly pushed it away. He couldn't afford to think about her now. Dinah's death was his fault. She had been his responsibility, and he had failed her. He couldn't repeat that mistake. The fear of failure pestered his soul, a constant reminder of the price of a lapse in vigilance.

The door to his bedchamber opened, and his short, light-haired valet, Watkins, entered with a grave expression. Watkins was more than a mere valet. He was Wesley's confidant and a fellow agent of the Crown.

Wesley turned to face him, his voice tense. "What did you discover?"

"Nothing," Watkins replied, frustration evident in his tone.

"That is not the least bit helpful," Wesley muttered.

Watkins offered him an apologetic look. "The guests should be arriving tomorrow, and Lady Dallington sent for the dancing master. Mr. Durand doesn't seem to pose a threat despite his eccentricity."

Wesley frowned. "We will need to remain alert. I cannot lose Lady Melody," he said with steely determination.

"Have you considered this might be a waste of time?" Watkins asked. "After all, there was a leak at the agency, but that doesn't mean Lady Melody's cover has been compromised."

"I won't risk it. We will remain here for the time being," Wesley declared.

Watkins tipped his head. "Yes, my lord." He paused. "If I may, if this situation is about Dinah…"

Wesley cut him off sharply. "I don't want to talk about Dinah."

A look that could only be construed as pity came to Watkins's face. "You never do. But her death wasn't your fault," he attempted.

"Whose fault was it, then?" Wesley demanded. "After all, I was the one that recruited her to the agency."

Watkins sighed heavily. "Yes, but Dinah knew the risks…"

Wesley put his hand up, stilling Watkins's words. "I should have protected her," he said. "I won't make the same mistake with Lady Melody."

"Yes, my lord," Watkins responded with a resigned look.

Walking to the door, Wesley said, "I will be up to change for dinner." He didn't bother to wait for a response before he exited his bedchamber. He knew Watkins was only trying to help, but he couldn't let history repeat itself.

As Wesley moved through the corridors searching for Melody, he spotted her emerging from a nearby corridor—or so he thought. Upon closer inspection, the slight sprinkling of freckles across the bridge of her nose gave her away. It wasn't Melody but her twin sister, Lady Elodie. It was just one of the many subtle differences he had begun to notice about the two sisters.

He bowed. "Lady Elodie," he acknowledged.

Elodie stopped in front of him and curtsied briefly. "My lord. I must assume that you are looking for my sister."

"I am," he admitted.

She gestured towards a nearby door. "You will find her in the music room with the dancing master. She has kindly agreed to pretend to be me for the lesson."

"And why, may I ask, would she do that?"

A sheepish smile came to Elodie's face. "I am a terrible dancer, and I couldn't take one more moment with Mr. Durand. The man despises me."

"I doubt that is true," Wesley attempted.

"Oh, he absolutely does," Elodie replied. "He had me twirling around the room like a performing monkey, and when he got distracted, I simply danced my way out of the room."

Wesley found himself curious about one thing. "Does Lady Melody often switch places with you?"

"More often than you would expect. Most people can't tell us apart, so we take advantage of it when possible." Elodie tilted her head thoughtfully. "How is it that you can?"

"You forget we have met before," Wesley reminded her.

"I haven't forgotten, but we were only introduced on that one occasion," Elodie responded.

Wesley tipped his head in acknowledgment. "That is true, but I have spent more time conversing with your sister. Over time, the differences between you both become rather obvious."

Elodie regarded him with newfound respect. "I must admit that I may have underestimated you, my lord. You are far more observant than I gave you credit for."

"I shall take that as a compliment," Wesley said.

"You should," Elodie remarked with a smile. "Well, I think I will slip away to my room before my mother realizes I have escaped."

Wesley bowed once more. "I wish you luck, my lady."

As she walked away, Wesley found himself deep in thought. The twins' similarities could be a danger. If someone were targeting Melody, it wouldn't take much for someone to mistake Elodie for her. He would need to watch both sisters closely to ensure their safety.

With that thought, he made his way to the music room. As he approached, the gentle sound of the violin drifted through the partially open door. He stepped inside to find Melody gracefully moving across the room. The dancing master stood at the center, absorbed in his playing as his violin filled the air with a lilting melody.

Wesley leaned against the door frame, watching in admiration as Melody danced. Her movements were effortless, her grace undeniable, and Wesley couldn't help but wonder if there was anything she couldn't do.

Melody's eyes widened when she saw him, and she stopped dancing abruptly. "Lord Emberly," she said, surprise evident in her voice. "What brings you here?"

Not wanting to reveal that he had come in search of her, he replied, "I heard music and I found myself curious."

"Well, as you can see, there is nothing to see here," Melody said, gesturing around the room with a sweeping motion.

Wesley knew he should leave and let her continue her lesson in peace, but something kept him rooted to the spot. He wasn't ready to let her out of his sight just yet. Deciding to play along, he changed tactics with a sly smile. "You are an excellent dancer, *Lady Elodie*," he said, adding a wink to let her know he was in on the ruse.

The dancing master clapped his hands together and turned his attention to Wesley. "My lord, you have arrived at the perfect time! Lady Elodie requires a dancing partner."

"I do believe Lady Elodie is managing just fine on her own," Wesley attempted.

Mr. Durand waved off the suggestion with a dismissive gesture. "Nonsense! Dancing is always better with a partner. It allows you to feel the music flow between the two of you."

Wesley glanced at Melody, who looked equally uncomfortable at the idea. "I… um… I'm not much of a dancer," he stammered.

The dancing master stepped forward with determination. "If you will, my lord."

Wesley cast Melody an apologetic look before he went to stand by her. She leaned closer to him and whispered, "Thank you for not revealing me."

Understanding her gratitude for keeping her identity a secret, he slightly nodded in response.

Mr. Durand approached them and declared, "Excellent. Let us attempt the waltz."

"The waltz?" Melody repeated, her words holding uncertainty.

The dancing master seemed unbothered by her hesitation. "Are you familiar with the dance?" he asked, addressing Wesley.

Wesley nodded. "I am."

"Good, that will save us considerable time," the dancing master said. "Will you take Lady Elodie in your arms, and we will begin?"

Turning to face Melody, Wesley asked, "Are you agreeable, my lady?"

A myriad of emotions flittered across Melody's face before she lifted her chin slightly. "I am," she said.

Wesley offered her an encouraging look before taking her hand in his. He gently placed his other hand on her waist. He could feel how tense Melody was, and he didn't blame her. He didn't want to dance with her, either. But as he held her, he had to admit their closeness was oddly comforting. She almost felt like she belonged in his arms.

Mr. Durand clapped loudly, startling them both. "Dance!" he ordered.

As the dancing master began to play the violin, they started dancing around the room and Wesley felt Melody slowly relaxing in his arms.

In a hushed voice, Melody said, "I am sorry about this."

"There is no reason to apologize."

"You should have saved yourself," Melody remarked. "I have to be here, but you don't."

He smirked. "Who says I don't want to be here?"

Melody shot him a look of disbelief. "We are dancing the waltz, and I suspect Mr. Durand is a drill sergeant for Napoleon."

Wesley chuckled. "The dancing master doesn't seem so terrible."

"I'm afraid he is far worse," Melody responded. "At least my sister is safe from Mr. Durand."

He found himself curious about one thing. "Why did you switch places with your sister?" he asked, his voice low enough to keep their conversation private.

Melody's eyes darted towards Mr. Durand, who stood in the center of the room. "I worry about Elodie. She is struggling to find her place in the world."

"And you feel you must protect her?"

"If not me, then who?" Melody asked. "I am her older sister. It is what I am supposed to do."

Wesley offered her a reassuring smile. "I do not doubt that Lady Elodie will find her way. She will likely take the Season by storm, attracting more suitors than she will know what to do with."

"I do hope so," Melody murmured, though her tone was far from convinced.

"Isn't that what you want, as well? For yourself, I mean?"

"All I truly want is for my sister to be happy."

"You are a good sister," Wesley pressed. "But I suspect you will be quite sought after in the marriage mart."

A silence fell between them, and Melody's expression shifted, her usual confidence waning for a moment. "I do want to marry," she admitted. "But I worry that if I do, I will have to give up my work as a spy."

"That is a decision only you can make. However, I know the agency would be disappointed to lose someone as skilled and dedicated as you."

Melody studied him for a moment. "And what of you? Do you intend to marry?"

He glanced away briefly. "I do, eventually, but being a spy complicates things. It puts my family, anyone I love, at risk."

Before Melody could respond, Mr. Durand clapped his

hands loudly, his voice booming through the room. "Well done! That was brilliant."

Wesley released Melody and took a step back. "Thank you for dancing with me," he said with a slight bow.

Melody dropped into a curtsy. "The pleasure was mine, my lord," she murmured.

"I think that is enough for one day," Mr. Durand stated as he met Melody's gaze. "I will expect to see you and your sister tomorrow. Now, it is time for me to rest. Good day to you both."

With that, Mr. Durand departed from the room, his departure as abrupt as his commands. As the door closed behind him, the tension in the air seemed to dissipate.

Melody offered him a faint smile. "If you will excuse me, I think it is best if I retire until dinner," she said before she walked swiftly out of the room.

Wesley debated if he should follow her to ensure she arrived at her bedchamber safely, but he thought better of it. With a quiet sigh, he let her go, trusting that she would be safe —at least for now.

Chapter Three

The sun was setting as Melody sat in the library, staring intently at the coded message in front of her. The secret message seemed to mock her, but it was only a matter of time before she deciphered it. She had never failed before and didn't intend to start now.

Melody leaned back in her seat, feeling a wave of discouragement washing over her. Perhaps she was just distracted. Her thoughts drifted back to the unexpected dance she had shared with Lord Emberly. She had always kept her distance from him, finding his demeanor infuriatingly arrogant. He may be deucedly handsome, but she had no interest in him beyond their professional interactions as spies.

So why did she feel so comfortable in his arms?

No.

She refused to think there was anything more to it than two people sharing a dance. It may have been the waltz, but she had danced it before without a second thought.

The door swung open and Elodie stepped into the room with a determined stride. "There you are," she said. "I have been looking everywhere for you."

"Well, here I am," Melody said, hastily slipping the coded paper into the folds of her dress.

Elodie settled into the chair beside her, her eyes curious. "What were you doing?"

"I was just reading a letter from Josephine," Melody replied, hoping the explanation would satisfy her sister's curiosity.

Fortunately, it did, because Elodie did not press her. "How did the dancing lesson go?" she asked.

"It went well," Melody said.

Elodie's expression turned skeptical. "I saw you were dancing the waltz with Lord Emberly. That must have been awful for you."

Melody shrugged one shoulder. "It wasn't as terrible as I thought it would be."

"Is it because he is so handsome?" Elodie teased.

With a blank look, Melody asked, "Is he? I suppose some people might consider him handsome."

"And you are not one of those people?"

"Absolutely not!" Melody lied, a little too forcefully. "I have no interest in Lord Emberly."

Elodie leaned back, a satisfied smile playing on her lips. "You can still find someone handsome, even if you have no interest in them. You protest too much, making me think you find him handsome."

Melody gave her sister an exasperated look. "Is there a point to this conversation?" She didn't dare reveal that she found Lord Emberly to be the most handsome of men with his dark hair, strong jaw, and straight nose.

"No, but I do think Lord Emberly isn't as boring as I thought he was," Elodie responded. "He has the uncanny ability to tell us apart, despite only being acquainted with us. It is impressive, to say the least."

"I do think you are giving Lord Emberly far too much credit," Melody said, trying to dismiss the topic.

"Or you are not giving him enough."

Before Melody could reply, their mother entered the room and met Elodie's gaze. "How did the lesson go with the dancing master?"

"It went well," Elodie said.

Their mother didn't look convinced. "Truly? I only ask because Mr. Durand informed me that Lady Elodie dances like an angel. Which we both know isn't true."

Elodie's mouth dropped, feigning outrage. "Why is it so impossible to believe I dance like an angel?"

"You dance like a wounded duck," her mother replied matter-of-factly.

Melody couldn't help but giggle. "It is true, Elodie."

Elodie shot her a frustrated glance. "I will have you know that I have improved significantly."

Their mother smiled indulgently. "I'm sure you have, but I must assume you two switched places again."

Melody knew there was no point in lying, especially since her mother was no simpleton. "We did, but it was only for this afternoon."

"It better be," her mother said. "Elodie needs to be proficient in dancing if she ever hopes to secure a match."

Elodie rolled her eyes. "Yes, because dancing is more important than my intellectual prowess."

Her mother stepped closer to Elodie. "My dear child, you will debut with many other eager debutantes who are all searching for the same thing—a husband. You must stand out."

"I play the pianoforte," Elodie attempted.

Melody gave her sister a knowing look. "That means little, since every debutante plays the pianoforte."

"What if I learn the bagpipes?" Elodie asked.

Her mother did not look amused. "Your father would never allow such a thing," she replied. "Furthermore, bagpipes are not played in the drawing room."

"What if—" Elodie started.

"No," her mother said, cutting her off.

"You don't even know what I was going to say," Elodie declared.

Her mother lifted her brow. "I know you, and I am sure it was something nonsensical."

Elodie smirked. "It was, actually."

The faint sound of the dinner bell could be heard in the distance, beckoning them all to the drawing room.

Her mother turned her head towards the door. "Come along, girls. We mustn't keep anyone waiting for dinner."

"You mean Lord Emberly," Elodie said.

With a slight nod, her mother responded, "Yes, he is our guest, after all."

Melody rose from her chair. "Why did you have to invite him to remain here?"

"I only thought it was prudent," her mother replied. "His mother is a dear friend of mine, and I thought it was best if we all became better acquainted with him."

Rising, Elodie said, "Well, I think it would be best to lock our doors and pretend we are not home when the other guests arrive."

"That would hardly work. Besides, think of the fun we will have," her mother remarked with a flourish of her hand.

As they made their way to the corridor, Elodie leaned closer to Melody and whispered, "Moo."

Melody laughed. "We are not cattle," she responded.

"Then why do I feel like Mother just wants to marry us off to produce offspring?" Elodie asked.

Her mother's chiding voice came from behind them. "Why must you insist on being so dramatic about everything?"

"Mother isn't wrong," Melody pointed out.

Turning her head, Elodie spoke over her shoulder, addressing her mother. "We all know that Melody will be the diamond of the first water and I will just fade into the background."

"I did not raise you to blend in," her mother responded. "I daresay that you are not giving yourself enough credit."

"You have to say that because you are my mother," Elodie countered. "You have to pretend I am the greatest thing since the discovery of biscuits."

Melody placed a hand on her stomach. "I do enjoy a good biscuit."

"As do I," Elodie said. "My favorite is the millefruit biscuit. I should ask the cook to make us some for tomorrow."

"I think that is a splendid idea," Melody agreed.

Her mother sighed. "You two digress, as usual," she said. "I am your mother, which means I am your biggest supporter, but I am aware of your flaws, as well."

Elodie looked stunned. "I have flaws?" she asked. "As in, more than one? Why haven't you said something before now?"

"You are hopeless, Child," her mother muttered.

Melody started to descend the stairs as she remarked, "Everyone has flaws. Some are just more obvious than others."

Her mother bobbed her head. "Well said, Melody," she praised. "I do hope that you both will behave while our guests are here."

"How is that possible, considering I just learned I have flaws?" Elodie insisted. "My whole world has been turned upside down."

As they reached the bottom of the stairs, Melody noticed Lord Emberly standing in the entry hall, his gaze fixed on them. He offered a polite bow as they approached.

"Good evening, ladies," he greeted.

Her mother responded with a gracious nod. "Good evening. I trust you are finding everything to your satisfaction?"

"Indeed, Lady Dallington," he replied.

Melody's heart gave an unexpected flutter at the sight of him, but she quickly reminded herself of her resolve. She had no interest in him. None at all.

"Shall we wait in the drawing room?" her mother suggested, gesturing towards the door just off the entry hall.

They entered the drawing room, and Elodie addressed Lord Emberly. "Were you aware that I have flaws?"

Lord Emberly furrowed his brow, clearly puzzled by Elodie's question. "I was not."

"I was just as surprised as you were," Elodie quipped.

Lady Dallington pressed her lips together, saying, "Child, please do not bother Lord Emberly with this nonsense."

Elodie brought a hand up to her chest. "Oh, no! Did I just let one of my flaws show?"

Lord Emberly turned his attention towards Melody. "Did I miss something?"

Taking pity on him, Melody replied, "You did. Elodie is just upset that our mother said that she had flaws. Apparently, it is news to her."

"I see," Lord Emberly said.

Her father stepped into the room with his usual commanding presence. He was a tall man with a stern countenance softened by kind eyes. His gaze landed on Lord Emberly and a smile spread across his face. "Welcome to our manor," he greeted.

Lord Emberly bowed. "Lord Dallington, it is an honor to be here."

Her father tipped his head in acknowledgment. "It is good to see you looking so well. Last I saw you was at your father's funeral, which was some time ago."

"I have been rather busy running my estate," Lord Emberly explained. "I must admit that my father made it look easy, considering he spent so much time away serving as an admiral in the Royal Navy."

"Your father was a good man," Lord Dallington expressed, a touch of sadness in his voice. "But enough of such talk. We have many things to be grateful for."

Elodie spoke up, a teasing lilt in her voice. "Not me. I have too many flaws."

Lady Dallington groaned, her patience clearly wearing thin as she pinched the bridge of her nose. "Grant me patience with this child," she muttered. She then straightened, regaining her composure. "Let us adjourn to the dining room."

After Lord and Lady Dallington departed from the drawing room, Wesley stepped forward and offered his arm to Melody. "May I have the honor of escorting you to the dining room?" he asked.

Melody's lips tightened into a thin, white line as she accepted his arm. "Thank you, my lord," she responded, though her tone lacked enthusiasm.

As they moved through the dimly lit corridor, Wesley leaned closer, lowering his voice so only she could hear. "Were you able to decipher the code that was sent to you?"

"Not yet," she replied, her voice equally hushed. "But I will."

"I believe you."

Melody looked sideways at him, her brow slightly furrowed. "You do?"

Wesley's lips curved into a smile. "I am not sure why you are surprised. You have successfully deciphered every code the agency has ever given you."

"One of the more common codes is when letters of the alphabet are shuffled in a particular sequence, and I just have to work out the key," Melody said. "But this particular coded message is proving to be more complicated."

"You will figure it out," Wesley assured her. "You always do."

Melody met his gaze briefly. "Thank you for the vote of confidence."

They entered the dining room, the rich scent of roasted meats and herbs filling the air. Wesley led her to her seat at the long, rectangular table, pulling out the chair with a smooth, practiced motion. As she settled herself, he made his way around to his place at the table, directly across from Lady Melody and Lady Elodie.

A comfortable silence enveloped the room as the footmen moved quietly, placing delicate bowls of steaming soup in front of each of them. The flickering candlelight danced off the silverware, casting a warm, golden glow across the table.

Wesley picked up his spoon and began eating, content to observe in silence, but his reprieve was short-lived.

Lady Dallington shifted in her seat, her gaze landing on Wesley. "I do hope your bedchamber is to your liking," she inquired.

He placed the spoon down and dabbed the sides of his mouth with his linen napkin. "It is, very much so. Thank you, my lady."

Lady Dallington's smile widened, satisfaction evident in her expression. "We are rather pleased you decided to join us for these few days," she said. "I hope your mother won't miss you terribly while you are here."

Wesley's expression softened at the mention of his mother. "I doubt it, since she is rather independent."

"Yes, I do remember that about her," Lady Dallington said. "Does she still wear trousers to ride horses?"

Wesley chuckled softly. "No, I'm afraid her days of riding horses are long over. These days, she spends most of her time reading."

"A fine pastime to have," Lady Dallington remarked approvingly.

"It is," Wesley agreed, "though I could do without the cats. She has two rather dysfunctional cats, Bella and Tiger. She adores them, but they rule the manor."

Lady Dallington laughed. "I do recall her fondness for cats. She snuck one into our room when we went to boarding school. The headmistress did not find it amusing, but she somehow convinced the woman to let the cat remain with us until we went home."

Elodie leaned forward and interjected, "Can we have a cat, Mother?"

Lord Dallington, who had quietly observed the exchange, spoke up with a faint frown. "We already have a cat, Elodie. He is in the barn where he belongs."

"But I want a cat that I can cuddle with in the mornings," Elodie pressed, her tone imploring.

Lord Dallington's frown deepened. "If you want something to cuddle, get yourself a husband."

Elodie gave her father an exasperated look. "That is hardly the same thing."

With a disapproving shake of her head, Lady Dallington went to take control of the conversation. "Perhaps we can discuss this later," she suggested, her tone firm with a hint of warning.

"Yes, Mother," Elodie muttered.

"Why don't we go around the table and share one thing that we have learned recently?" Lady Dallington suggested.

Melody let out a soft groan. "I hate this game. I never know what to say."

Lady Dallington offered her daughter an encouraging smile. "Yet you always find something to say, don't you? Who would like to start?"

An awkward silence descended as Lady Dallington's gaze swept around the table, waiting expectantly. Wesley racked his brain for something to contribute but was at a loss for what he should say. Discussing estate management seemed dreadfully dull, and he certainly wasn't about to divulge anything from his covert activities as a spy.

Finally, Lord Dallington cleared his throat, breaking the silence. "I will start." He paused. "The price of a bushel of hay has gone up... again."

"That is... interesting," Lady Dallington remarked, her tone indicating it was anything but.

Elodie raised her hand.

Lady Dallington sighed. "Yes, Elodie?"

"I have one," Elodie replied. "I recently discovered that ostriches run faster than horses."

"Truly?" Melody asked. "They don't appear that fast."

"That is because you have only seen them at the Royal Menagerie in cages," Elodie explained. "They run extraordinarily fast in the wild, and the males can roar like lions."

Lord Dallington raised a skeptical brow. "I believe they are fast, but to roar like lions? Where did you hear such nonsense?"

"I read it in a book," Elodie replied.

"You can't believe everything you read in a book," Lord Dallington said.

Elodie shrugged. "I could always ask one of the keepers at the menagerie when we go to London for the Season."

"Yes, you could, but until then, we have no reason to doubt the authenticity of your information," Lady Dallington said. "Do we, Dear?" She gave her husband a pointed look.

Lord Dallington pressed his lips together. "No, we don't."

"Wonderful," Lady Dallington declared with satisfaction. "Shall we move on to Melody?"

Melody winced. "I... uh... can you come back to me?" she asked. "I need more time to think."

Noticing her discomfort, Wesley decided to step in. "I might have something of interest."

All eyes turned towards him, and Wesley shifted uncomfortably in his seat, hoping his contribution would suffice. "For successful childbirth, Pliny the Elder recommended putting the right foot of a hyena on a pregnant woman to help with the delivery."

"Why the right foot?" Melody asked.

"The left foot meant death," Wesley informed her.

Melody reached for her glass, taking a small sip as she considered his words. "How did you learn of this?"

Wesley offered a brief smile. "My mother lost two children before she finally had my sister and me," he explained. "My father was desperate for an heir and willing to try anything the doctors suggested."

"I can respect that, but that seems rather illogical," Melody said.

"That is precisely what my mother said," Wesley shared. "My mother didn't believe in those superstitions, but I know she was greatly affected by losing those two children."

Lady Dallington nodded, her eyes holding empathy. "Any mother would be."

Elodie chimed in. "What do you think would happen if pregnant women put the right foot of an ostrich on them during delivery?"

"Nothing would happen. It is just quackery," Melody remarked.

Elodie tapped her lips thoughtfully with her finger. "But what if it made their child an incredibly fast runner? I think that is worth looking into."

Lady Dallington leaned to the side as the footmen collected their bowls. "Melody?" she prompted gently. "Have you thought of one yet?"

Melody bit her lower lip. "I have been reading about the spymaster, Sir Francis Walsingham. Under the authority of Queen Elizabeth, Walsingham used his unique set of skills to protect the interests of the Crown. It was through his efforts that Mary, Queen of Scots, was executed."

"Why would you read such a thing?" Lord Dallington asked. "Spying is such a distasteful thing to do, especially for someone of good breeding."

"I found it rather interesting," Melody admitted.

"You should stick to reading books that are more appropriate for a young woman," Lord Dallington chided.

Wesley felt a surge of protectiveness for Melody and did not like how Lord Dallington was talking down to her. "I find it admirable that Lady Melody is interested in the history of our country." "History is just fine for a young woman to read, but spying…" Lord Dallington's voice trailed off. "It is not something I could ever condone."

"Spies have been used since the beginning of time," Wesley remarked.

Lady Dallington interrupted, drawing everyone's attention. "I heard the most wonderful news today," she started, her tone full of excitement. "A very handsome and very unattached vicar has just arrived in the village."

Cocking her head, Elodie asked, "And why exactly is that 'wonderful news'?"

"Mr. Bramwell, the vicar in question, is the grandson of a marquess. He comes highly recommended, according to Lord Wythburn," Lady Dallington shared.

Melody raised an eyebrow. "I must assume you heard this news from Mrs. Walker, the village busybody."

With a dismissive wave of her hand, Lady Dallington brushed off the remark. "It matters not where the information came from. Besides, you two are missing the point."

"What exactly is the point?" Lord Dallington asked. "I sincerely hope you are not implying that our daughters should be interested in a mere vicar."

"There is nothing wrong with being a vicar," Lady Dallington defended.

Lord Dallington nodded in agreement, though his expression remained unconvinced. "I do not dispute that, but our daughters are in a position to make a much more brilliant match this Season."

"It is true," Melody said, her tone teasing. "Elodie might even snag a prince."

Elodie let out an exaggerated, unladylike huff. "Good heavens, I would make a terrible princess. The last thing I want is to be locked away in some dreary castle."

"Princesses are not exactly locked up, but they do lose certain freedoms we often take for granted," Lady Dallington pointed out.

Elodie's eyes gleamed mischievously. "What if they put a unicorn foot on me during childbirth?"

Wesley knew he would regret saying this, but he said it, nonetheless. "Unicorns aren't real."

Elodie didn't look convinced. "Just because no one has seen a unicorn doesn't mean they don't exist."

"Usually, that is precisely what that means," Wesley countered.

Undeterred, Elodie continued with even more enthusiasm, her hands growing more animated as she spoke. "Regardless, if I use a unicorn foot, that will most likely grant my children magical powers! They might even grow up to be powerful sorcerers."

Wesley didn't quite know what to say at this precise moment. He wasn't entirely sure if Elodie was joking or if she truly believed in her fantastical ideas. His gaze shifted to Melody, who was smiling at her sister, clearly amused by the whimsical turn of the conversation.

One thing was certain—he had never had such an interesting—or decisively odd—conversation over dinner before.

Chapter Four

The morning sun streamed through the windows as Melody went down to the dining room. Today was the day her mother's guests would arrive—an event she dreaded. She knew exactly what her mother was planning: matchmaking. The thought alone made her stomach twist with unease. She had no intention of marrying any man her mother paraded in front of her, no matter how eligible.

She wanted love and a family of her own, but she knew that would come at a great cost to her. She couldn't bear the thought of giving up her work as a spy, the one thing that gave her life purpose and excitement.

As she reached the bottom of the stairs, White, the ever-dutiful butler, stood by the entry hall. His expression was as impassive as ever, though she could swear there was a flicker of warmth in his eyes. Perhaps it was his way of smiling.

"Good morning, my lady," he greeted her in his usual composed manner.

"Good morning," Melody replied as she passed by him.

Entering the dining room, her heart dropped as she saw Lord Emberly seated at the table, engrossed in the newssheets.

Drats.

He was the last person she wanted to see that morning.

Melody hesitated in the doorway, contemplating a quiet retreat. Maybe if she moved slowly enough, she could slip away unnoticed. But just as she was about to make her escape, Lord Emberly spoke without lifting his eyes from the newssheets. "Are you truly trying to escape from me?"

Melody knew how ridiculous she was being, but she didn't want to converse with the infuriating lord, at least not at such an early hour. Perhaps a cup of chocolate would help her mood. That had always helped before.

Stepping forward, she replied with a feigned air of nonchalance, "I was merely being considerate. I thought you might prefer some solitude during breakfast. If anything, you should be thanking me for being so courteous."

Lord Emberly placed the newssheets down and stood, his eyes meeting hers with a knowing glint. "Your consideration is noted, but I find I prefer your company. It allows me to keep a watchful eye on you."

Melody raised an eyebrow. "How noble of you. Because I am in such dire danger here at the breakfast table," she mocked as she took her seat.

"One can never be too cautious. You will have to grow accustomed to my presence," Lord Emberly responded, returning to his seat.

"Oh, wonderful," Melody muttered under her breath.

At that moment, Elodie swept into the room, her face full of enthusiasm. "Good morning, Sister. Lord Emberly."

Lord Emberly pushed back his chair and stood once again. "I trust that you slept well, my lady?"

"I did indeed," Elodie responded as she settled into her chair opposite of Melody. "I have decided that I am going to seize the day."

Melody tilted her head. "And how do you intend to do that?"

Elodie leaned in conspiratorially, her voice dropping to a

whisper. "Mother's guests are set to arrive any time, and I refuse even to consider marrying the buffoons that she is presenting us with." She stopped speaking and had the decency to look slightly ashamed as she shifted her gaze to Lord Emberly. "My apologies, my lord. I am not referring to you."

Lord Emberly waved off her apology with a slight nod. "I did not take offense. Please, continue."

Elodie's smile returned, and she pressed on with renewed vigor. "As I was saying, Lord Belview and Mr. Artemis Nelson may be eligible, but they are—"

"Buffoons," Lord Emberly interjected, his lips curling into a smirk.

"Precisely. Which forced me to devise a plan," Elodie declared.

Melody reached for her chocolate cup and brought it to her lips. "What is this devious plan?"

Elodie's eyes twinkled with amusement. "That is the beauty of it, Sister. There is nothing devious about it," she revealed. "I am simply going to be the perfect daughter, the perfect hostess—essentially, I will pretend to be you."

Placing the cup back down, Melody protested, "I am hardly perfect. And how, pray tell, would that deter Mother from her relentless matchmaking?"

Elodie leaned back, a self-satisfied smile on her face. "No gentleman wants a perfect wife," she responded.

Melody wasn't sure whether to feel insulted or amused by her sister's remark. "So, in this scenario, I'm considered perfect?"

"Well, I daresay that you have never made a misstep before," Elodie said.

"That doesn't mean I am perfect," Melody countered.

Elodie shrugged. "No, but there is not one thing you are not good at. It can be rather grating for us 'normal' people."

Melody sat back in her seat, folding her arms. "Regardless,

I do not see how you pretending to be like me will help the situation."

"Trust me," Elodie said.

She shot her sister a dubious look. "I am not sure that I should, since you just soundly insulted me."

Elodie picked up a knife and spread butter on her toast. "I did not mean to offend you. I meant to offer you the highest of compliments."

Melody frowned. "It didn't exactly sound like one."

"Well, I must have said it wrong," Elodie said, placing the knife down. "You know you are my favorite sister."

Lord Emberly grinned. "I do believe Lady Elodie's plan is flawless."

Elodie flashed him a triumphant smile. "Thank you, my lord."

Turning towards Lord Emberly, Melody asked, "Why are you encouraging her? My mother will not be amused with Elodie's antics."

"You seem to doubt my acting abilities," Elodie said with a flourish of her hand. "I could have a career in the theater if I so desired."

Melody sighed. "I see that I am outnumbered. I wish you luck."

Elodie mimicked her sister's tone, her voice full of mock seriousness. "I wish you luck."

"What are you doing?" Melody asked.

Elodie placed her toast down and brushed the crumbs from her hands. "I am practicing being you." Lowering her voice in an exaggerated manner, she repeated, "I wish you luck. There. That was much better."

Melody looked heavenward. "I do not sound like that, and this conversation is utterly ridiculous. Mother will see through what you are attempting to do."

Just then, White stepped into the room and met Melody's

gaze. "Mr. Bramwell is requesting a moment of your time, my lady."

Elodie perked up. "The new vicar?" she asked. "Why is he here, and why does he want to see you?"

"I don't know, but I intend to find out," Melody said, rising from her chair.

Lord Emberly stood as well, offering his hand to assist her. "If you have no objections, I shall accompany you."

"I do have objections," Melody said, her tone firm as she pulled her hand back.

Unperturbed, Lord Emberly offered his arm instead, a teasing glint in his eyes. "I shall accompany you anyway. I have a great appreciation for vicars."

Melody bit back a retort, deciding it wasn't worth the effort to argue further. "Very well, but do not make a nuisance of yourself."

"That is something I strive for," Lord Emberly quipped.

Resigned, Melody took his arm, and they approached the drawing room. As they entered, she released his arm and stopped abruptly. Mr. Bramwell, the new vicar, stood tall and strikingly handsome with jet-black hair and a long, angular face. His straight nose gave him an air of quiet dignity.

Mr. Bramwell's face lit up with a warm smile as he bowed respectfully. "Lady Melody, I do apologize for calling at such an early hour."

She dipped into a curtsy. "There is no need to apologize. You are always welcome in our home."

"That is kind of you to say," Mr. Bramwell said, his gaze shifting briefly to Lord Emberly before returning to Melody.

Sensing the need for introductions, Melody gestured towards Lord Emberly. "Allow me to introduce Lord Emberly to you. He is a... family friend," she said, tripping over her last words.

Mr. Bramwell inclined his head politely. "My lord, it is a pleasure to meet you."

Lord Emberly returned the gesture with a respectful nod.

Bringing his gaze back to Melody, Mr. Bramwell said, "I understand you have a lovely singing voice."

"I am merely proficient," Melody responded, brushing off his praise.

"That is not what Lord Wythburn told me," Mr. Bramwell countered. "He said you have the voice of an angel, and I was hoping to convince you to sing at our next church service."

Melody's smile faltered slightly. "I am flattered, truly, but as I have told him, I only sing for friends and family."

"Are we not all friends?" Mr. Bramwell asked, spreading his hands out.

She shifted slightly, feeling the weight of his kind but insistent gaze. "I appreciate the sentiment, but I do not enjoy being the center of attention. It makes me somewhat uncomfortable."

Mr. Bramwell's eyes softened with understanding. "I would never wish to cause you discomfort, my lady. I merely wanted to extend the invitation."

Melody nodded, grateful for his consideration. "Thank you for your understanding."

"I do hope that one day I might earn a place in your circle of friends," Mr. Bramwell said before he bowed. "Now, if you will excuse me, I must prepare for my first sermon at this parish."

After Mr. Bramwell departed from the drawing room, Lord Emberly said, "My sister did say that you had a lovely voice."

"It is nothing special, I assure you."

Lord Emberly turned to face her. "Why do you do that?" he asked.

"Do what?"

"You deflect every compliment that comes your way," Lord Emberly replied, his tone more curious than accusatory.

Melody moved past him, unwilling to delve into the topic. "I don't need to explain myself to you, my lord."

Lord Emberly easily caught up to her and met her stride. "That is true, but you are doing yourself a disservice."

Her patience was wearing thin, but she decided to ask the question anyway. "Why am I doing myself a disservice?"

Lord Emberly paused for a moment, as if choosing his words carefully. "Accepting a compliment honors both you and the person giving it. It is a way of acknowledging their sincerity and their effort to offer you praise."

Melody stopped and turned to face him. "It is much easier for me—and what I do—if I remain unnoticed."

"I can appreciate that sentiment, but singing in a church isn't exactly the kind of attention that will disrupt your life," Lord Emberly remarked.

Melody narrowed her eyes at him. "Has anyone told you that you are an infuriating man?"

A smirk tugged at the corners of Lord Emberly's mouth. "Not to my face. People tend to be rather nice to me, given that I am an earl."

"Well, I am not one of those people. I think you are a complete muttonhead," Melody said.

Lord Emberly's smirk grew. "Are you trying to flirt with me, Lady Melody?"

Melody's mouth dropped in sheer disbelief. "Heavens, no! I would never flirt with you. Ever."

But Lord Emberly was not deterred. His grin only grew more smug. "I don't know. It seems like you are flirting with me, even if you won't admit it," he teased. "I must say, I am flattered, but perhaps we should keep our relationship purely professional."

Melody could only stare at him, stunned by his audacity. Without another word, she shook her head in exasperation and turned on her heel, walking away from Lord Emberly.

She couldn't help but wonder how much longer she had to endure his insufferable presence.

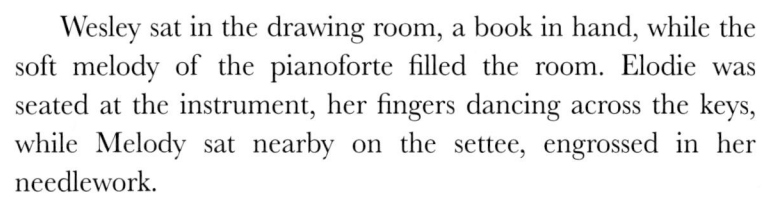

Wesley sat in the drawing room, a book in hand, while the soft melody of the pianoforte filled the room. Elodie was seated at the instrument, her fingers dancing across the keys, while Melody sat nearby on the settee, engrossed in her needlework.

As the afternoon light streamed through the large windows, Wesley's gaze drifted towards the sprawling gardens of Brockhall Manor. The lush greenery reminded him of his estate, where countless responsibilities awaited him. Yet, far from home, he was bound by a duty that transcended any obligation to his estate. His priority was ensuring Melody's safety, whether she appreciated his presence or not. Her reluctance didn't matter. He had vowed to protect her and would see it through, no matter the costs.

The music abruptly ceased as Elodie lowered her hands from the keys. "I would hope that is enough playing to satisfy my mother."

Wesley glanced over at Elodie. "Do you not enjoy playing?"

Elodie sighed, a hint of frustration in her tone. "Every young woman in the *ton* plays the pianoforte. I want to play the bagpipes."

"Then why don't you?" Wesley asked.

"My father would never approve," Elodie responded.

Still focused on her needlework, Melody looked up and teased, "When has that stopped you before?"

"True, but I am trying to be perfect," Elodie said. "I keep asking myself, 'What would Melody do?'"

"You should just be true to yourself," Melody suggested.

Before they could continue the conversation, Lady Dallington swept into the room and announced, "The dancing master is ready for your lessons."

A bright smile came to Elodie's face. "Wonderful. I was thinking it was time for me to dance," she said, her enthusiasm almost too earnest.

Lady Dallington eyed her daughter curiously. "Are you being facetious?"

"No, Mother, I do enjoy a good dance," Elodie said, her smile intact. "Dancing is my favorite pastime."

Turning towards Melody, her mother asked, "What has gotten into Elodie?"

Melody shrugged. "Who knows?"

Lady Dallington still seemed unconvinced, but she decided to let it go. "Shall we adjourn to the music room, then?" she asked. "I do not want to keep the dancing master waiting."

Leaning forward, Melody placed her needlework onto the table and rose. "How many more lessons must we endure?"

"I suppose it depends on what the dancing master recommends," Lady Dallington responded.

Suddenly, a knock echoed from the main door, drawing everyone's attention.

Lady Dallington's face lit up with a delighted smile. "How wonderful! Some of our guests have arrived," she said, her tone filled with anticipation.

"Mooo," Elodie muttered under her breath.

Lady Dallington lifted her brow. "What was that, Dear?"

Elodie quickly adopted an innocent expression. "I said, 'Marvelous.' I do so adore having guests over."

Wesley couldn't help but grin at Elodie's antics, though he quickly brought his gloved hand to his mouth to hide his amusement. It wouldn't do to show too much approval of her irreverent behavior.

Moments later, the butler entered the room and

announced, "Mr. and Mrs. Nelson and their son, Mr. Artemis Nelson, have arrived."

A tall, heavy-set man appeared with a silver-haired woman by his side. Mrs. Nelson smiled at Lady Dallington. "Catherine, it has been far too long."

Lady Dallington approached the woman and embraced her warmly. "I am so pleased that you have arrived. We have much to discuss." She turned her attention to Mr. Nelson. "Adam, you are looking well."

Mr. Nelson patted his ample belly. "It is only because of my wife. She insists I do not overindulge myself these days."

"That is because I want you to live a long, healthy life," Mrs. Nelson responded, exchanging a look of love with her husband.

"Where is Lionel?" Mr. Nelson asked, glancing around the room.

Lady Dallington waved her hand in front of her. "Where else is my husband but in the study? He is always working, I'm afraid."

Mr. Nelson chuckled. "I am glad that my brother is alive and well. I have no desire to become an earl and take on all that responsibility."

Gesturing towards Wesley, Lady Dallington said, "Speaking of earls, have you met Lord Emberly? He was most gracious to join us."

Wesley stepped forward and offered a polite bow. "Mr. and Mrs. Nelson. It is an honor to meet you," he said.

Mrs. Nelson's eyes shone with kindness as she returned the greeting. "Are you acquainted with our son, Artemis?" Her eyes roamed the room, suddenly realizing something. "Where is he?"

Mr. Nelson cleared his throat, a hint of impatience in his voice. "Pardon me for a moment," he said before quickly exiting the room.

A short time later, Mr. Nelson returned with a tall, blond-haired man by his side. "This is Artemis," he said. "He was admiring the plants. He is quite passionate about botany."

Artemis bowed stiffly, his expression as flat as his tone. "Thank you for inviting me to your lovely home," he said, his words sounding more like a formality than genuine gratitude. "You are a most gracious host."

Mrs. Nelson swatted at her son's sleeve. "We agreed that you would be pleasant at Brockhall Manor," she whispered sharply. "Now, do greet Lady Melody and Lady Elodie politely. It has been ages since you have seen them last."

Artemis cast a brief, disinterested glance in their direction before bowing. "My ladies, it is a pleasure to see you again."

"Haven't they grown to be beautiful young women?" Mrs. Nelson asked.

"I suppose so," Artemis said as he approached the large window overlooking the gardens. "May I tour your gardens? From the coach, they were rather impressive to look upon."

"You are welcome to—" Lady Dallington began, but Artemis was already out the door before she could finish her sentence.

Mrs. Nelson's lips pressed into a tight line as she watched her son go. "He is trying, but he is far more interested in botany than the marriage mart," she confessed.

"With any luck, he will find a young woman that shares his passion," Lady Dallington said kindly before shifting to face her daughters. "Girls, would you be so kind as to give Artemis a tour of the gardens?"

"But what about the dancing master?" Elodie asked.

"The lessons will have to wait. We must attend to our guests," Lady Dallington responded.

Wesley stepped forward, offering an arm to each of the sisters. "It would be my privilege to escort you to the gardens."

Elodie placed her hand on his with a playful smile. "I am unsure what is more exciting—dancing or looking at plants."

Melody took his other arm, and Wesley led them towards

the manor's rear. A footman opened the door and discreetly followed them outside, standing watch on the veranda.

As they strolled down one of the gravel paths, Elodie glanced around with a hint of concern. "Where do you suppose Artemis went?"

Melody scanned the surrounding gardens. "Not sure, but the gardens are extensive."

Elodie went to sit down on a bench. "I think I will rest while you search for him," she said. She settled in, and no sooner, a goat emerged from the bushes and hopped onto the bench, curling comfortably in her lap.

Wesley stared at the goat in surprise. "Where did that goat come from?"

Elodie lightly stroked the animal's fur. "This is Matilda, the Warrens' goat. She has a particular fondness for this bench and tends to claim it as hers. You can't sit here without her joining in."

"Do you like goats, my lord?" Melody inquired.

Wesley hesitated, considering the question. "I do not have a strong opinion either way," he admitted. "I own goats, but I leave their care to others."

"If you are lucky, you will see Matilda perched up in a tree," Melody shared. "Just don't sit under her for too long, or you might receive an unwelcome surprise."

Wesley smiled. "I shall heed your advice."

Still petting Matilda, Elodie said, "I think it would be fun to have a pet goat. Or perhaps a miniature donkey."

"If Father won't let you get a cat, I doubt he will let you have a pet goat or a miniature donkey," Melody pointed out.

"Good point," Elodie mused. "I shall have to make do with Matilda, then."

Wesley shifted his stance towards Melody. "If you could choose any animal to be your pet, what would it be?"

Melody considered his words for a moment. "I suppose I

would like a messenger hawk. It is practical and could be quite fun."

"I would pick a unicorn," Elodie declared.

"Again, unicorns are not real," Wesley reminded her.

Elodie smiled. "We shall have to agree to disagree on this."

Melody gave him a curious look. "What of you? What animal would you choose to be a pet?"

"None," he replied. "I am content alone, and I see no need to care for an animal, especially in the home."

"That sounds rather lonely," Melody said.

Wesley grinned. "You seem to forget that my mother has two cats and they are determined to follow me everywhere. It is as if they know I am not particularly fond of them, and they take great pleasure in tormenting me."

Melody studied him briefly before asking, "Are you close with your mother?"

"We used to be quite close, but my mother has become withdrawn since my father died," Wesley responded. "She is not the same vibrant woman she once was. Her eyes always seem so sad. I'm not quite sure what I can do to help her."

"Would your sister be willing to return home to care for her?" Melody asked.

Wesley huffed, the sound laced with frustration. "Rosella does what she wants when she wants. It has been this way since she was a little girl. No one can tell her what to do."

Elodie chimed in, "I think Rosella is brave. She defies convention and works as a teacher because she wants to."

"Sometimes I think my sister has something to prove, but I cannot say what that is," Wesley admitted.

"Do we not all have something to prove to others or ourselves?" Melody asked, her gaze growing distant.

Elodie rose gracefully from the bench and began to smooth down her gown. "My lady's maid won't be pleased by the amount of goat hair on my gown."

Melody laughed. "You brought it upon yourself by sitting on Matilda's favorite bench."

"It was worth it, though," Elodie replied.

As she uttered her words, Artemis appeared from behind a hedge, his expression as solemn as ever. "Who is responsible for your gardens?" he demanded.

Melody furrowed her brow at his sudden question. "The gardeners, I suppose."

"I need a name," Artemis insisted, his voice firm. "Some fool planted butterfly weed right next to impatiens."

Elodie gasped dramatically, covering her mouth with her hand. "The horror!" she exclaimed. "I understand why that is wrong, but I doubt my sister does. Will you kindly explain it to her in the most layman's terms?"

Artemis pressed his lips together. "These plants may attract pollinators, but they have different growing needs. One thrives in full sun, while the other prefers shade. It is a basic gardening principle that should never be overlooked."

With a bob of her head, Elodie said, "We can't let such an error stand. I will speak to the head gardener at once and see to it that this grievous mistake is corrected."

Artemis nodded approvingly. "Thank you," he said before continuing down the garden path, his focus already shifting back to the plants around him.

Watching him go, Wesley turned to the ladies with a bemused smile. "Which one of you was responsible for inviting Mr. Artemis Nelson to this house party?"

Melody groaned softly. "That would be me," she admitted. "When we were children, Artemis and I would play together. My mother has this misguided notion that our childhood friendship might blossom into something more."

Wesley chuckled. "I must say, you two would make quite the pair."

"As long as you don't put butterfly weed next to impatiens," Elodie quipped. "I am fairly certain even Parliament would grant a divorce on those grounds."

Melody placed her hand on her hip. "Are you two quite done?"

Elodie exchanged a mischievous glance with Wesley. "I am, are you?"

Wesley decided to take pity on Melody. "I am, as well," he said. "Since Mr. Nelson is nowhere to be found, should we go inside?"

"Yes, I would greatly appreciate that," Melody remarked. Without waiting for Wesley to offer his arm, she headed towards the manor at a brisk pace.

Coming to stand next to him, Elodie said, "Give her time."

He turned his attention towards Elodie. "Pardon?"

"Melody doesn't like to be teased, but she will come around," Elodie responded. "But, if you don't mind, we should go inside before we give my mother any matchmaking ideas."

Wesley tipped his head in acknowledgment as he offered his arm.

Chapter Five

With quick, determined steps, Melody descended the grand staircase, her gaze fixed ahead as she made her way towards the rear of the manor. She had one goal in mind: escape, if only for a little while, from the infuriating Lord Emberly. She wanted to be alone, a chance to clear her thoughts without his incessant presence. Despite being a spy, the man seemed to have nothing better to do than to shadow her every move. Surely, he had more pressing matters to attend to.

As she approached the stables, she sighed in relief, grateful that she had not encountered anyone along the way. The familiar scent of hay and manure greeted her as she pushed open the heavy stable door, bringing with it a sense of comfort. But that comfort was short-lived. She heard the unmistakable sound of Lord Emberly's voice reach her ears, and she froze, her heart sinking.

Of course, he was here.

Curiosity curbed her instinct to flee, and despite herself, she ventured further into the stables, her booted footsteps echoing softly in the quiet. There he was, saddling his horse with a practiced ease that surprised her. Why was he performing such a menial task himself? Did he not know that the grooms were there for precisely this reason?

Lord Emberly tightened the strap on his saddle but paused as he saw her. A slow, knowing smile spread across his face. "Lady Melody, I was wondering when you would join me for a ride."

Taken back by his assumption, she crossed her arms over her chest. "I am not joining you for anything."

His smile didn't falter. "I was under the impression that you go on a ride around this time each day."

"I do," she replied curtly, "but I ride alone."

"Well, today is your lucky day," he said, his cheerful tone grating on her nerves. "You won't have to ride alone. I will accompany you."

She narrowed her eyes at him. "I do not wish for your company."

He clucked his tongue in mock disapproval. "What kind of protector would I be if I allowed you to go alone?"

Melody tilted her chin defiantly. "You, sir, are not my protector. As I have told you countless times, I can take care of myself."

"Be that as it may, I want to ensure you are safe," Lord Emberly responded with maddening calm. "If that means keeping my distance, so be it."

"You are infuriating," Melody muttered.

Lord Emberly's lips twitched. "I have been called much worse. By you, no less."

Before she could reply, the groom approached and cleared his throat. "My lady, your horse is ready," he said, gesturing to the gelding that awaited her.

"Thank you, Jack," Melody responded.

"Perfect timing," Lord Emberly remarked as he opened the stall door. "My horse is ready as well."

Biting back the sharp retort that hovered on her tongue, Melody walked over to her horse. There was no point in arguing further with Lord Emberly. He would do as he pleased regardless of her wishes. It only aggravated her more that he didn't seem to believe she could protect herself.

The groom placed a small stool by the horse, and Melody stepped up gracefully, settling into the saddle. She didn't wait for Lord Emberly. Instead, she urged her horse into a swift gallop, eager to put some distance between them. The familiar feeling of the wind whipping against her face brought a sense of freedom and exhilaration, which she cherished during her solitary rides.

But today, she wasn't alone.

Lord Emberly's horse easily kept pace with hers, his presence a constant reminder of her frustration. She reined in her horse at the top of a hill, her breath catching slightly as she took in the sweeping view of the valley below. It was a sight that never failed to stir something profound within her.

Lord Emberly came to a stop beside her, his gaze following hers. "You are a magnificent rider," he said, his voice holding a note of genuine admiration.

"You sound surprised," she remarked.

"No, nothing about you surprises me anymore," Lord Emberly said. There was something almost akin to a compliment in his words, though she couldn't be sure.

Melody kept her gaze on the horizon. "How long do you intend to stay here?"

"As long as it takes," he replied, his voice firm.

She turned her head towards him. "That doesn't answer my question."

"I suppose it is rather vague, but I must ensure you are safe."

"I am safe," she insisted.

Lord Emberly's face grew solemn, his usual teasing demeanor replaced by something much more severe. "You may think you are, but the French want you dead. And the agency can't afford to lose you."

Melody tightened her grip on her reins. "I can take care of myself. I have proven it before and will do so again—without hesitation."

"With all due respect," Lord Emberly said, his tone almost gentle, "what do you know about making hard calls when the situation demands it?"

A heavy silence fell between them before Melody spoke again, her voice quieter now. "My aunt was being abused by her husband, and I knew there was only one choice in the matter. He had to die."

Lord Emberly's eyes widened slightly in surprise. "You have killed before?"

"It was either my aunt or my uncle," Melody replied, her voice steady though the emotions churned inside of her. "I do not regret my choice, but I still am haunted by that decision."

"Taking another person's life is not something you will ever get over, but it does get easier with time," Lord Emberly said.

Melody turned towards him as she studied his face. His expression was guarded, but the way his jaw tightened told her that the memories he carried were as raw as her own. "You seem to speak from experience."

"I do," he said, his words clipped as if each one was drawn from a well of pain he had long tried to bury. For a moment, the mask he wore so well slipped, revealing a flicker of vulnerability before he quickly turned his face away.

She heard the unspoken sorrow in his tone, the kind that only someone who had been through the same harrowing ordeal could recognize. A surprising wave of empathy washed over her, and for the first time in a long while, she didn't feel so entirely alone.

"It is ironic," she said, "that we write so much to one another, yet we know nothing about each other."

"It is, but that is the nature of our work," Lord Emberly acknowledged.

"I do not contest that," Melody said, her eyes searching his. "But don't you ever get lonely? Doing what we do, always on guard, never able to share our true selves with anyone?"

Lord Emberly's gaze flickered away. "It is simpler that way," he remarked as if trying to convince himself as much as her.

Melody could see the truth in his words but also the weight they carried. And for reasons she couldn't quite explain, she felt a sudden urge to reach out to him, to offer some measure of comfort. "Will you tell me one thing about yourself that no one knows?"

Lord Emberly's brow furrowed. "And what would be the purpose of that?"

"There is no harm in getting to know one another, is there?" Melody asked. "After all, you are a guest at Brockhall Manor."

It seemed he would refuse her request for a moment, but then, to her surprise, he relented. "On occasion," he began, his voice carefully measured, "I will garden with my mother."

"You, a gardener?" Melody asked.

"I never said I was good at it," he corrected her with a faint smile. "But I do it to appease my mother. It brings her joy."

A playful grin tugged at Melody's lips. "I daresay that you and Mr. Artemis Nelson will get along quite nicely."

Lord Emberly returned her smile. "The worst part is, I agree with him. You should never plant butterfly weeds next to impatiens."

"I know very little about gardening, but I can appreciate our well-maintained gardens," Melody said.

His gaze softened as he turned the conversation back to her. "What about you? What secrets are you keeping?"

Melody huffed. "I feel like all I do is keep secrets," she confessed. "No one truly knows me because I am afraid of letting anyone in."

"That is to be expected."

"Perhaps," she murmured, "but it is hard to lie to my family. I understand why I must, but it is difficult, hiding a part of myself from them."

There was a brief pause before Lord Emberly responded. "I am most fortunate that my sister knows the truth about me. It is a comfort not having to shoulder everything alone."

His admission piqued Melody's curiosity. "How did it come to pass that Rosella became a spy?"

Lord Emberly's expression shifted, his face becoming unreadable once more. "That is not my story to share, and that is all I will say on the matter."

Recognizing the firmness in his voice, Melody decided to let the matter drop… for now. "Shall we return to Brockhall Manor now?"

"We can, but only after you tell me one thing about yourself that no one knows," Lord Emberly said.

Melody took a moment to consider her response. "I can brew my own beer. Our cook taught me how to make spruce beer, and I have perfected the recipe over the years."

A flicker of amusement danced in Lord Emberly's eyes. "I shall have to try some of this beer."

"I would not get your hopes up since it is nothing special. I use loads of molasses for a sweeter taste."

Lord Emberly held her gaze. "I am sure you are not giving yourself enough credit," he said, his voice low and sincere.

The way he looked at her—his eyes filled with a quiet appreciation—unnerved Melody, stirring an unfamiliar sensation within her. She felt an overwhelming urge to flee, to distance herself from whatever was happening between them. She didn't need—or want—his approval. They weren't even friends. So why did she feel this inexplicable desire to learn more about him?

This would not do. She needed to keep Lord Emberly at arm's length. It was safer that way—for both of them.

In a steady voice, Melody said, "I will race you back to the stables." Without waiting for his response, she kicked her horse into a gallop, the wind whipping through her hair as she sped away, determined to leave her confusing emotions—and Lord Emberly—far behind.

As Wesley led Melody from the stables, a comfortable silence settled between them, each retreating into their own thoughts. He couldn't help but find Melody intriguing, though he would never dare admit it—to her or anyone else. Her beauty was undeniable, but it wasn't what captivated him. Her sharp intellect and the way her mind worked genuinely fascinated him. Melody was far more than others perceived her to be, a fact that was partly his doing. He had been the one to recruit her into this shadowed life, and with that thought came the familiar pang of guilt. He knew all too well the sacrifices required of an agent of the Crown, the loneliness that could seep into one's soul.

They had just reached the back of the manor when the door swung open, and Elodie slipped out with a dramatic wave of her hand. "It is too late for me, but save yourself," she declared, her tone exaggeratedly grave.

Melody dropped her hand from Wesley's arm, her brows knitting in concern. "What is wrong?"

Elodie began to stride down the garden path. "Lord Belview has arrived and he is as vexing as ever. I am leaving, and I might never return."

"Where will you go?" Melody asked, her tone half-amused, half-concerned.

"Does it matter?" Elodie asked, speaking over her shoulder. "I will create a new life for myself in the woodlands, where only the creatures will be my friends."

Wesley turned to Melody, his voice low as he inquired, "Dare I ask what this is about?"

Melody's lips quirked. "Elodie has quite the aversion to Lord Belview—"

"An aversion?" Elodie interrupted, spinning around to face them. "No, it is far more than that. Lord Belview used to torment me relentlessly when we were younger. Do you remember when we played hide and seek?"

"We were young—" Melody started.

Elodie threw her hands up in the air, her expression one of exasperation. "I would hide, but Lord Belview would never 'seek.' Once, I was up in a tree for hours until my nursemaid found me."

Wesley chuckled, the image of a young Elodie stranded in a tree amusing him more than it should have. "I do believe Lord Belview has changed his ways. We studied at Oxford together and never once played hide and seek."

"A cheetah cannot change its spots," Elodie stated.

A deep, familiar chuckle came from the doorway, and Wesley turned to see Lord Belview leaning against the door frame, a smile playing on his lips. "What nonsense are you spouting, Elodie?"

Elodie tilted her chin, meeting his gaze with defiance. "I am only telling the truth."

"*Your* truth," Lord Belview corrected, "is a slightly different version of the actual truth."

Wesley approached his friend, extending a hand in greeting. "Belview, it is good to see you. It has been far too long since we last saw one another."

"It has," Lord Belview agreed, his tone more serious. "My father is in poor health, and I have been running the estate in his place."

"I am sorry to hear that," Wesley acknowledged.

Melody stepped forward, her voice gentle. "Were your parents able to accompany you on the journey?"

Lord Belview shook his head. "No, but they insisted I come. I hope that is not an inconvenience."

"Not at all—" Melody began to assure him, only to be cut off by Elodie muttering, "Yes."

Lord Belview's eyes sparkled with amusement as he turned his gaze back to Elodie. "Please don't say that. I came all this way to see you, Elodie. I wouldn't dare deny you the pleasure of my company."

"Well, you have seen me. You may go home now," Elodie said.

Melody shot her sister a pointed look. "You are being rude to Anthony. He must be tired after his long journey."

"Thank you for your concern, but the journey was rather uneventful," Lord Belview said. "However, I could use a drink."

Wesley seized the opportunity to lighten the mood. "I could use a drink, as well."

"There is a drink cart in the drawing room," Melody offered. "I would show you there, but Elodie and I need to start dressing for dinner."

"No, I am running away to start a new life with woodland creatures," Elodie huffed.

Melody grinned, clearly used to her sister's dramatics. "Yes, but if you run away, there won't be any biscuits for you to eat."

Elodie paused, considering her sister's words. After a moment, she sighed dramatically. "I suppose I could stay for a little while longer."

After the ladies disappeared into the manor, Wesley lifted his brow at Lord Belview. "Should I even ask what is happening between you and Lady Elodie?"

Lord Belview held up his hands defensively. "Absolutely nothing, I assure you. But Elodie seems to find my mere presence to be insulting."

"Well, if it is any consolation, Lady Melody feels the same way about me," Wesley confessed with a wry smile.

"At least I am in good company, then," Lord Belview quipped. "Let us get that drink, shall we?"

As they strolled down the corridor, Wesley glanced at his friend and asked, "How is your brother?"

Lord Belview sighed heavily, his frustration evident. "Stephen is still as useless as ever. I honestly don't know if he will ever grow up."

"Give him time," Wesley suggested, hoping to offer encouragement.

"That is all I have given him, and he never fails to disappoint," Lord Belview shared with a pained expression. "I do worry he will drive my father into an early grave if he doesn't change his ways."

Entering the drawing room, Wesley made his way to the drink cart. He picked up a crystal decanter and poured two generous glasses of brandy. "Your father is a good man," he said, handing one of the glasses to Lord Belview.

"He is," Lord Belview agreed, taking a sip. "And he doesn't deserve the heartache Stephen is causing him."

"I truly hope things improve," Wesley offered sincerely.

"You and me both, my friend," Lord Belview replied.

A tall, brown-haired woman entered the room but halted abruptly when she saw them. "Pardon me," she murmured, turning to leave.

Before she could exit, Lord Dallington strode into the room, his face lighting up with delight. "Sarah, you came," he exclaimed, his arms outstretched in welcome.

Sarah smoothed her hands nervously over her simple blue gown. "I do not know why you insisted I come. I hardly have anything suitable to wear."

"Nonsense, you look perfect," Lord Dallington reassured her. He then turned to the other men in the room. "Gentlemen, let me introduce you to my sister, Lady Sarah."

Wesley bowed respectfully. "A pleasure, my lady," he greeted.

"It is an honor to meet you," Lord Belview said.

Sarah dropped into a curtsy, her eyes flickering towards the door as if searching for an escape.

Lord Dallington walked over to the drink cart and poured himself a drink. "The ladies should be down shortly."

Sensing Sarah's discomfort, Wesley tried to put her at ease. "How are you finding Brockhall Manor, Lady Sarah?"

"It is slightly overwhelming," Sarah responded, her tone reserved, making it clear she wasn't in the mood for small talk.

Lord Dallington picked up his glass. "You will have to excuse my sister. She tends to avoid these types of social gatherings."

"It is true," Sarah admitted.

The dinner bell rang, echoing through the manor and summoning everyone to the drawing room.

Lady Dallington glided into the room, and her eyes lit up when she saw Lord Belview. "Anthony," she said warmly. "I am so pleased that you decided to come."

Lord Belview bowed slightly. "Thank you for inviting me."

"You are always welcome in our home, you know that," Lady Dallington declared with a smile. "I trust Elodie has been behaving herself?"

A smile came to Lord Belview's lips. "She behaved exactly as I anticipated."

Lady Dallington's smile faltered slightly, concern creasing her brow. "Oh, dear. That does not sound very promising."

"I assure you, Lady Elodie is a delight," Lord Belview responded.

"I think you are being far too generous in your assessment of my daughter, but thank you nonetheless," Lady Dallington said.

As the other guests filtered into the room, Wesley's attention remained fixed on the doorway. He was waiting for

Melody, driven by a sense of duty more than anything else—or so he told himself.

What felt like an eternity passed, though it was likely only moments before Melody finally appeared. She entered the drawing room, dressed in a deep, rich green gown accentuating her graceful figure. Her hair was arranged into an elegant chignon, and she looked nothing short of beautiful.

Lord Belview leaned closer to Wesley and whispered, "You are staring."

Wesley quickly averted his gaze and turned to his friend. "I was just lost in thought for a moment."

"Did those thoughts involve the lovely Lady Melody?" Lord Belview teased.

Wesley's grip tightened around his glass, his voice firm. "No. Lady Melody and I are merely acquaintances."

"Acquaintances that go on rides together," Lord Belview remarked with a knowing look.

"I would not read anything into that," Wesley insisted.

Lord Belview smirked. "Very well. I shall take you at your word."

"Thank you," Wesley said, hoping that would end the conversation.

But Lord Belview wasn't quite finished. He added in a low voice, "You could do much worse than Lady Melody. And I suspect she won't have trouble securing a suitor this Season."

"That is the least of my concerns," Wesley said, feigning indifference. But he did care, and that is what irked him the most.

Chapter Six

Melody was utterly miserable as she sat between Artemis and Lord Emberly at the grand rectangular dining table. Her placement seemed more like a punishment than anything. The lively hum of conversation filled the room, but Melody didn't feel like making idle chit-chat. She knew what was expected of her. It was her duty to converse politely with those closest to her, but tonight, that was the last thing she wanted to do, especially with these two gentlemen.

The footmen glided forward with practiced grace, placing steaming bowls of soup before the family and guests. Melody eagerly picked up her spoon, hoping that by keeping her mouth busy, she could avoid the tiresome obligation of small talk. But her plan was quickly thwarted.

Lord Emberly turned towards her and asked, "It is a fine night this evening, is it not?"

The weather? Truly? Was that the best he could come up with? It seemed so. "Yes, the weather is quite agreeable."

But Lord Emberly wasn't content to leave the conversation there. Leaning slightly closer, he lowered his voice. "I quite enjoyed our ride earlier. Perhaps we could go for another tomorrow?"

Melody inwardly groaned. The last thing she wanted to do was go on another ride with Lord Emberly. "I'm afraid I am rather busy tomorrow."

"Busy, you say?" Lord Emberly asked, his amusement evident.

She nodded quickly. "Yes, I have loads to do."

Lord Emberly, far from deterred, turned more fully towards her, his eyes sparkling with curiosity. "Dare I ask what those things are?"

Desperately grasping for an excuse, Melody blurted out, "Needlework. It has been ages since I have done so."

"Ah, yes. Needlework is of the utmost importance," Lord Emberly retorted.

Melody knew how ridiculous she sounded but wasn't about to back down. "It is," she insisted. "Every accomplished young woman is proficient at needlework."

Lord Emberly grinned. "By my calculation, needlework shouldn't take up your entire day. Surely, you will have time for a ride?"

"I'm afraid I have many other tasks to attend to. I am quite busy."

Lord Emberly's gaze softened, and he asked gently, almost teasingly, "Are you trying to avoid me, my lady?"

Melody knew there was only one thing to do, and that was to tell the truth. "Yes," she responded. "Is it so obvious?"

"Very much so."

Knowing she owed him an explanation, Melody said, "We just have spent so much time together lately and I do not want my mother to think there is anything more to it than that." She glanced at her mother, who sat at the head of the table, watching them with a keen eye.

Lord Emberly followed her gaze before saying, "It is just one ride. No harm will come from it."

Melody gave him a small smile, though her mind still raced with thoughts. Despite his reassurance, she could not shake the feeling that things were becoming more complicated than she would like.

Artemis cleared his throat, drawing Melody's attention away from her thoughts. "You enjoy flowers, do you not?" he inquired, his tone unusually earnest.

"I do," Melody replied.

"Do you have a favorite flower?" Artemis pressed.

Melody hesitated for a moment, considering her response. "I would have to say marigolds. They are bright and cheerful."

Artemis bobbed his head thoughtfully, a hint of enthusiasm creeping into his voice. "'Marigold' is an English name taken from the common name used for flowers from different genera, such as *Calendula* or *Tagetes*," he revealed. "The flower is used in reference to the Virgin Mary, hence the name 'Mary gold.'"

"That is rather interesting," Melody responded.

Artemis's eyes lit up. "Did you know there's a flower with your name in it?" he asked, leaning slightly closer as if sharing a secret. "It is the Dahlia 'Melody Gipsy.' Botanists who boarded the ships of the Spanish conquistadors discovered this remarkable flower nearly a hundred years ago."

Melody leaned to the side as a footman collected her bowl. "Did you study botany at university?"

"I did," Artemis confirmed with a proud smile. "We can learn so much from plants. Sometimes, I find myself lying beside them, simply imagining what they might be trying to tell me."

Before Melody could respond, Elodie's voice cut through the conversation from across the table. "I do something similar with chocolate. I stare at it, hoping it will reveal all its secrets. Why is it so delicious? What does it want me to feel?"

Melody fought the urge to laugh, knowing that Elodie was just being facetious, but Artemis missed the humor entirely.

"I'm not sure what chocolate might be saying, considering

the cocoa beans are ground down in the process," Artemis said.

In a mock-serious voice, Elodie leaned forward, her eyes twinkling with mischief. "I do believe the chocolate is saying, 'Drink me. Drink me.'"

Artemis blinked, clearly not amused by her playful antics. "Chocolate does not say anything."

Mrs. Nelson, sitting nearby, discreetly nudged her son's shoulder and whispered, "Behave, Son. You promised."

Artemis responded in a hushed, slightly frustrated tone, "But Elodie is being so difficult."

Melody listened to the exchange with barely concealed amusement, her lips twitching as she tried to suppress a smile. Letting anyone know how much she enjoyed this unexpected exchange would not do.

Artemis, now focusing on Elodie, asked, "Do you have a favorite flower, my lady?"

"Yes, my favorite plant is the cuckoopint," Elodie said, clearly savoring the absurdity of the name. "I just like saying that name—cuckoopint."

Artemis frowned. "The technical name for that plant is *Arum maculatum*, which is quite poisonous. I would advise caution if you ever come into contact with it."

Elodie grinned. "I like to live dangerously," she quipped.

"It is also referenced in Nicholas Culpeper's herbal book," Artemis revealed.

"Did you know that 'pint' is shortened from the word 'pintle', which means—" Elodie started to share.

Before she could finish, her mother interjected, her voice laced with exasperation. "Good heavens, Elodie, that is hardly appropriate dinner conversation. You must remember yourself."

Artemis seemed unconcerned by the subject matter. "We were merely discussing technical terms. There is no need to be embarrassed by using such words."

"Surely, there is something else you can discuss," her mother said, casting a beseeching glance at Melody.

Understanding the unspoken request, Melody dabbed the corners of her mouth with her napkin before speaking. "Has anyone read anything particularly interesting?"

Lord Belview, who had been sitting quietly, shared, "I recently finished reading *Groundwork of the Metaphysics of Morals* by Immanuel Kant."

"That is much too serious for the ladies at this table," Lord Dallington said.

Elodie lifted her brow. "I can be serious, Father."

Lord Dallington let out a slight huff of amusement. "Says the young woman who still believes in unicorns."

"Regardless, why can't I read Kant?" Elodie asked. "Are you afraid it will cause me to think too much?"

"No, I'm afraid you will start forming opinions contrary to how a young woman should think and behave," Lord Dallington replied, his tone more serious.

Her mother pressed her lips together. "Oh, dear," she murmured.

Elodie straightened in her chair, her posture rigid with defiance. "I am entitled to opinions," she challenged. "I wouldn't wish to marry a man who didn't want me to express my thoughts and desires freely."

Lord Dallington cast a wary glance around the table before responding. "We shall discuss this later… preferably in private."

Her mother smiled, albeit appearing forced. "Has anyone else read anything of note? Perhaps something a little less controversial?"

Lord Emberly tipped his head thoughtfully. "My sister convinced me to read the book by 'A Lady.' I found it to be rather enjoyable."

"We are quite the admirers of the books written by 'A Lady,'" Lady Dallington remarked.

"There is more than one?" Lord Emberly asked.

Lady Dallington laughed. "There are two," she replied. "*Sense and Sensibility* and *Pride and Prejudice*, which was recently published."

"A woman writer?" Lord Dallington scoffed. "What nonsense."

Melody shook her head subtly, knowing her father took perverse pleasure in ruffling Elodie's feathers, almost as if he relished the debates that inevitably followed.

As expected, Elodie chimed in, "Women make excellent writers. They have been writing books for years."

"They may have been writing them, but very few get published," Lord Dallington argued.

"That is only because people are afraid of a woman who knows her voice," Elodie declared.

Lord Dallington didn't look convinced. "Or perhaps it is because they find that women have nothing of substance to say."

Elodie opened her mouth, undoubtedly ready to continue the debate, but their mother spoke first. "It seems you now have two things to discuss later," she said, her tone carrying a clear warning.

Reaching for his glass, Lord Dallington said, "Very well."

As the tension slowly dissipated, Lord Emberly leaned closer to Melody and asked in a low voice, "Is it always like this?"

"Worse, my lord," Melody replied with a small smile.

A brief, comfortable silence settled over the table as the guests resumed their meal. However, it was broken when Artemis abruptly pushed back his chair, the wooden legs scraping loudly against the floor. All eyes turned towards him.

"My apologies," Artemis said, his voice weak. "I am not feeling well. I should go lie down."

Melody noticed his pale complexion and the unsteady way

he stood. Concern tightened her chest, and she instinctively half-rose from her seat, unsure how best to assist him.

Before Artemis could take a step, Lord Emberly was on his feet, moving swiftly to his side. He caught Artemis's arm with a firm grip, steadying him before he could falter. "I have you," he said firmly.

"Thank you," Artemis responded, his voice barely audible, as though even speaking required more effort than he could muster.

Lord Belview quickly came around the table, joining Lord Emberly in supporting Artemis. "We should send for the doctor," he suggested.

Lady Dallington, her expression now filled with worry, placed her napkin down on the table with deliberate care. "I shall have White send for him at once," she said, rising swiftly from her seat and leaving the room.

"We will see you to your bedchamber," Lord Emberly stated. His tone brooked no argument as he and Lord Belview guided Artemis towards the door gently.

As the men carefully escorted Artemis from the room, Mrs. Nelson rose from her chair. She followed them, her worry etched on her face with every step and her hands nervously clasped as she closely watched her son.

Melody wasn't sure what she could do to help at this moment, but she knew the situation was being handled. Unfortunately, the unease in her chest would not dissipate.

Wesley sat in the drawing room, the relentless ticking of the long clock in the corner filling the heavy silence. The room had fallen into a contemplative hush as everyone retreated into their thoughts, anxiously awaiting news about Artemis. The doctor had arrived what felt like ages ago, and the longer they waited, the more the uncertainty gnawed at Wesley's nerves.

He couldn't shake the uneasy feeling that had taken root in his mind. How had Artemis grown so sick, so suddenly? The notion that he might have been poisoned flittered through Wesley's thoughts. It was far-fetched, but impossible to dismiss entirely.

Wesley glanced across the room at Melody and Elodie, who sat side by side on the settee. Melody's brow was furrowed in concern, and Elodie's usual vivacity had dimmed. The gravity of the situation had stifled any desire for conversation. All anyone could think about was Artemis.

Lady Dallington stepped into the room, her presence drawing everyone's attention. "Artemis should be just fine," she announced. "Doctor Anderson believes he may have accidentally poisoned himself while studying the plants in the gardens."

A collective sigh of relief rippled through the room, though Wesley's unease lingered.

Melody spoke up. "Does the doctor know which plant could have caused Artemis's symptoms?"

Lady Dallington shook her head slightly. "He said it could have been any number of plants in the gardens or a combination of them," she replied. "The most important thing is that Artemis is resting comfortably."

"We did see Artemis touching and sniffing the plants," Melody remarked, her tone thoughtful.

With a faint smile returning to her lips, Elodie quipped, "And this is exactly why I do not study plants."

Lord Belview, standing by the window, let out a chuckle. "Yes, that is the reason," he teased, glancing at Elodie.

"Regardless, we must focus on the positive," Lady Dallington said, clasping her hands together. "Mr. and Mrs. Nelson are with their son, as is the vicar."

"Why is Mr. Bramwell here?" Melody asked.

"I sent for him on Mrs. Nelson's behalf," Lady Dallington informed them. "They wanted Mr. Bramwell to pray over their son."

"I haven't met Mr. Bramwell yet, but I doubt he could ever live up to Lord Wythburn. He was our vicar for as long as I could remember," Elodie said.

Lady Dallington's expression softened with understanding. "Yes, but Lord Wythburn has moved on, and so must we," she encouraged. "I want you to be nice to Mr. Bramwell when you see him."

Elodie feigned innocence. "How else would I greet him? He is a man of God, after all."

Lady Dallington didn't quite look convinced, but she let the matter pass. "Just be on your best behavior."

Wesley caught Melody's eyes across the room, and the unspoken question in her gaze mirrored his own concerns. Did she suspect there was more to Artemis's sudden illness? He needed to speak to her, but not in front of the others.

Melody must have had the same thought because she stood and smoothed her gown. "It is late," she said. "I think I shall collect a book from the library and retire for the evening."

Wesley seized the opportunity. "That is a fine idea. May I accompany you to the library?"

"Yes, if you would like," Melody replied.

He crossed the room, extending his arm to her. She took it, and together they quietly exited the drawing room. As they walked down the dimly lit corridor, Melody leaned in closer, her voice barely above a whisper. "Do you think Artemis was poisoned?"

"I don't rightly know, but I do believe it is possible," Wesley said.

"If Artemis was indeed poisoned, what would be the reason?" Melody asked.

Wesley shrugged. "I cannot think of one. However, I can't help but think that perhaps you were the intended target."

Melody shook her head. "I truly doubt that."

"Even so," Wesley urged, his voice firm, "if I were you, I would trust no one, not even your servants, until we know more."

"My household staff is loyal to me," Melody stated.

He lifted his brow. "Then how would you explain what happened to Artemis?"

Melody hesitated, her confidence wavering. "We don't know for certain that he was poisoned. The doctor might be right. It could have been an accident while he was examining the plants."

"Do you truly believe that?" Wesley asked.

"It seems much more likely than someone in my household staff trying to kill me," Melody replied.

"I find it utterly unbelievable that a man who has studied botany would accidentally poison himself."

"It does seem rather unlikely, but, as I have said before, I tend to deal in facts."

As she spoke, Mr. Bramwell appeared at the end of the corridor, his eyes lighting up as they fell on Melody. Or was that just Wesley's imagination? "May I have a word, Lady Melody?" the vicar asked.

Melody slipped her arm off Wesley's and nodded. "You may," she replied.

Mr. Bramwell cast Wesley an expectant look, clearly hoping for privacy, but Wesley had no intention of leaving. Not when he suspected that Melody's life could be in danger.

A flicker of annoyance passed through Mr. Bramwell's eyes before he shifted his attention back to Melody. "I wanted to see how you were faring," he said, his tone compassionate.

"I am well, thank you," Melody responded.

Mr. Bramwell moved closer to her, still maintaining a

respectful distance. "It is understandable to be alarmed when someone falls ill so suddenly."

"I truly appreciate your concern, but I am confident that Artemis is in capable hands," Melody said. "Thank you for coming when you did. I am certain your presence provides great comfort to Artemis and his parents."

Mr. Bramwell smiled. "It is the least I can do for you and your family. If there is anything you require, please let me know."

"I will. Thank you," Melody said.

With a brief glance at Wesley, Mr. Bramwell murmured his goodbyes and offered a polite bow.

As the vicar walked away, Wesley's eyes followed him, a flicker of doubt crossing his mind. He couldn't quite pin down what it was about the man that unsettled him.

Melody, however, seemed to have no such reservations. "Shall we adjourn to the library for that book?"

Wesley tipped his head in agreement, and they made their way towards the library. Once inside, Melody approached the bookshelf, her fingers grazing the spines before selecting a book seemingly at random.

"Goodnight, Lord Emberly," Melody said as she turned to leave.

He quickly stepped forward, his hand outstretched to stop her. "Allow me to walk you to your bedchamber."

"No, you won't," Melody responded, her voice taking on a firmer edge. "If you did such a thing, then people would talk."

"I don't care what people say. I only care about keeping you safe," Wesley insisted.

Melody squared her shoulders. "I can assure you that I am safe in my bedchamber."

Wesley wasn't ready to back down. "If Artemis was poisoned—"

"We don't know that for certain," Melody interrupted.

"... but if he was, then you must be overly cautious," Wesley pressed on. "Besides, you are my responsibility—"

Melody's eyes flashed with anger as she cut him off. "I am no one's responsibility but my own."

"I am just trying to keep you safe. Surely, you must know that," Wesley remarked.

Some of the anger faded from her eyes, though not entirely. "I do know that, but how far do you intend to do so?"

Wesley hesitated, knowing how absurd his next words would sound but feeling compelled to say them anyway. "I would marry you if I had to."

Melody's eyes widened in shock. "Are you mad?" she whispered fiercely. "Do not say such things, especially with my mother under the same roof."

"I am in earnest."

"No, you aren't," Melody countered.

But the more Wesley thought about it, the more the idea made sense. "If we were married, I could protect you all the time, and you could continue working as a spy."

Melody gave him an exasperated look. "I am not going to marry you. Quite frankly, you are the last person I would ever consider marrying."

"I am an earl," Wesley pointed out.

"That doesn't mean much to me," Melody responded. "I want to marry for love or not at all."

Frustration flared in Wesley, and he ran a hand through his hair, struggling to find the right words. "This could be a solution to all of our problems."

"No, this is a solution to *your* problems, not mine," Melody said, her voice unwavering.

"Just be reasonable—" Wesley began, but Melody immediately cut him off.

"Me, be reasonable?" she asked. "You are the one proposing marriage as if it is some business arrangement. And, just for the record, your proposal was poorly done."

Wesley knew he had not approached the topic correctly but still believed it was a practical solution. He could protect her in ways he couldn't as just a friend.

"If you will excuse me, I have had enough foolishness for one night," Melody declared as she turned to leave.

"Just think about what I have said," Wesley urged.

Melody pressed her lips together. "I will not think on it," she replied. "It would be best to pretend that this conversation never happened."

"But it did happen."

"What happened?" Melody asked, her tone light and airy. "See how easy that is?"

"You are being impossible," he muttered under his breath.

In a steady, calm voice, Melody said, "You may think that you want to marry me, but you know nothing about me. How do you know we would even suit?"

"I know enough about you to admire you," Wesley responded earnestly.

A sad smile came to Melody's lips. "I want more than to be admired," she said. "Goodnight, my lord."

"Wesley," he corrected gently. "You have more than earned the right to call me by my given name."

"Then you must call me by mine," Melody said.

Wesley reached for her hand and brought it up to his lips. "Goodnight, Melody," he murmured, the name slipping from his lips with a familiarity that felt oddly comforting.

Melody's eyes searched his as if trying to decipher the emotions behind them.

With some reluctance, he lowered their hands and released hers. "Be sure to lock your door behind you," he advised.

"You need not worry," Melody said. "I sleep with a pistol under my pillow."

"Doesn't everyone?" he joked, feeling the need to lighten the mood.

Melody's lips twitched slightly. "Goodnight, Wesley," she replied, taking a step back.

Wesley didn't know what had come over him, but he found he wasn't quite ready to say goodnight. But it was the right—and honorable—thing to do. "I hope you sleep well, my lady," he said with a slight bow.

She dropped into a curtsy before turning to leave the room.

Even after Melody had departed, Wesley's eyes remained fixed on the door. A tangle of conflicting emotions churned within him. A small part of him wished Melody would agree to the marriage, if only to keep her safe. But as much as he wanted to believe that was the only reason, he couldn't deny there was something more—a feeling he wasn't yet ready to confront.

Chapter Seven

With the morning sun streaming through the windows, Melody sat at her writing desk, her fingers absentmindedly tracing the edges of the coded message before her. She was so close to deciphering it; she was sure of that. Yet, despite her determination, her thoughts were straying from what lay in front of her. Instead, her mind kept wandering back to Wesley. It was infuriating. He was a distraction, a nuisance, so why did she allow him to occupy any space in her thoughts?

She shook her head, frustrated with herself. She needed to focus. She was a spy, not a love-craved debutante. Lives depended on her ability to crack and replicate this code to confound the French. Unfortunately, no matter how hard she tried, Wesley's face kept creeping into her mind, breaking her concentration.

Melody sighed deeply and was about to tuck the coded message into the desk's top drawer when something caught her eye. A pattern she hadn't noticed before emerged from the seemingly random letters. Her heart skipped a beat. She quickly placed the paper back on the desk and reached for the quill to transcribe the message:

I
AM
COMING
FOR
YOU

Melody's quill slipped from her fingers as the final word formed on the page. She leaned back in her chair, her mind racing. There was no doubt in her mind that this was the message, but its meaning was a mystery that sent a chill down her spine. Who was coming, and for whom? For her? Could it possibly be a coincidence? No, she didn't believe in those.

A knock at the door pulled her from her thoughts.

"My lady, may I enter?" Lydia asked.

Melody pushed back her chair and rose, quickly locking away the coded message before crossing the room to unlock the door. "Good morning, Lydia," she greeted, opening the door wide.

Her lady's maid entered with a bemused expression. "Dare I ask why you started locking your door?"

Not wanting to reveal the true reason, Melody responded, "With guests in the manor, I thought it prudent."

"Are you concerned about a particular guest?"

"No, but it is better to be safe than sorry," Melody responded, knowing how ridiculous she must sound to Lydia.

Fortunately, Lydia didn't press the issue but moved towards the wardrobe instead. "Shall we dress you for the day?"

"I think that is a fine idea."

Lydia selected a pale green gown and held it up for her inspection. "Will this do?"

"It will," Melody said as she removed her nightgown.

Once dressed, Melody sat down at the dressing table and removed her cap on top of her head. Lydia picked up a brush and began arranging her hair into an elegant chignon.

As Lydia stepped back to admire her handiwork, she remarked, "You seem troubled this morning, my lady."

"Do I?" Melody asked, feigning innocence.

"Is everything all right?"

Melody rose and turned to face her lady's maid. "Yes, everything is just fine. I was merely woolgathering."

A knowing smile came to Lydia's lips. "Were you thinking about Lord Emberly?"

"Heavens, no!" Melody exclaimed, a little too quickly. "He is the absolute last person I would think of."

Lydia put her hands up in front of her in mock surrender, her smile widening. "My apologies," she said, though her words lacked sincerity.

Melody crossed the room to her bed, slipped her hand under her pillow, and retrieved the small pistol she had started keeping there. She held it at her side as she turned back to Lydia.

Lydia glanced at the gun with a curious expression. "Do you intend to practice your shooting at this early hour?"

"I do," Melody confirmed.

"Are you not concerned about waking up Lady Elodie?"

Melody glanced at the clock on the mantel. "It is almost time for breakfast. My sister should be awake for the day."

"Very well," Lydia said, tidying the room as Melody made her way to the door.

As she stepped out of the bedchamber, Melody slipped the pistol into the folds of her gown. She needed time to think. If someone was truly coming for her, she needed to be ready to defend herself. But what if that person was already here, within the walls of the manor?

Determined to clear her mind, Melody hurried out of the main door and headed towards the side of the manor where her servants had set up targets for her shooting practice. She positioned herself in front of one of the targets and aimed, firing a shot that hit dead center.

A footman stepped forward and asked, "Would you like me to reload your pistol, my lady?"

Melody handed the weapon to him without a word, her thoughts still occupied by the message she had deciphered.

Once the pistol was reloaded, the footman extended it back to her.

"Thank you," Melody acknowledged, taking the weapon from him.

As she went to aim again, something in the woodlands beyond the targets caught her eye. She turned, her grip tightening on the pistol, only to see a tall, dark-haired figure stepping out from the covers of the trees. Jasper, the Bow Street Runner, raised his hand in greeting.

Melody lowered her pistol. "Whatever are you doing here?" she asked. "I thought you had returned to London."

"I had every intention to, but Lord Winston asked me to remain here while he was on his wedding tour," Jasper explained, stepping closer. "He wanted to ensure his family remained safe, despite my many objections."

Melody felt a subtle sense of relief knowing Jasper had remained behind, but she didn't dare reveal her thoughts to him. She had to keep too many secrets, even from those she trusted. She noticed Jasper's approving gaze as he glanced at the target she had just hit.

"You are an excellent shot, my lady," he praised.

Melody waved off the compliment. "I have had plenty of practice."

Jasper turned his attention back to her. "I daresay that Lady Sarah could learn a great deal from you."

"You have done a fine job of teaching her how to handle a pistol," Melody replied, offering him a small, sincere smile.

"Yes," Jasper agreed, but his eyes showed a trace of regret. "But it is time that I pass the torch, so to speak."

"I would be happy to teach my aunt everything I know, assuming she is interested."

Jasper looked away, his expression turning serious. "Now that the immediate danger has passed, it is best for me to spend as little time as possible with her—for propriety's sake."

Her smile dimmed. "Is that what Sarah wants?"

Jasper didn't answer, instead choosing to change topics. "I heard that Mr. Nelson managed to poison himself through his carelessness last night."

Melody kept her face expressionless. "I am not entirely sure what happened."

With a lifted brow, Jasper asked, "Do you think there was something more to it than that?"

She bit her tongue, knowing that revealing her suspicions could lead to trouble. Without any real evidence, there was no point in alarming anyone.

Melody shrugged, feigning indifference. "What more could it be?"

Jasper studied her closely as if trying to discern the truth from her composed expression. "Indeed," he murmured, his tone skeptical.

Feeling uneasy under his scrutiny, Melody shifted her body slightly, putting a little more distance between them. "I should head in for breakfast," she said. "Would you care to join me?"

Jasper scoffed lightly. "A Bow Street Runner sharing your dining table? I am sure your father would have plenty to say about that."

Before Melody could respond, her sister's voice called down from above. "What are you two yammering about outside of my window?"

Melody looked up to see Elodie leaning out the window, her hair still tousled from sleep. "We are not yammering," she retorted.

"Regardless, I do hereby declare that you cannot practice shooting until after breakfast," Elodie exclaimed. "I nearly had a heart attack when the pistol was discharged."

"You should have been out of bed already," Melody countered.

Jasper cleared his throat, drawing Melody's attention back to him. He subtly pointed towards the manor, and Melody turned to see Wesley approaching, his expression stern and his gaze fixed intently on Jasper.

Wesley stopped a short distance away, his eyes narrowing slightly as he looked Jasper up and down. "Who are you?" he asked, his tone clipped.

Melody shook her head, exasperated. "You are in a fine mood this morning, my lord," she remarked dryly. She gestured towards Jasper. "This is Jasper. He is a Bow Street Runner my brother hired to watch over us."

"For what purpose?" Wesley asked.

In a low voice, Melody replied, "He was hired to protect my aunt from her abusive husband."

Realization dawned on Wesley's face, and his expression softened slightly. "My apologies," he said, his tone more measured. "I found it disconcerting that you were speaking to a man that I was not acquainted with."

Jasper inclined his head politely. "It is a pleasure to meet you, my lord."

"You know who I am?" Wesley asked.

An amused look came to Jasper's face. "I make it my business to know all about the guests staying at Brockhall Manor."

Wesley shifted his gaze to Melody. "Why didn't you wait for me to escort you outside?"

"There was no need. I did not think I needed an escort in my own gardens," she replied. "Besides, I have a pistol."

Wesley's expression darkened with disapproval. "You think you are safe…" He trailed off, his voice dropping to a tense whisper. "May I speak to you privately?"

From above, Elodie chimed in, "Don't go. I was just starting to enjoy the show."

Melody glanced up to see her sister munching on a biscuit

as she leaned out the window. "Where did you get that biscuit?"

"I keep one on my nightstand for situations like this," Elodie replied with a grin.

Jasper chuckled softly. "If you will excuse me, I have matters to attend to," he said, bowing slightly before turning to leave.

Wesley reached for Melody's arm, guiding her a short distance away from the manor before releasing her with a grim look. "You are being too careless with your safety."

"A little louder, please!" Elodie shouted from her perch.

Melody bit her lip to suppress a smile, but it was a losing battle. Wesley, however, was far from amused by her sister's antics. "You can't go traipsing around—"

"I am not traipsing around," Melody interrupted, placing a hand on her hip. "I merely stepped outside to practice my shooting."

"That was foolishness on your part," Wesley stated bluntly.

"You do not get to have an opinion on the matter, my lord," she shot back. "I will do what I want, when I want."

"That is a sure way to get yourself killed," Wesley said, his frustration evident. "And I won't allow it."

Melody's brow arched. "You won't allow it?" she repeated back slowly.

Wesley held his ground, his expression resolute. "I won't. From now on, you will listen to what I have to say."

"Are you sure you want to try to order me around when I have a pistol in my hand?" Melody asked, bringing her pistol up.

He reached out and gently pressed down the pistol, lowering it back to her side. "You are the most maddening woman I have ever known."

"Thank you," Melody replied.

"It wasn't a compliment."

Melody was tired of this conversation. Wesley had no right

to order her around. Without saying another word, she turned on her heel and headed towards the manor.

Wesley watched as Melody walked away, knowing he had reacted poorly. He shouldn't have yelled at her, but his frustration and fear had gotten the better of him. Melody was far too reckless with her safety, and it was his duty to keep her safe. But could he fulfill that duty when she resisted him at every turn?

He should just let her walk away and give them both time to calm down. Instead, he found himself following her towards the manor.

"Melody," he called after her.

She kept walking, ignoring him.

He raised his voice, more insistent. "Melody!"

At last, she stopped but didn't turn around. "Yes, my lord?" she responded, her voice curt.

Wesley quickened his pace until he was in front of her, forcing her to meet his gaze. "It is Wesley, if you don't mind," he said, the sharpness in his voice softening. "I'm sorry."

Melody crossed her arms over her chest, her expression unreadable. "For what?" she asked, her voice laced with a challenge.

Wesley winced inwardly, knowing she wasn't going to make this easy. "I'm sorry for yelling at you."

"Are you also sorry for ordering me around when you had no right to?" Melody asked.

"You must understand. It is for your own good," Wesley replied, frustration edging into his voice.

Melody let out a huff, clearly unimpressed. "That didn't sound like an apology," she said.

"Melody—"

Before he could finish, she uncrossed her arms and moved to brush past him. He reached out and gently grasped her arm. "I can't lose another agent," he said in a low voice.

Melody gave him a curious look. "Another agent?"

Wesley nodded, the weight of past memories heavy on his shoulders. "Yes. I was assigned to protect another agent before you, and she was murdered."

Compassion crept into Melody's eyes. "May I ask what happened?"

No.

He didn't want to tell anyone.

Wesley hesitated, the memory still too raw, too painful. He didn't want to talk about it or revisit the darkness that had haunted him since. But he knew he owed her some explanation. "The details are not important," he finally said, his voice tight. "Dinah is dead. That is all that you need to know."

Melody shook her head. "You are never going to let me in, are you?"

"That is amusing, coming from you," Wesley replied. "You have kept me at arm's length since I arrived here."

"That is only because you are making a nuisance of yourself," Melody shot back, her tone defensive.

Wesley held her gaze. "I want you to trust me."

"Trust is to be earned," Melody countered. "And you have given me no reason to trust you."

The worst part was that he knew Melody wasn't entirely wrong. He had kept a part of himself hidden from her—from everyone. He gestured towards a bench on a nearby path. "Will you sit with me for a moment?"

Melody glanced towards the manor, uncertainty clouding her expression. "We should be going in to breakfast."

"It won't take long," Wesley encouraged.

After a brief pause, Melody relented and walked over to the bench. She sat on the far edge, leaving a significant gap between them, as if still wary of him. Wesley took a deep breath, knowing he needed to open up, even a little, to gain her trust. He needed her to understand the gravity of the situation they were in.

"Dinah was an agent much like you," Wesley began, his voice tinged with sorrow. "She deciphered enemy codes, just as you do, until one day, she was found dead in her bedchamber."

"How did she die?" Melody asked.

Wesley took a deep breath before revealing, "She was found alone in her bed. The door was locked, the windows were closed and there were no marks on her body."

"Then how do you know she was murdered?"

"Dinah was thirty years old and in perfect health," Wesley replied. "The doctors claimed she passed away in her sleep, but I do not believe so. I think she was poisoned."

Melody arched an eyebrow, her skepticism evident. "Did the coroner do an investigation?"

"Yes, but he came to the same conclusion as the doctors," Wesley replied. "But Dinah's death was eerily similar to two other agents who have also died in the past few years."

"It could be a coincidence," Melody suggested, though her tone lacked conviction.

Wesley shot her a disbelieving look. "Do you believe in coincidences?"

"No, I do not," she replied with a shake of her head. "Which is why I have a problem." She frowned. "I deciphered the code that was sent to me this morning."

He straightened in his seat. "What did it say?"

In a steady voice, Melody replied, "*I am coming for you.*"

Wesley leaned back, his mind racing through all the possibilities. Someone was coming for Melody, and he had a sinking feeling that whoever it was might already be among them, watching, waiting for the perfect time to strike. He could see that Melody was trying to remain brave, but there was a flicker of fear in her eyes that she couldn't completely hide.

"It will be all right," he said, though he wasn't sure who he was trying to convince—her or himself.

"How?" Melody asked. "We don't know who is coming or when. What if the person is already here and poisoned Artemis by mistake?"

"We don't know anything for certain, but I think it would be best if you left Brockhall Manor," he said, his mind working quickly. "We could go to my estate, where my staff is loyal to me."

Melody reared back. "I am not leaving my home."

"It isn't safe for you here," he argued.

"Why do you think the person wouldn't follow me to your estate?" Melody asked. "Besides, my reputation would be ruined if I left with you."

"Not if we married," Wesley suggested, the words slipping out before he could stop them.

Melody rolled her eyes. "Not this again," she muttered.

But Wesley wasn't ready to let it go. He knew his suggestion was unconventional, even absurd, but it was the only solution that made sense to him. He needed to protect her. The only way to do that was to keep her close. He just had to find a way to make her see that.

Wesley shifted in his seat to face her, his expression serious. "I will not stand back and let anything bad happen to you. I will protect you."

"Wesley—" she began, but her words were abruptly cut off when a goat suddenly jumped onto the bench beside her, its head nestling comfortably in her lap.

Wesley tried to push the goat off the bench, but the animal responded with a loud bleat of protest, clearly unappreciative of his efforts.

"Oh, you can't push Matilda off," Melody said, her tone light. "This is her bench."

"How can a goat claim a bench?" Wesley asked.

Melody shrugged. "I don't make the rules."

"But you let the goat dictate your actions?" Wesley countered.

"The goat was here before me."

Wesley couldn't believe he was having this conversation, especially when far more pressing matters were at hand. He decided to cut through the nonsense and get to the point. "Marry me, Melody."

"No."

"No?" Wesley repeated. "You haven't even considered it."

Melody kept her gaze fixed ahead of her, her voice calm but firm. "We will find another way."

"There is no other way," he insisted.

"Then we aren't very good spies," Melody said. "I am not going to enter a marriage of convenience. It wouldn't be fair to either of us."

Wesley looked heavenward as he tried to calm his anger. She was being so stubborn, and he was determined to make her see reason. He would get Melody to marry him if it was the last thing he did.

Melody shifted her gaze towards him. "I know you think you are doing what is right, but I won't let you throw your life away for me."

"I am an agent of the Crown. That is where my duty lies," Wesley said. "You are my responsibility—"

She cut him off with a glare. "I swear if you say that one more time, I will shoot you."

"It is merely the truth."

As if to emphasize Melody's point, the goat turned its head and let out a loud bleat, almost as if it were agreeing with her.

Melody grinned. "The goat has deemed you unworthy to sit on her bench."

"You speak goat now?"

"I do."

Wesley carefully shifted the goat away from him before rising to his feet. He dusted off the stray goat fur from his trousers. "I am beginning to hate goats."

Melody covered Matilda's ears. "Do not let Matilda hear you say that."

The back door of the manor opened, and Lady Dallington stepped out into the gardens. Her eyes landed on them, and she headed towards them. "There you two are," she said. "It is time for breakfast."

Wesley wondered why Lady Dallington hadn't sent a servant to relay that message, but he didn't dare question it. "Thank you, my lady," he responded.

Lady Dallington stopped a short distance away, her eyes twinkling with amusement. "You two have been spending a considerable amount of time together. It is very encouraging," she mused with a smile. "Come along. I am calling a family meeting and Lord Emberly is welcome to join us."

Melody gently moved the goat to the side before standing. "What is this family meeting about?"

"You shall have to find out for yourself," Lady Dallington responded before turning on her heel and heading back towards the manor.

Wesley offered his arm to Melody. "May I escort you inside?"

She accepted his arm, and they followed Lady Dallington into the manor. Once inside, Melody leaned in close, her voice a hushed whisper. "Be careful. I do believe my mother is attempting to play matchmaker with us."

"I am not opposed."

"But I am," Melody said firmly.

They entered the dining room, where Wesley pulled out a chair for Melody before taking the seat next to her. Across from them, Elodie was meticulously buttering a piece of toast.

Lady Dallington clasped her hands in front of her at the

head of the table. "I have called this family meeting because today will be spent with the dancing master."

Elodie groaned in protest. "I do not like this family meeting."

"Nor do I," Melody said. "I have things I must see to."

Lady Dallington held up a hand to silence their complaints. "The dancing master has traveled a long way, and you both must become proficient dancers."

"But I will never be a proficient dancer," Elodie argued. "Why can I not be an *okayish* dancer?"

"Do you not wish to get married?" Lady Dallington asked pointedly.

Elodie held up her toast. "If my husband only cares about my dancing abilities, then he is not the man for me."

Lord Belview's voice came from the doorway. "I can personally attest that Lady Elodie is a remarkable dancer. Do you remember the time you read about the dance that was supposed to summon rain?"

Elodie huffed. "Good heavens, I can't believe you are bringing that up. I was ten."

"Yes, but you danced in that circle all morning until it finally started raining," Lord Belview said, approaching the dining table.

Elodie did not look the least bit amused. "It is England. It rains all the time."

"Or perhaps it rained because of your dance," Lord Belview teased. "I guess we will never know."

Taking a bite of her toast, Elodie narrowed her eyes at Lord Belview, as if to silence him with her eyes.

Lady Dallington took control of the conversation by saying, "If the gentlemen have no objections, they are welcome to join my daughters in their dancing lesson today."

Wesley resisted the urge to groan. The thought of dancing for hours was far from appealing, but it would allow him to keep a close eye on Melody, which was reason enough.

Lord Belview, on the other hand, seemed more than willing. "I'd be delighted," he said. "I have been told that I am quite the accomplished dancer."

"By whom, your mother?" Elodie quipped.

Lord Belview's grin widened. "This may come as a surprise to you, but loads of women prefer my company. It is a burden I must bear."

Elodie placed her toast back on her plate, wiping her hands clean of breadcrumbs. "I am not one of those women."

"Elodie!" Lady Dallington exclaimed, her words holding a reprimand. "Be nice to Anthony. He is our guest, after all."

Lord Belview's grin didn't falter as he held Elodie's gaze for a moment longer, a playful glint in his eyes before she looked away, clearly uninterested in engaging further.

The footmen stepped forward and placed plates of food on the table. In a swift, almost instinctive motion, Wesley switched plates with Melody.

When he noticed the curious looks from those around the table, Wesley offered a quick explanation. "I preferred the portions on Lady Melody's plate."

"But they appear to be the same portions," Elodie pointed out.

Melody spoke up. "They aren't," she said. "Thank you for switching plates with me, my lord."

As they began to eat, Wesley couldn't help but feel a twinge of unease. He hoped this wouldn't be his last meal, but if it were, the knowledge that he had protected Melody, even in this small way, made it worth the risk.

Chapter Eight

Melody sat heavily in the chair and rubbed her tired, aching feet. The hours of dancing had weighed on her, and she wasn't sure how much more she could endure. There were far more pressing matters demanding her attention, yet here she was, trapped in a seemingly endless dance lesson.

Wesley took a seat beside her and offered an approving nod. "You are a remarkable dancer," he said, his voice warm with admiration.

"Thank you, and so are you," Melody responded, straightening in her chair despite her fatigue. "But how much longer do you think Mr. Durand will keep us here?"

Looking at the long clock in the corner, Wesley replied, "I think we have only just begun."

She groaned, leaning back in her chair. "Do not tell me that."

Wesley's expression softened with a hint of sympathy. "It is merely the truth," he said, gazing at Elodie on the dance floor. "The only good thing is the dancing master seems to focus all his attention on your sister."

Melody followed his gaze, watching as the dancing master

critiqued her sister's every move. "Elodie has never quite taken to dancing," she remarked.

"And yet you have," Wesley observed, looking back at Melody. "How do you seem to excel at everything you do?"

"That is hardly true."

Wesley gave her a pointed look, his eyebrow raised in challenge. "Name one thing you are not good at."

Melody paused, considering his words. After a moment, she replied, "I am not very good at taking a compliment."

"That is fair," Wesley conceded with a smile, "but what else?"

She sighed, her eyes drifting back to the dance floor where Elodie was now twirling in Lord Belview's arms. "I am boring."

"Pardon?"

Melody met his gaze and repeated, "I am boring."

"You are hardly boring."

"No, it is true," Melody said. "I follow the rules and do what is expected of me. Even Elodie thinks I am boring."

Wesley pressed his lips together. "You are many things, but boring is not one of them. Stubborn. Maddening. Thinking you know what is best—"

Melody spoke over him, her tone edging towards irritation. "Do you have a point, my lord?" She wasn't entirely sure whether to feel insulted or not, but she was leaning towards being insulted.

He chuckled. "I do," he replied. "You have a certain charm about you that captivates the attention of everyone around you."

Melody turned away, dismissing his words with a wave of her hand. "Now, I think you are just attempting to flatter me."

Wesley reached out, gently touching her arm to recapture her attention. "I would not say it if I did not mean it," he replied earnestly. "I find you to be irresistibly engaging and I have cherished every letter you sent me."

"Those letters mean nothing," Melody insisted.

"To you, perhaps," Wesley said, letting his hand drop from her arm. "I have kept every letter you have sent."

Melody blinked, surprised. "Why?"

A smile came to Wesley's face. "Because they came from you."

Melody stared at Wesley, trying to decipher his meaning. Their correspondence had been mostly business-coded messages with little personal sentiment. Yet, something in his eyes suggested those letters held more significance to him than she had realized.

Her thoughts were interrupted by a loud clap from the dancing master, who had appeared beside them. "Why are you not dancing?" Mr. Durand demanded.

Perhaps it was exhaustion, or maybe she was fed up, but Melody was no longer in the mood to comply. "I am done for the day," she announced firmly.

Mr. Durand's eyes widened in disbelief. "I think not!" he exclaimed, his voice rising. "I will tell you when you are done, and you are not done. Now, dance!"

Melody rose slowly, her movements deliberate. "No. You will have to go on without me," she said, her voice resolute.

Mr. Durand's nostrils flared in anger. "Lady Melody, you are under my tutelage—"

She took a step closer to him, her gaze unwavering. "I have had enough for one day, and I am going to my bedchamber to rest."

Elodie, who had been observing the exchange from across the room, took the opportunity to chime in. "If Melody is done, can I be done as well?"

"No one is done!" Mr. Durand declared, gesturing dramatically with his hand. "Not until I say it is so."

Melody knew her mother would likely have words for her later, but she was beyond caring at this point. "Good day, Mr.

Durand," she said, turning on her heel and starting to walk away.

"Lady Melody, if I may…" Mr. Durand began, his frustration evident.

She spun around, her patience wholly gone. "No, you may not!" she snapped. "Save your breath, sir. Nothing you say will change my mind."

"Mine, either," Elodie added quickly, hurrying to join her sister.

As Melody exited the music room, Elodie followed closely behind, her expression one of admiration. "That was the most interesting thing you have ever done. Well done, Sister."

"I am going to take a nap," Melody said as she headed towards the grand staircase.

Elodie moved to walk beside her, a hint of concern creasing her brow. "Are you all right?"

"I am," Melody answered, though her voice lacked conviction.

"I have just never seen you so… feisty before," Elodie said with a small smile. "I think I like it."

Melody wasn't in the mood for Elodie's antics. "Do you have a point?"

Elodie reached out, gently stopping her at the base of the staircase. "You seem rather agitated."

"I am fine," Melody said, not wanting to give anything away. She was stressed. Exhausted. And someone was trying to kill her. She was anything but fine, but she couldn't bring herself to tell her sister that.

Elodie studied her closely, clearly unconvinced. "I do not believe you."

Melody brushed past her, eager to end the conversation. "It is the truth," she lied.

"Well, I am here if you wish to talk," Elodie said, remaining rooted in her spot.

"Thank you," Melody responded over her shoulder. She

knew her sister was in earnest. Despite her quirks and odd remarks, Elodie had always made time to listen, and for that, Melody was grateful.

Once she reached her bedchamber, she quickly locked the door behind her and collapsed onto the bed, her body heavy with exhaustion. Perhaps a nap would help ease her troubled mind as she nestled into the soft covers. But just as she began drifting off, she noticed something that sent a jolt of alarm—someone was trying to turn her door handle. The slow, deliberate movement was unmistakable.

She reached for the pistol under her pillow and jumped out of bed. Thankfully, she'd locked the door and knew no one could enter. But who had been trying to?

Her pulse quickened as she quickly unlocked the door and, in one swift motion, yanked it open, her pistol raised and ready.

But the corridor was empty.

She stepped out cautiously, her eyes scanning the long corridor. There was no sign of anyone. Had she imagined it? No, she was certain of what she had seen. The door handle had definitely moved.

With her pistol still in hand, she hurried down the corridor. She had just reached the top of the stairs when she saw Wesley ascending them, his expression immediately turning serious as he noticed the pistol in her hand.

His eyes sharpened with concern. "What has happened?" he asked in a low voice, stopping before her.

Melody slipped the pistol into the folds of her gown, not wanting to attract any further attention. "Someone tried to break into my room," she informed him.

Wesley's face darkened with worry as he moved closer. "Are you all right?"

"I am, but it was rather unnerving," Melody admitted.

"I have no doubt," Wesley declared. "I am going to

London to secure a special license. You will come with me, of course."

Melody's brows knitted in frustration. "I am not going to London with you, nor am I going to marry you," she asserted.

Wesley looked unpleased, his jaw tightening. "Melody—"

"Please, can we not discuss this now?" Melody interrupted, bringing a hand to her forehead. "I am tired and in desperate need of a nap."

He exhaled, clearly reluctant to let the matter drop, but he nodded. "All right," he conceded. "But I am not going to give up."

"I wish you would. My answer won't change," Melody said.

Wesley gently placed his hand on her sleeve, his touch light but reassuring. "All I want is for you to be safe. Nothing else matters."

Melody met his gaze and saw the sincerity in his eyes, a warmth that made her heart flutter despite herself. "Thank you," she said, unsure of what else to say.

"When you awake from your nap, we need to create a list of people who could harm you," Wesley said.

"I can't think of one person."

"But you must," Wesley asserted. "Someone is here to kill you."

Melody tossed her hands up in the air. "Why me?" she asked. "All I do is decipher codes. I am the least interesting person at the agency."

"That is not the least bit true. Your contribution is vital to the war efforts," Wesley said.

As he spoke, Melody realized that his hand was still resting on her sleeve, providing a comforting presence that was far more reassuring than it should have been. Wesley seemed to realize it, too, as he quickly withdrew his hand, clearing his throat.

"You look tired," he remarked gently.

Melody pursed her lips, not sure whether to feel offended or grateful. "That is not very kind of you to say."

"Would you prefer I lie to you?" Wesley asked.

"No, I would not," Melody replied, glancing over his shoulder as her exhaustion caught up with her. The events of the day—the endless dancing, the strain of the situation, and the weight of her responsibilities—were wearing her down.

Wesley said in a soft, concerned voice, "Allow me to walk you back to your bedchamber."

"People will talk," Melody murmured.

A hint of a smile played on Wesley's lips. "Let them talk," he responded.

Melody reluctantly nodded, partially because she was too tired to argue. "Very well," she agreed.

As they returned to her bedchamber, Wesley glanced at her sideways. "I'm sorry that this is happening to you."

"It is not your fault," Melody said.

"Perhaps not," Wesley replied, his tone somber, "but I recruited you into this life."

Melody stopped outside of her door, turning to face him. "If I wanted a quiet, safe life, I would have turned you down. I wanted this."

Wesley smiled, but it looked tight, strained, lacking its usual warmth. "Be sure to lock your door behind you." He paused. "I would suggest you let me inspect your bedchamber for anything suspicious, but I have a feeling you would refuse."

"You are right. I would," Melody responded as she opened the door. She stood there for a moment, not quite ready to say goodbye. Wesley's presence was comforting and made her feel everything would be all right.

He must not have felt the same because he took a step back. "Enjoy your rest," he said.

Melody tipped her head in acknowledgment before she disappeared into her room, locking the door behind her. Dear heavens, what was happening to her? This would not do. She couldn't—no, she wouldn't—allow herself to develop feelings for Wesley.

With that resolution firmly in place, Melody placed the pistol under her pillow and slipped under the covers, determined to focus on her rest and not on the unsettling emotions swirling within her.

Wesley paced back and forth in his bedchamber, each step increasing his agitation. His mind raced with thoughts of Melody and the ever-growing danger surrounding her. He was responsible for her safety. But how could he protect her when she resisted him at every turn?

Why wouldn't she marry him? It made perfect sense, at least to him. It wasn't just about protection, though it was a significant part. No, there were also those pesky feelings he was beginning to develop for her.

Botheration.

His thoughts were interrupted when the door opened, and Watkins entered the room. The man held up a piece of paper, his expression serious. "I spoke to the butler and compiled a list of all the recently hired servants at Brockhall Manor."

Wesley extended his hand, eager to see the information. "Give it here," he ordered.

Watkins stepped forward and handed him the paper. "As you will see, a gardener and various household staff members were recently hired."

"Have you spoken to them?" Wesley asked, his eyes scanning the names and positions on the paper.

"Not yet," Watkins replied.

Wesley reviewed the list carefully, his mind working through the possibilities. "I want you to speak to each one of them discreetly. See if any of them arouse suspicion."

Watkins tipped his head in acknowledgment. "Yes, my lord."

As Wesley returned the paper to Watkins, he added, "Someone attempted to enter Lady Melody's bedchamber."

"I take it that they weren't successful."

"No, thanks to Lady Melody's foresight in locking the door," Wesley said. "I do not like this. Not one bit. I shudder to think what would have happened if someone had been successful in entering her bedchamber."

"The important thing is that Lady Melody is unharmed." Watkins folded the paper, tucked it into his jacket pocket, and spoke cautiously. "I did make some inquiries about Jasper, as you requested."

Now, Watkins had his full attention. "What did you discover?"

"No one is quite sure where he is staying, but he has been keeping close to Brockhall Manor, particularly near Lady Sarah," Watkins revealed. "I have overheard a few maids whispering that Jasper appears to be quite taken with Lady Sarah."

"That is hardly of interest," Wesley said.

"Beyond that, there is little information about Jasper," Watkins remarked. "He is an anomaly, at least to the household staff."

Wesley walked over to the window, looking out over the gardens, deep in thought. "I don't like that. I need to know if I can trust him."

Watkins observed him for a moment. "What did Lady Melody say about Jasper?"

"Not much, but she seems to trust him."

"Is that not enough, then?" Watkins asked.

Wesley leaned against the window frame, his arm propped up as he sighed heavily. "I don't know," he admitted. "In my opinion, Lady Melody is far too trusting. She has no idea what she is up against. The agency was so careful with her identity, associating her only with a number. Very few people even knew her true name."

"I just received word that the agent responsible for the leak was caught and interrogated, but he gave up nothing useful," Watkins said. "We don't know who he spoke to or what he might have revealed."

Pushing against the window, Wesley straightened, his expression grim. "Well, we know that someone sent Lady Melody a message, and I have no doubt they intend to make good on their threat."

"We will keep her safe, my lord," Watkins stated.

"How?" Wesley asked. "Lady Melody is intent on going about this whole thing on her own. How do I make her see reason?"

"If anyone can, you can," Watkins encouraged.

A knock at the door interrupted their conversation.

"Enter," Wesley commanded.

The door opened and a footman stepped inside. "You asked to be notified the moment Mr. Artemis Nelson awoke."

"I did," Wesley confirmed. "Thank you."

Once the footman had departed, closing the door behind him, Watkins turned to Wesley with a skeptical look. "Do not tell me that you actually intend to question Mr. Nelson?" he asked, his tone laced with doubt.

"What kind of spy would I be if I didn't investigate him?" Wesley retorted.

Watkins didn't look convinced. "You truly believe he might have poisoned himself just to divert suspicion?"

Wesley shrugged. "It is not completely unheard of."

"He nearly died," Watkins argued. "That is quite a risk to take."

"True," Wesley conceded, "but he is a botanist. He knows precisely how much poison to administer to bring himself to the brink without crossing the line into death."

Watkins put his hand up in surrender. "If you think Mr.

Nelson is so dangerous, would you like me to accompany you when you interrogate him?"

"There won't be an interrogation," Wesley replied, crossing the room to the door. "I am simply going to ask him a few questions and see if I can deduce whether he is lying."

"That doesn't answer my question," Watkins said.

Wesley paused with his hand on the door handle. "No, I do not need your assistance. I can handle the botanist."

Watkins's expression remained wary. "Very well, but I won't be far off if you need assistance."

Stepping out into the corridor, Wesley walked to Mr. Artemis Nelson's room. He knocked firmly on the door, his mind already focused on the task ahead.

A moment later, the door opened slightly, and a servant peeked out, his expression cautious. "Yes, my lord?"

"Is Mr. Nelson available to speak for a moment?" Wesley asked, his tone polite but firm.

"Give me a moment," the servant said. "I will see if he is up to speaking."

The door closed briefly before it opened again, this time wider, as the servant gestured for Wesley to enter.

Wesley stepped into the bedchamber, his gaze immediately falling on Artemis, who was sitting up in bed, propped against the wall with a look of irritation etched across his face.

Artemis did not look pleased to see him. "To what do I owe this grand honor, my lord?"

"I came to see how you were faring," Wesley replied.

With a huff, Artemis replied, "How do you think I am faring? The doctor just informed me that he believes I poisoned myself when I was examining the plants."

"And did you?" Wesley prodded, his eyes narrowing slightly as he watched for any telltale signs of deceit.

A flash of annoyance flickered in Artemis's eyes. "How can you ask that question? I can assure you I know how to handle plants. It is my passion, my livelihood."

Wesley took a few steps closer to the bed, his gaze steady. "Then how do you account for your sudden illness?"

"I don't know, but it was through no fault of my own," Artemis declared, his voice rising with indignation. "Just the insinuation is insulting to me."

Knowing he needed to proceed carefully, Wesley asked, "Do you think someone might have poisoned you?"

"Me?" Artemis asked, furrowing his brow. "Are you mad? Why would someone wish to poison me?"

"It is merely a question," Wesley replied. "One that needed to be asked."

"No one has a reason to poison me," Artemis said, crossing his arms over his chest. "I have no enemies, at least that I know of."

Wesley nodded, seemingly satisfied with the answer. "Very good. Although I do have one more question."

Artemis looked mildly bored but gestured for Wesley to continue. "Yes, my lord?"

"Could your symptoms be explained by inhaling a plant from the gardens here?" Wesley asked.

"I suppose a few plants located in the gardens could have caused similar symptoms, but as I said before, I did not poison myself," Artemis insisted. "I am good at what I do. I wouldn't want my associates to know I mishandled a plant."

Wesley raised an eyebrow, his curiosity piqued. "You handled a plant?"

"Yes, but I wore gloves," Artemis remarked, his tone almost defensive. "I am not an idiot, my lord."

"Which plant?" Wesley pressed.

Artemis hesitated, a look of discomfort crossing his face before reluctantly admitting, "An oleander plant."

Satisfied, Wesley's expression softened slightly. "Thank you for your time," he said. He briefly glanced at the servant in the corner before moving to the door.

As Wesley stepped into the corridor, he found Watkins waiting for him. "Well, what did you discover?" he asked.

Wesley motioned for Watkins to follow him as they made their way back to his bedchamber. Once inside, Wesley spoke quietly, "Mr. Nelson admitted to handling an oleander plant, which could explain the symptoms he experienced."

"Do you truly believe he poisoned himself?" Watkins asked.

Wesley sighed, running a hand through his hair in frustration. "I am unsure, but I cannot dismiss him as a suspect. He has the knowledge and means to kill someone with plants."

Watkins gave him a pointed look. "There are likely a dozen ways someone could be poisoned in the gardens of Brockhall Manor, and I suspect most of the servants are aware of that."

Wesley tensed. "I can't make a misstep. Not again," he said, his voice hardening with determination.

"My lord, Dinah—" Watkins began, his tone gentle.

He cut his valet off with a sharp gesture. "No. I do not want to discuss her."

"You never do, but her death was not your fault," Watkins asserted.

"You keep saying that, but it does not make it any less true," Wesley retorted. "I should have taken the threat on her life more seriously."

Watkins stared at him, his eyes filled with disbelief. "You did everything you could."

Wesley's voice rose, the pain and guilt he carried breaking through his calm façade. "Everything but save her life! I failed, and I won't make that same mistake again with Lady Melody."

Walking over to the wardrobe, Watkins reached for a black dinner jacket. "We should get you dressed for dinner. The dinner bell should be ringing shortly."

Wesley knew that Watkins was just trying to help him, but

he had lost the only woman he had ever loved. She was gone, and it was because of him.

The faint chime of the dinner bell echoed through the hall, pulling Wesley from his thoughts.

Watkins approached him with a look of sympathy. "My lord—"

Wesley cut him off, not wanting to hear anything more, not wanting pity. Nothing could bring Dinah back, and the memory of her loss was a constant reminder of why he should remain alone. "I don't have time for this. I need to leave for dinner."

"Yes, my lord," Watkins said, his voice resigned.

As Wesley dressed for dinner, his mind retreated into the familiar haze of regret. He had been recruited out of Oxford by the spymaster, eager to do more with his life than simply inherit a title. But what did he have to show for it? Nothing. He couldn't even protect the agents entrusted to him.

The guilt was a shadow that clung to him, one he feared would never fade.

Chapter Nine

The moonlight streamed through her window as Melody lay in bed. Though it was late, sleep eluded her. Her mind whirled with the ever-present reminder that she was in danger. From whom, she still did not know.

Wesley had urged her to trust him, to rely on him, but fear held her back. He was a good man, that much was clear, but she had learned to depend on herself rather than others. It was much easier that way.

Dinner had been a somber affair. Mr. and Mrs. Nelson had dined with their son, Artemis, and Wesley had hardly spoken a word to her. Not that she minded. She needed to keep him at arm's length to avoid deepening these inconvenient feelings for him.

A sudden knock at the window startled her, snapping her out of her thoughts. She instinctively reached for the pistol she kept under her pillow, gripping it tightly.

Another knock.

Melody turned her head slowly, her breath catching as she saw a figure's shadow outside the window. Who would knock at her window at this hour, and for what purpose? She cautiously rose from the bed, her pulse quickening with each step she took towards the window.

As she drew closer, the figure became more apparent in the moonlight—Wesley. Relief mixed with confusion as she hurried to open the window. "What are you doing?" she whispered.

"Isn't it obvious?" Wesley replied, matching her hushed tone. "I am here to protect you."

"From what?" she asked, still trying to comprehend the situation.

Wesley shifted his grip on the window frame, his expression solemn. "Can we have this conversation inside your bedchamber?"

Melody's eyes widened in shock. "Are you mad?"

"No," he answered, a slight smirk on his lips. "Surprisingly, that is not the first time someone has asked me that today."

"You can't come in here. I would be ruined if anyone discovered you were in my bedchamber," Melody protested.

Wesley gave her a pointed look. "Well, I can't stay outside your window all night."

Melody glanced nervously at the door, torn between propriety and practicality. With a resigned sigh, she conceded, "Fine. You may come in, but only until we settle the matter."

"Thank you," Wesley said as he climbed through the window.

Melody hurried to slip on her wrapper, tying it securely in the front. "What do you think you are doing?" she demanded, being mindful to keep her voice low.

"You already asked that," Wesley replied, amusement in his eyes.

"I know, but I cannot fathom what you were thinking. Do you not care for my reputation?"

Wesley brushed off his trousers, his expression earnest. "I

care greatly for your reputation, which is why I waited until now to climb the ivory walls to your bedchamber."

Melody walked over to the window, peering out into the night. "How were you able to climb up here so easily?"

"It wasn't easy," Wesley admitted, "but I used to sneak out of my bedchamber at my country estate all the time. It is all about finding your footing on the bricks jutting out."

She closed the window and turned back to Wesley. "You should have told me what you were planning to do."

"If I had, you would have said no," he pointed out, a knowing look in his eyes.

"Of course, I would have," she retorted. "I am perfectly safe in my bedchamber with the door locked."

"Locks can be picked," Wesley countered, his tone matter-of-fact.

Melody held up her pistol, her grip steady. "Which is why I have my pistol with me."

"A pistol only has one shot."

"You seem to forget that I have remarkably good aim," Melody remarked, a touch of defiance in her voice.

"I have yet to see it," Wesley said.

Melody slipped her pistol under the pillow. "What now?" she asked.

Wesley settled into a chair by the window. "I will stay here and make sure you are safe," he informed her, his tone leaving no room for argument.

"You intend to watch me sleep?" Melody asked in disbelief.

"Yes."

Melody bit her lower lip, a flicker of embarrassment creeping in. "What if I snore?"

"Do you snore?" he asked, raising an eyebrow.

She shrugged. "I don't rightly know."

Wesley's smile widened. "I do not care if you snore."

"You might not, but I do," Melody declared.

He chuckled softly. "Is that your only concern?"

"Yes, but it is a *big* concern."

Reaching behind him, Wesley drew a pistol and placed it on the table beside him, the metal gleaming faintly in the dim light. "I am only here to keep you safe—nothing more," he assured her, his voice unwavering.

Melody knew she was fighting a losing battle but couldn't help but voice her thoughts. "You do realize I can take care of myself, don't you?"

"There is no need, not when I am here," Wesley said, leaning his head back against the wall. "You should get some sleep."

Melody glanced over her shoulder at the bed. Could she really sleep with Wesley in her bedchamber? The mere thought sent a shiver of unease through her. What was he thinking, putting them both in such a precarious position? Surely, he understood the implication of being here.

But she suspected he did.

Reluctantly, Melody moved to the settee and sat down, trying to gather her thoughts. "I understand that you spoke to Artemis," she said, her tone cautious.

"I did," Wesley confirmed.

"May I ask what you discussed?"

Wesley straightened in his chair, giving her his full attention. "I was curious as to how conveniently he was poisoned."

"Conveniently?" Melody repeated. "Can anyone be 'conveniently' poisoned?"

"If he was sent here to kill you, he might have poisoned himself to deflect suspicion," Wesley explained.

Melody stared back at Wesley. "I have known Artemis since he was young. He was not sent here to kill me."

"What do you truly know about him?" Wesley challenged.

Melody pressed her lips together. "I know that he studied botany at university and he is socially inept. He has always been high-handed, even arrogant at times, but he is not a killer."

"If it was indeed an accident, then how did a trained botanist manage to poison himself?"

"I can't answer that," Melody admitted. "Didn't we surmise that the person who poisoned Artemis might have intended to poison me?"

"That is one theory, but I prefer to deal in facts," Wesley remarked, using her previous words against her. "The only thing we know for certain is that you received a threatening message."

Melody yawned, quickly bringing her hand up to cover her mouth. The exhaustion from the long day was finally catching up with her.

"It is late," Wesley said gently. "You need to get some sleep."

"I don't know if I can," Melody confessed. "I haven't slept in the same room with someone since I was in the nursery with Elodie."

Wesley's lips curved into a smile. "Your sister is quite a force to be reckoned with."

"She is high-spirited," Melody agreed.

"That is one way to put it."

Melody rose, her thoughts lingering on her sister. "Elodie may say outlandish things, but she is my dearest friend. Sometimes, I worry that Society will stifle her spirit."

"But not yours?"

Walking over to her bed, Melody sat down on the edge of the mattress. "I know the part that I am expected to play, but I don't know what my future holds for me."

Wesley considered her for a moment before asking, "Knowing what you know now, would you still accept my offer to become an agent?"

"I have never once regretted my choice, but I do know it

would bring shame to my family if the truth ever came out," Melody said.

"I won't let that happen," Wesley promised.

Melody slowly removed her wrapper, folded it neatly and placed it at the foot of the bed. "Sometimes, things are out of our control," she said quietly, her tone laced with resignation.

Wesley settled back in his chair, watching her with a thoughtful expression. "Like you, I know the role I must play."

"We make quite the pair, don't we? Two people playing parts in a world that demands so much from us." She hesitated for a moment, then asked, "May I ask you a question?"

"I suppose it is only fair."

Melody lay on the bed, propping herself up slightly to keep her gaze on him. "How did you become an agent?"

Something flickered in Wesley's eyes for a moment, an emotion she couldn't quite identify. "I was recruited at university by the spymaster."

"Why you?" Melody pressed.

His lips twitched. "Why not me?" he asked, clearly finding her question amusing.

Melody sensed that he was intentionally being vague, guarding himself from revealing too much. But she wanted to understand him better, especially the parts of himself that he kept hidden.

"You picked me because of my linguistics background," Melody began, her tone probing. "What did the agency want with you?"

Wesley's expression grew solemn. "It runs in the family, I suppose. My father also worked for the agency when he was in the Royal Navy."

"Is it not unusual for an earl to not only serve in the Royal Navy but also be a spy?" Melody asked.

He leaned forward slightly as if contemplating how much to share. "My father was the second son," he explained. "He had already established a career in the Royal Navy when his brother died unexpectedly. He refused to give up that part of his life, leaving my mother to manage the estate in his absence."

Melody could feel her eyelids growing heavy, but she had one more thing to say. "Thank you."

Wesley tilted his head, his expression bemused. "For what?"

Melody offered him a weak smile. "For trusting me enough to tell me the truth."

"I do trust you," Wesley stated, his voice firm. The words hung in the air, a quiet acknowledgment of the fragile trust they were building in a world filled with secrets and danger.

Slowly, her eyelids grew heavy, and as she drifted off to sleep, the last thing she felt was the reassuring sense of safety that Wesley's presence brought. The darkness outside seemed a little less daunting with him there, and for the first time in days, Melody allowed herself to surrender to the quiet peace of sleep, trusting that with Wesley nearby, she was truly safe.

Wesley departed from his bedchamber and made his way down the corridor, his footsteps echoing softly against the polished floors. As he reached the top of the grand staircase, he noticed Melody standing near the iron railing, her gaze fixed intently on the entry hall below. She caught sight of him approaching and quickly brought a finger to her lips, signaling for him to remain silent.

Intrigued, Wesley moved closer, positioning himself beside her as he followed her line of sight. Below, in the entry hall, Elodie and Lord Belview were locked in what appeared to be a heated argument, their voices low but clearly agitated.

Wesley leaned in closer to Melody. "Can you hear what they are saying?" he whispered.

Melody nodded, her eyes sparkling with amusement. "They were just fighting about how Lord Belview doesn't enjoy poached eggs for breakfast."

"That is an odd thing to argue about."

"I know, which makes it all the more entertaining," Melody said with a giggle.

Wesley chuckled softly and placed his hands on the railing to watch the scene unfold. "How long have you been eavesdropping?"

"About five minutes now," Melody confessed. "I don't dare interrupt them, especially since I am most curious to see how it all ends."

"Are you not the least bit famished?" Wesley asked.

Melody turned her gaze from the scene below to Wesley, considering his question. "You make a good point. Perhaps I will ask my lady's maid to bring a tray to my room."

Wesley grinned. "That is ridiculous."

"Do you have a better idea?"

Before he could respond, Elodie's voice rang out from below. "Are you two quite finished?" she asked, clearly aware of their presence. "Mother has called a family meeting in the dining room."

Melody groaned softly. "I do not like family meetings. No good ever comes from them."

Wesley offered his arm. "May I escort you to the dining room?"

"Very well," Melody agreed, slipping her hand into the crook of his arm.

As they began descending the grand staircase together, Wesley glanced at her with a gentle smile. "Did you sleep well?"

"I did, actually," Melody said. "When did you leave?"

Wesley kept his voice low, leaning slightly closer. "Before dawn," he replied. "I didn't think it was prudent to stay much longer."

"That was wise."

He smirked. "You sound surprised."

"Well, sneaking into my bedchamber could have had disastrous consequences," Melody pointed out.

Wesley couldn't resist teasing her. "By the way, you don't snore," he said, his grin widening.

Melody looked relieved by his admission, but her cheeks flushed with a hint of embarrassment. "That is a relief."

"But you did snort a few times," Wesley joked. "I was a little worried for you."

A deeper blush spread across Melody's cheeks, and she ducked her head. "A gentleman wouldn't comment on such things."

He patted her hand reassuringly. "I promise I won't tell anyone."

"You'd better not," she warned with a mock-serious tone. "If you did, everyone would discover the truth."

At that moment, Elodie appeared beside them, her sudden presence catching both of them off guard. "What truth?" she asked.

Melody quickly withdrew her hand from Wesley's arm. "We were just talking about…" She hesitated briefly. "The weather."

"The weather?" Elodie repeated, raising an eyebrow. "You don't actually expect me to believe that, do you? No one really talks about the weather."

"The weather is a perfectly acceptable topic of conversation," Melody said with a slight shrug of her shoulder.

Elodie shook her head, clearly unconvinced. "Fine. Do not tell me, but I will discover the truth eventually."

As Elodie disappeared into the dining room, Wesley leaned closer to Melody and whispered, "That was impressive."

Melody frowned, glancing after her sister. "I do believe my

sister is a ninja. I didn't even see her. I will need to be more careful."

With a smile, Wesley gestured for Melody to enter the dining room first. He followed her inside and moved to pull out a chair for her, ensuring she was situated before taking the seat beside her. Across the table, Lord Belview and Elodie were already seated, their earlier argument seemingly forgotten, though the tension between them still lingered.

Lady Dallington swept into the dining room with a bright smile lighting up her face. "Wonderful, you have all assembled."

Elodie, reaching for her cup of chocolate, looked up with mild amusement. "You did call a family meeting," she remarked dryly.

"Yes, I did, and that is what I wish to discuss with everyone," Lady Dallington acknowledged, moving to the head of the table. "I have arranged for the four of you to go on a carriage ride this morning."

"Wonderful," Elodie muttered under her breath, her tone lacking any genuine excitement.

Lady Dallington ignored Elodie's lackluster response and continued, her voice full of cheer. "I thought you would enjoy a ride through the countryside. The fresh air, the scenery—it will be quite refreshing."

Elodie raised her hand.

"Yes, Dear?" Lady Dallington sighed.

"May we take the coach?" Elodie asked.

Lady Dallington shook her head. "I thought a carriage would be more pleasant, allowing you to enjoy the countryside as you pass through."

Elodie raised her hand again.

Lady Dallington glanced heavenward, clearly exasperated. "You don't need to raise your hand."

"I would still prefer the coach," Elodie insisted. "I seem to attract bugs, and I would rather not spend the entire ride swatting them away."

Lord Belview puffed out his chest. "It would be my honor to protect you from the bugs, my lady."

Elodie shot him a skeptical look. "You say that now, but wait until you swallow one. It is most unpleasant."

"Then I suggest keeping your mouth closed during the ride," Lady Dallington remarked.

As the footmen stepped forward to place plates of food before them, Wesley instinctively went to switch his plate with Melody's, but she gently placed a hand on his arm to stop him.

Leaning closer, she whispered, "What if someone anticipated that we would switch plates?"

Wesley paused, considering her point. "You are right. Perhaps we should eat what is on our own plates."

"I think that is wise," Melody agreed.

Elodie spoke up. "Take Lord Belview's plate away," she ordered. "It has a poached egg on it, and he has made it quite clear he does not care for those."

Lord Belview waved the footman off with a slight chuckle. "That is not what I said."

"That is what I heard," Elodie retorted.

"I am beginning to think you have selective hearing," Lord Belview said. "You only hear what you want to hear."

Elodie picked up her knife, carefully buttering her toast with precision. "That is not true."

Melody chimed in, "I do think Anthony has a point."

"Traitor," Elodie declared, though her voice was more playful than accusatory. "I should have known that you would take his side since you are not particularly fond of poached eggs either. It is a poached egg conspiracy!"

Lady Dallington put her hands up. "Elodie, you digress, as usual. There is no conspiracy, and you should be nicer to Anthony. He is our guest, after all."

Lord Belview smirked. "Did you hear that, Elodie? You should be nicer to me."

Elodie rolled her eyes dramatically. "When pigs fly."

With a glance at the toast in her hand, Lord Belview remarked, "Why do you take such care to butter your toast?"

"Because, my lord," Elodie drawled, "a piece of toast must have the perfect ratio of butter to bread in each bite. Anything less would be a culinary tragedy."

Wesley couldn't help but notice that Melody was absent-mindedly pushing her food around on her plate, seemingly uninterested in eating. It was not surprising, given the circumstances. Not knowing if someone was trying to poison you had a way of dampening one's appetite. He realized he wasn't particularly hungry, either.

Elodie seemed to notice the same thing about her sister. "Are you not hungry, Melody?"

Melody set her fork down. "I must admit that I am not."

"Well, if you find that you are hungry later, there will be plenty of bugs to eat on our carriage ride," Elodie quipped.

Lady Dallington let out a slight huff. "A lady does not eat bugs," she declared, clasping her hands with practiced grace.

"That is not entirely true," Elodie responded. "Some people consider bugs a delicacy."

Melody abruptly rose from her seat, causing the gentlemen to stand. "Excuse me for a moment," she murmured before departing from the dining room.

Wesley's gaze lingered on the door through which Melody had just departed, his mind racing with worry. What had prompted her sudden exit? He couldn't shake the feeling that something was wrong.

As Wesley returned to his seat, Lord Dallington entered the room, the newssheets tucked neatly under his arm. "Good morning," he greeted, planting a quick kiss on his wife's cheek before heading to his seat at the table.

Lord Dallington laid the newssheets on the table with a

practiced motion, but Elodie reached for them before he could begin reading. Her father quickly pulled them back. "What do you think you are doing, young lady?"

Elodie looked unperturbed by her father's rebuke. "I was hoping to read the newssheets."

Lord Dallington's response was immediate and firm. "I think not. Genteel women do not read the newssheets."

With a defiant spark, Elodie asked, "Why, Father? Are you afraid I will start forming my own opinions, or worse, that I won't share yours?"

Lord Dallington let out a scoff. "You haven't shared my opinions in quite some time," he said, pulling a page from the bundle. "You can read the Society page."

Elodie didn't bother to reach for the paper. Her disapproval was evident. "Oh, yes, because I care what someone was wearing or who attended which event."

"What happened to you?" Lord Dallington asked, his tone serious but the glint in his eyes betraying his mirth. "You used to be such an agreeable young woman."

Wesley found the exchange entertaining, but his thoughts kept drifting back to Melody. As much as he tried to focus on the lighthearted banter at the table, concern gnawed at him. Where had she gone so suddenly? He wanted to find her, to ensure she was all right, but propriety caused him to remain seated.

Chapter Ten

Melody descended the rickety, uneven stairs to the kitchen, the wooden steps creaking under her weight. Her stomach growled, reminding her just how hungry she was, but the thought of eating the breakfast served earlier, with the ever-present fear of it being poisoned, had made it impossible to eat. Now, she was seeking something simple and safe.

As she stepped off the last stair, she nodded politely to the servants she passed. The warm, yeasty aroma of freshly baked bread filled the kitchen, drawing her attention to Mrs. Meek, the portly cook, who was kneading dough on the countertop.

Mrs. Meek looked up and greeted Melody with a warm smile. "Good morning, my dear. What brings you down to the kitchen?"

"Do you have any bread ready?" Melody asked.

The cook's smile faltered slightly. "Was something wrong with the food I sent up with the servants?"

Melody quickly shook her head, trying to ease the cook's worry. "No, nothing was wrong with it, but I find I am craving some fresh bread."

Mrs. Meek's expression softened again, and she gestured

towards the large wooden table in the center of the room. "Take a seat, and I will bring you some," she offered.

As Melody moved further into the kitchen, she saw her Aunt Sarah sitting quietly in the corner with a cup of tea cradled in her hands. "Good morning, Sarah," she said, approaching her with a smile.

Sarah returned her smile, but it didn't quite meet her eyes, the weariness she carried evident in her gaze. "Good morning, Melody."

Melody took a seat across from her aunt, curiosity tugging at her. "Why didn't you join us for breakfast this morning?"

With a glance at her tea, Sarah replied, "I was busy." But the answer felt hollow, lacking conviction.

Melody wasn't convinced and decided to pry a little deeper. "We have missed you these past few days," she said gently.

Sarah waved her hand dismissively. "You don't need—or want—me around your other guests."

"And why not? It has hardly been uneventful," Melody remarked with a wry smile. "Mr. Artemis Nelson has taken ill, presumably poisoned by handling a plant."

"Regardless, it is best if I don't come around," Sarah said.

"Why do you say that?"

Sarah's expression turned solemn, her voice softening with old pain. "I gave up that life when I eloped with Isaac. I do not belong in that world anymore."

Melody frowned. "That is not the least bit true. You are still the daughter of a marquess."

"But my station in life has changed dramatically," Sarah countered. "I married a scoundrel, and I am now living off my brother's good graces."

"You will always be a part of our family," Melody insisted, leaning forward, her voice filled with sincerity.

Sarah offered her a weary smile in return. "You are kind, but I am sure your guests don't feel the same way."

Melody met her aunt's eyes with determination. "Who cares what they think? I certainly don't."

Sarah sighed, her fingers tracing the rim of her teacup. "I just don't want to embarrass your family, especially after everything you have done for me."

"If you truly wanted to thank me, you would come upstairs and save me from my mother's matchmaking schemes," Melody encouraged.

Sarah hesitated, clearly torn. "I know what you are trying to do, but I don't belong."

"You do. You just have to believe it."

Before Sarah could respond, the door to the kitchen creaked open, and Jasper stepped inside, his arms full of firewood.

"Where would you like the wood, Mrs. Meek?" Jasper asked.

Mrs. Meek gestured towards the hearth. "Right there will do, thank you. You are a godsend," she said with a grateful smile.

Jasper moved to place the firewood down, and as he did, Melody noticed the way Sarah's eyes followed him, a look of longing softening her features. But as soon as he turned around, Sarah quickly ducked her head, a faint blush coloring her cheeks.

He tipped his head in greeting, his eyes first meeting Melody's. "Lady Melody," he acknowledged before shifting his gaze to her aunt. "Lady Sarah."

Sarah lifted her eyes, her voice soft. "Jasper."

"I trust that you slept well last night?" Jasper asked.

"I did," Sarah replied, managing a small smile. "And you?"

Jasper nodded. "I did. I noticed that your son is outside playing with the other children. He seems to be getting along just fine here."

A hint of pride and warmth crept into Sarah's voice. "Yes,

it is true. For so long, Matthew had no one to play with. It warms my heart to see him making friends."

"Perhaps I can take him out hunting tomorrow, assuming you have no objections," Jasper suggested.

"I have none. He really enjoyed it the last time you took him," Sarah responded.

For a moment, Jasper lingered, his eyes locked on Sarah's as if wanting to say more. But then he cleared his throat and broke the connection. "I should be going," he said before he turned to leave.

As he departed, Melody couldn't quite believe what she had just observed between Jasper and Sarah. It was evident that there was more to the story than either was willing to share.

Mrs. Meek walked over with a slice of bread and placed it down in front of her. "Enjoy," she encouraged.

Melody had so many questions as she reached for the bread. Did she dare ask them? It was, after all, none of her business. But her curiosity got the best of her. She met Sarah's gaze. "Do you have an understanding with Jasper?"

Sarah's reaction was immediate, her eyes widening in shock as her mouth fell open. "Good heavens, no!" she exclaimed. "Why would you think such a thing?"

"But you fancy him, don't you?" Melody pressed.

Sarah placed her teacup down with a slight clatter, her hands trembling ever so slightly. She began to rise from her seat. "I should be going. My son needs his lessons…"

Before she could leave, Melody interrupted her. "Please, don't go. I am sorry. I had no right to pry."

Sarah's shoulders slumped as she slowly returned to her seat. "I know you mean well, but you must understand that the life I once dreamed of—the future I envisioned—is all gone. Marrying Isaac destroyed those dreams."

Melody's heart ached for her aunt, but she wasn't ready to

give up so easily. "Then maybe it is time to find a new dream," she urged.

Her aunt looked at her with a sad smile. "You are young and kind, but I live in a far less forgiving world. A world that doesn't easily accept those who defy convention," she replied. "And besides, you are wrong about Jasper. He was there to protect me from Isaac—nothing more."

Despite her aunt's words, Melody couldn't shake the feeling that there was more between Sarah and Jasper than her aunt was willing to admit. She had seen how they looked at each other, the spark that flickered when they were near. It was a spark that could grow into something much brighter with a bit of encouragement. But first, she needed to convince Sarah to see it for herself.

As Sarah rose to leave, she said, "I do need to go, but thank you for your kind words. I am grateful to have you in my life."

Melody watched as Sarah left the kitchen, a heavy silence settling over the room. It was Mrs. Meek who finally broke it, her voice filled with quiet sympathy. "Poor woman. She has been through so much and she doesn't have much to show for it."

"How can we help her?" Melody asked.

Mrs. Meek shrugged. "I don't know if there is much we can do," she responded. "Lady Sarah is trying to find where she belongs, but it isn't easy. She is caught between two worlds, neither of which seems to accept her fully."

At that moment, Wesley appeared in the doorway, his presence filling the room. "There you are," he said, a note of relief in his voice. "I have been looking everywhere for you."

"Here I am," Melody responded, gesturing to the seat beside her.

Wesley sat down next to her, glancing at the slice of bread on the table. "I can understand now why you retreated to the kitchen."

Mrs. Meek approached him with a plate of bread, placing it in front of him. "It is fresh from the oven."

Wesley took a bite, savoring the simple offering. "Thank you. It is delicious."

"I shall have to send more bread up for breakfast," Mrs. Meek said, her voice trailing off as she busied herself in the kitchen.

Melody shifted in her seat to face Wesley, feeling determined. "I want to help my Aunt Sarah. She seems so sad, and I know the perfect way to cheer her up. We will play matchmaker."

Wesley arched an eyebrow. "We?"

"Do you have anything else pressing at the moment?" Melody asked with a playful challenge in her voice.

Wesley shot a glance at Mrs. Meek before lowering his voice. "How about the threat on your life?"

Undeterred, Melody's enthusiasm didn't waver. "We can handle both," she insisted. "I want to do this. No, I *need* to do this. Will you help me?"

Wesley sighed. "All right. Just tell me what you would like me to do."

Melody felt the corners of her lips curving upwards. "I don't have a plan just yet. But I will, in time."

Brushing the crumbs from his hands, Wesley gave her a knowing smile. "Well, I do not think it will take much effort," he remarked. "My valet informed me just this morning that the gossip around Brockhall Manor is that Jasper is quite taken with Lady Sarah."

"That is my conclusion as well," Melody said. "But how, exactly, does one go about playing matchmaker?"

"You could always ask your mother," Wesley suggested.

A shudder ran through Melody at that thought. "Heavens, no. There must be another way."

Wesley pushed back his chair as the legs scraped lightly

against the wooden floor. "Regardless, we have a carriage ride awaiting us that Lady Dallington has so graciously arranged," he said, rising to his feet and extending a hand to assist her.

Melody accepted his hand, standing with a graceful nod of thanks. "A carriage ride could be the perfect opportunity to gather some ideas."

Wesley sat uncomfortably in the carriage, the heat of the morning sun bearing down on him as sweat trickled down his back. He wasn't entirely sure why he had agreed to the carriage ride, but he couldn't deny the small pleasure he found sitting so close to Melody. The delicate scent of lavender drifted off her person and he had to force himself not to lean in closer. He needed to remain a gentleman despite the temptation.

Sitting across from him, Elodie swatted with a dramatic flair at the air. "Yuck, bugs," she complained. "I do not know why Mother insisted on this open-drawn carriage. A coach ride would have been perfectly acceptable."

Melody had a fan open in front of her, gently waving it back and forth to ward off the bugs. "Just use your fan, Elodie," she suggested.

Lord Belview chuckled from his seat beside Elodie. "That would be far too simple, and Elodie does not like to do things the simple way."

Elodie shot Lord Belview an annoyed look. "Says the man who is constantly pettifogging."

"I do not pettifog," Lord Belview retorted.

"You do. You are a pettifogger," Elodie declared.

Lord Belview's smile widened, clearly enjoying the conversation. "Fine, I will admit that, on occasion, I might pettifog.

However, it takes one pettifogger to know another, does it not?"

Elodie straightened in her seat, her posture rigid. "You think you are so clever," she remarked.

"I do, actually," Lord Belview responded. "Besides, it is rather easy to vex you. I think I could do it in my sleep."

Elodie's eyes narrowed. "Please do not think of me when you are sleeping. In fact, I would prefer if you did not think of me at all."

Lord Belview leaned back, chuckling softly. "You take issue with me dreaming about you?"

"Yes, I do," Elodie stated. "I forbid it."

Lord Belview chuckled again. "You cannot forbid someone from dreaming about you. It doesn't quite work that way."

Melody shifted towards Wesley, her words light. "The weather is quite pleasant, is it not?"

Wesley caught the hint and nodded, adjusting his top hat as he replied. "It is, though the sun is particularly strong."

"I would agree," Melody said, her fan continuing its steady rhythm.

Elodie leaned closer to Lord Belview, lowering her voice. "I do believe they want us to stop arguing."

"Were we arguing?" Lord Belview asked, feigning innocence. "I thought we were merely engaging in a lively debate."

Elodie shook her head. "You are an infuriating man," she muttered.

Lord Belview's gaze lingered on Elodie a moment longer than was proper before turning his attention towards Melody. "Are you excited for the upcoming Season?"

Melody hesitated slightly before answering. "I am, for the most part," she replied, though her voice lacked enthusiasm.

"Why did that not sound convincing?" Lord Belview joked.

Melody brought a smile to her lips, but it did not fool Wesley. "I have been looking forward to the Season for so long that I do hope I will not be disappointed."

Sensing her apprehension, Wesley decided to step in. "You won't be," he assured her. "Besides, I will be there to help you—if you so desire."

"You will?" Melody asked.

He nodded. "We are friends, are we not?"

Something flickered across Melody's face for a moment—an emotion Wesley couldn't quite decipher. "We are," she agreed.

Wesley nudged her shoulder gently with his. "And friends help one another."

A genuine smile spread across Melody's face, and this time, it reached her eyes. "That sounds wonderful."

As the carriage continued its leisurely journey through the countryside, Wesley couldn't help but feel that, despite the heat and discomfort, this moment—sitting beside Melody, sharing these quiet words—was worth every bead of sweat on his back.

Suddenly, the sharp crack of a rifle shot echoed through the air, cutting through the peaceful countryside like a knife. Without thinking, Wesley acted on instinct, throwing himself over Melody, shielding her with his body as his heart raced.

A moment later, Melody's muffled voice came from beneath him, her tone surprisingly calm. "You can get off me now, my lord."

Wesley straightened quickly, feeling slightly embarrassed, as he adjusted himself back into the seat. He noticed that Melody's hat had been knocked askew. "I am terribly sorry," he stammered, struggling to regain his composure. "I heard the shot, and I just reacted."

Melody raised her hand to adjust her hat. "It is all right," she assured him. "No harm done."

Across from them, Elodie eyed Wesley with a mixture of curiosity and suspicion. "May I ask why you reacted in such a fashion?" she inquired. "Surely, you have heard a rifle discharging before."

Wesley met her gaze, knowing he had to offer a plausible explanation. "I have, of course," he replied, knowing how foolish he must sound. "But it was so close…"

"Why would you think someone was shooting at Melody?" Elodie asked.

Wesley should have known that Elodie wouldn't let the matter drop. "It was merely a lapse of judgment on my part."

Lord Belview spoke up in Wesley's defense. "I think it was brave."

"As do I," Melody said. "Now, can we let the matter drop?"

Elodie's lips were pursed as if she had more to say. But, after a moment, she gave a reluctant nod. "Very well," she said. "We are almost home anyway."

Lord Belview turned to Elodie with a playful grin as if to lighten the mood. "Will you play the pianoforte for me when we return?"

"No," Elodie responded flatly.

Lord Belview clucked his tone in mock reproach. "I do believe your mother told you that you should be nicer to me. I am a guest, after all."

Elodie shifted in her seat to face him fully, her expression one of exaggerated disdain. "You are merely an annoying gnat, my lord."

Lord Belview placed a hand over his heart, feigning deep hurt. "You wound me, my lady. All I strive for is your approval."

Elodie gave him an exasperated look. "You should have a career in the theater."

As the carriage approached Brockhall Manor, Wesley's eyes were drawn to Jasper, who stood out front, watching their approach with a serious expression. He wasted no time in exiting the coach to speak with him.

Jasper met him with a quiet intensity, his voice low as he asked, "Is everyone all right?"

"We are," Wesley confirmed, though a new wave of concern washed over him as he watched Jasper's actions. The man moved purposefully along the side of the carriage, his hands trailing over the wood as if searching for something.

Wesley turned back to the coach to help the ladies out, his mind racing with possibilities. He knew what Jasper was looking for but didn't want to alarm the ladies.

Melody must have noticed Jasper's odd behavior and looked at Wesley with a questioning gaze. "What is Jasper doing?"

Wesley forced a calm smile, though his mind was anything but at ease. "Why don't you go inside with your sister?" he suggested gently. "I will join you shortly after I speak to Jasper."

Melody seemed ready to argue, but after a brief pause, she conceded. "All right," she agreed, though her reluctance was apparent.

Once Lord Belview escorted the ladies inside, leaving Wesley alone with Jasper, he turned back to the man with a sense of urgency. "Did the carriage get hit?"

Jasper turned back to face him. "It did, but the shot landed near where you sat."

Wesley reared back slightly. "Me? Why would someone shoot at me?" he asked, knowing full well there were plenty of reasons why someone might want him dead. However, revealing that to Jasper was an entirely different matter. Wesley wasn't certain he could trust the Bow Street Runner and wasn't about to tip his hand.

Jasper's eyes narrowed slightly as if deep in thought. "Why, indeed?" he said. "That is what I intend to find out."

Wesley, careful to keep his expression neutral, gave a

casual shrug. "Well, when you do find out, please let me know." He turned to leave, hoping to end this conversation.

But Jasper's next words caused him to pause. "What are your intentions towards Lady Melody?"

Wesley turned to face Jasper. "Pardon?"

"Your intentions, my lord?" Jasper repeated, his voice firm. "It is a simple enough question."

Keeping his face impassive, he replied, "We are friends."

Jasper took a deliberate step closer to him, his scrutiny intensifying. "I find that hard to believe. You seem to follow her wherever she goes. Why is that?"

"I do not answer to you."

"No," Jasper conceded, "but Lord Winston asked me to watch over his family while he was away, and I intend to do just that."

Wesley knew he didn't owe Jasper an explanation, but revealing just enough might keep the Bow Street Runner at bay. "I can assure you that my interest in Lady Melody is honorable," he said, his tone measured.

Jasper crossed his arms over his chest, his expression skeptical. "Just know, I will be watching you, my lord."

"I have no doubt," Wesley said before entering Brockhall Manor.

Once he stepped into the entry hall, he immediately spotted Melody waiting for him. Her face was calm, but her eyes held curiosity as she approached him. "What was Jasper searching for?" she asked in a hushed voice.

Wesley lowered his own voice to match hers. "A bullet, which he found. Apparently, someone was shooting at me."

"Good heavens," Melody muttered.

"Jasper also wanted to ensure my intentions towards you were honorable." He paused, studying her reaction. "Do you trust Jasper?"

Melody didn't hesitate. "I do, wholeheartedly," she replied. "Don't you?"

A Shadowed Charade

He shrugged. "I am not quite sure yet."

"Jasper risked his life to save my aunt," Melody shared. "I do not doubt he would do the same for anyone in my family."

"That is his job, considering Bow Street Runners are for hire," Wesley pointed out.

Melody's expression tightened, clearly displeased by his remark. "I assure you that you can trust Jasper."

Wesley gave a slight nod, though doubt lingered in his mind. "I hope you are right."

"I usually am," she quipped.

He chuckled softly, feeling the tension ease slightly. "I forgot how humble you are."

Melody glanced towards the music room, where the faint sounds of the violin were drifting out. "You might want to save yourself. The dancing master is eager for us to begin our lessons."

"I do not mind accompanying you. I rather enjoy having you in my arms as we dance," Wesley said, surprised by his own admission. Why had he just said that out loud?

A charming blush spread across Melody's cheeks, and she quickly ducked her head. "You shouldn't say such things."

Wesley reached for her gloved hand, bringing it to his lips. "I can't speak the truth?"

She brought her gaze up, her eyes revealing a rare vulnerability. "Is it the truth, or are you just attempting to flatter me?"

"It is the truth," Wesley assured her. He allowed the words to linger for a moment before brushing his lips lightly against her hand.

Just then, Lady Dallington's voice came from the doorway of the music room. "Melody," she called, her tone holding impatience. "Mr. Durand is ready for you."

Wesley moved Melody's hand into the crook of his arm. "Allow me to escort you."

As they walked together towards the music room, Wesley

couldn't help but notice the tightening in his chest. The feelings he had so carefully tried to ignore, to push aside as mere distractions, were beginning to stir and awaken.

One thing was clear: Melody was becoming more than just a friend or duty.

Chapter Eleven

Melody sat in the library, a book resting lightly in her hands as she waited for the dinner bell to ring. The quiet room was her sanctuary, where she could retreat from her relentless thoughts. Yet, as much as she tried to focus on the words before her, her mind wandered, half-hoping that Wesley might appear. The thought was absurd, she knew. She shouldn't want to spend more time with him, especially when each moment they shared seemed to deepen the feelings she had tried so hard to suppress.

Determined to shake the thought, Melody focused on the page, forcing herself to concentrate. She just needed to read for a moment to forget about Wesley and the confusing emotions he stirred within her.

Elodie entered the room and promptly greeted her. "Good evening, Sister. I thought I might find you here."

Melody held up her book with a small smile. "I am just reading a book."

"Anything interesting?" Elodie asked, moving to stand beside her.

"Not particularly," Melody replied, lowering the book to

her lap. She knew Elodie well enough to sense that her sister had something on her mind. "What is it?"

Elodie feigned innocence, bringing a hand to her chest. "Whatever do you mean?"

Melody wasn't fooled. "You can drop the act."

A smile tugged at Elodie's lips as she gracefully sank onto the settee beside her. "I just want to ask you a few questions."

"What kind of questions?" Melody inquired.

"Oh, nothing too difficult," Elodie said with a shrug. "At least, not for you. Just respond with whatever comes to your mind first."

Melody knew she would most likely regret this, but she conceded. "Very well. Ask your questions."

Elodie straightened, her words taking on a more serious tone. "Cats or dogs?"

"Dogs," Melody answered.

"Summer or winter?"

"Winter."

Elodie bobbed her head. "Soirees or balls?"

"Soirees."

Her sister paused, then with a gleam in her eyes, asked, "Lord Emberly or Artemis?"

Melody blinked, caught off guard. "Pardon?"

Elodie waved her hand dismissively. "It is a simple enough question. Do you prefer Lord Emberly or Artemis?"

A frown creased Melody's brow. "I am not going to answer that."

Undeterred, Elodie leaned closer. "Let me put it another way. Imagine you are on a boat, and both Lord Emberly and Artemis fall overboard. If you could only save one of them, who would it be?"

Melody leaned to the side and placed her book down on the table. "Why are you asking these questions?"

"I am merely curious," Elodie responded.

"Why?" Melody pressed, sensing there was more to it.

Elodie's eyes danced with amusement. "You have been spending an awful lot of time with Lord Emberly lately."

"We are friends," Melody replied firmly.

"Interesting," Elodie said. "Didn't you once say you would never be friends with Lord Emberly?"

Melody was done with this ridiculous conversation. "Things can change," she said, moving to stand.

But Elodie put her hand out, stilling her. "Do you hold affection for Lord Emberly?"

"We are merely friends," Melody insisted, her frustration seeping into her words. "Now, can you stop with this interrogation?"

Elodie lowered her hand, but she didn't relent. "I just find it odd that your face lights up when you see Lord Emberly the same way it does when you receive a letter from Josephine."

"It is hardly the same," Melody argued.

Leaning back in her seat, Elodie remarked, "Furthermore, you haven't received one letter from Josephine since Lord Emberly arrived, nor have you posted one to her."

Melody worked to keep her face expressionless, though her mind raced. "It is merely a coincidence."

Elodie's skeptical gaze lingered on her. "Perhaps, but I know how prolific a letter writer you are when it comes to Josephine. It just baffles me. Why stop writing now?"

As Melody struggled to concoct a plausible explanation, the distant chime of the dinner bell offered a welcome reprieve. "We should go down to dinner," she suggested, quickly rising.

Elodie stood slowly. "Yes, we should," she agreed.

Melody turned on her heel and started walking out of the library. Her sister caught up to her and they made their way to the drawing room together. Once they arrived, Melody's breath caught in her throat when she saw Wesley standing by the mantel, looking deucedly handsome. No man had the right to look that handsome.

Wesley met her gaze and a slow smile spread across his lips. Melody approached him, stopping just a short distance away. In a hushed voice, she said, "We have a problem."

He grew alert. "We do?"

"Yes," Melody replied, glancing around the drawing room to ensure no one was listening. "My sister has noticed that I have not received a letter from Josephine since you arrived."

Wesley's brow furrowed. "She took note of that?"

Melody nodded. "My sister is clever—more so than most people give her credit for."

"I will take care of it," he assured her.

Relief washed over Melody as she returned her gaze to Wesley. "Thank you," she murmured.

Wesley's eyes perused the length of her, and she could see the approval glinting in his eyes. "You look lovely this evening."

Melody was secretly pleased by his compliment, but she was determined not to let it show. "Flattery, my lord?"

"Can I not offer a compliment when the situation calls for it?" Wesley inquired.

"This situation does not warrant it," she countered.

Wesley looked amused by her response. "Pray tell, when would the situation warrant it?"

Before Melody could respond, her mother stepped into the drawing room and announced, "White has just informed me that dinner is ready to be served."

Wesley offered his arm. "May I escort you to the dining room?"

Melody placed her hand on his sleeve, feeling the warmth of his arm beneath her fingers as they departed the drawing room together. As they walked, she lowered her voice and said, "By the way, I never did thank you for protecting me in the carriage."

Wesley's gaze softened. "It was the least I could do."

Melody looked up at him, her heart betraying her as she

allowed herself to be vulnerable, if only for a moment. "I thought it was rather brave," she admitted.

"It is my duty to keep you safe," Wesley responded.

Duty.

There it was again—the word she had come to dread. To Wesley, she was merely a responsibility. Why did she allow herself to believe, even for a second, that his actions were driven by anything more than obligation?

Wesley must have noticed the shift in her demeanor because he asked, "Did I say something wrong?"

"No," she replied quickly, forcing a smile to her lips.

They stepped into the dining room, and she slipped her hand off his arm. Wesley rushed forward to pull out her chair, and she murmured her gratitude before taking a seat.

Across the table, Lord Belview's gaze met hers, and he offered a warm smile. "You look especially lovely this evening, my lady," he praised.

Melody inclined her head in acknowledgment. "Thank you, my lord."

Wesley leaned in slightly, his voice dropping to a whisper. "You accept his compliment and not mine?"

"He was more sincere," Melody murmured.

"It didn't sound more sincere," Wesley countered with mirth in his voice.

Melody reached for her glass, trying to maintain her composure. "Will you not drop it?"

Wesley's smile widened as he straightened in his chair. "I will, but only because you asked nicely."

The delicate clink of silverware against glass caught everyone's attention. Her mother, seated at the head of the table, announced, "I have the most wonderful news. Doctor Anderson informed me that Artemis has nearly recovered, and he will be joining us tomorrow."

Lord Dallington raised his glass. "That is indeed wonderful news."

"I have so many questions for Artemis," Elodie chimed in. "I find that I am most curious about poisonous plants, especially the ones in our gardens."

Melody gave her sister a quizzical look. "Is there a particular reason you are so interested in poisonous plants?"

A mischievous glint flashed in Elodie's eyes. "There might be a time that I need to poison someone."

Melody laughed. "And what purpose would that serve?"

Elodie's gaze flickered briefly to Lord Belview before she returned her attention to Melody, her expression one of innocence. "Oh, no particular reason."

Lord Belview furrowed his brow. "You don't intend to poison me, do you?"

Elodie gasped dramatically. "Heavens, no!" she exclaimed. "Why would you think that?"

Her mother quickly interjected. "No one is going to poison anyone, much less one of our beloved guests. Isn't that right, Elodie?"

Elodie nodded. "I wholeheartedly agree, Mother. I do not know why Anthony is so paranoid. It is not very becoming of him."

Lord Belview's eyes narrowed playfully. "Perhaps I have good reason to be paranoid," he said, his words light.

"I assure you, my lord, you are perfectly safe… for now," Elodie replied.

Melody settled back in her chair as she listened to Elodie. She knew that her sister would never actually poison someone —least of all Lord Belview. Despite her sister's frequent claims of despising him, Melody wasn't entirely convinced of such a thing. There was a spark in Elodie's eyes when she quarreled with Lord Belview, a liveliness that was absent when she interacted with anyone else.

A Shadowed Charade

Wesley gritted his teeth, trying to ignore the sharp pain in his hands as he scaled the rough stone wall of Brockhall Manor. Climbing at night was no easy feat—each ledge and crevice seemed designed to resist him—but there was no room for failure. Melody's safety depended on him, and he was willing to risk anything to protect her.

As he reached her window, he noticed it was ajar, the faint glow from within guiding him. He hoisted himself up and went through the opening. Straightening, Wesley was met with the sight of Melody seated near the hearth, bathed in the fire's soft glow. She was wearing a white wrapper, a book resting on her lap, and her expression was a mix of irritation and something far more resigned.

"Wonderful," she muttered. "You have decided to risk my reputation once more by sneaking into my room at this late hour."

"It is for your own good," Wesley said.

"Is it?" Melody asked, setting her book aside. "Because for all your noble efforts, we have made little progress in discovering who wants us dead."

Wesley crossed the room and settled into a chair in the corner. "I am working on it."

But she had a point, and Wesley knew it. He had no solid leads—nothing to connect the attempt on his life and the poisoning of Artemis. The frustration gnawed at him. He was missing something crucial, but what?

Melody leaned back in her chair, her expression softening, though worry still lingered. "What happens if we don't discover who is after me after the other guests have departed? What will be your excuse for staying?"

Wesley met her gaze, his voice steady. "I have already told you the lengths to which I would go to keep you safe."

Her lips twisted into a wry smile. "Yes, you have made that quite clear. You would marry me—out of duty."

"You say that as if it were a bad thing."

Melody turned her gaze to the fire, her voice filled with emotion. "I don't want to be a duty to anyone. I want to marry for love."

Wesley sighed. "I know you have grand delusions of love, but we could make a marriage work between us."

"I want more, Wesley."

At that moment, Wesley knew she deserved more than what he could offer. Melody had dreams of a future filled with love and hope, things he wasn't sure he could give her. If she chose him, she would be giving up those dreams, which wasn't fair—to either of them.

"I just want to keep you safe," he stated.

Melody's eyes sharpened, her determination shining through as she squared her shoulders. "Why don't you believe I can protect myself?"

Wesley had known this would be her response. Melody was strong, and capable of so much more than what Society gave her credit for. But his fear wasn't rooted in her abilities. "It is not that I don't believe in you. It is that I can't bear the thought of losing you."

"You won't lose me," she said firmly.

"I wish it were that simple," Wesley responded. How he wished he could silence the constant dread that gnawed at him, the fear that something would happen to her, that the life he had created for her would pull her into danger.

A silence fell between them before Melody tilted her head. "Will you tell me about Dinah?"

Wesley's entire body tensed at the sound of her name, and the air around them felt heavier. Dinah. The name alone was enough to bring the rush of guilt, pain, and regret flooding back. He didn't want to talk about Dinah, not with anyone, least of all Melody. "There is not much to tell," he replied, his voice tight.

"I think there is more to the story than her being murdered," Melody pressed, her gaze unwavering.

His hands balled up into fists as he fought to steady his breathing. The mere thought of Dinah stirred something dark and painful inside him, a wound that had never truly healed. Why did her memory always cut so deep?

Melody's voice turned almost pleading. "Let me in, Wesley."

"It is not a matter of letting you in," Wesley remarked. "I do not like speaking about Dinah. She was a very important part of my life—until she wasn't."

The fire crackled in the silence that followed. He could feel Melody's eyes on him, searching, wanting to understand, but some parts of his past were too dark to share, even with her.

In a soft voice, she said, "I'm sorry. I should have never asked about Dinah. Everyone has a right to their own secrets."

Wesley felt a wave of guilt wash over him. Melody had done nothing wrong. His regrets had stirred up the pain, not her curiosity. He felt like a jackanapes for making her feel uncomfortable. "You do not have to apologize."

"I do."

"No, you don't. You did nothing wrong." He hesitated, the words heavy on his tongue. Could he trust himself to speak about Dinah, to let Melody glimpse the grief he carried? After a deep breath, he continued. "Dinah was more than an agent to me."

Melody's eyes widened as realization dawned. "You loved her?" Her words were tentative, more a question than a statement, as though she were trying to tread carefully.

He nodded. "I did," he admitted. "I still do, in some way. I thought we were going to build a life together, but she was taken from me far too soon."

"That is awful," Melody whispered.

Wesley turned his attention towards the crackling fire. "I have tried to forget about her, but I can't. When you have truly loved a woman until the end, you have known the deepest love. And the deepest pain."

Melody moved to sit on the edge of her seat. "I can only imagine," she replied. "But you keep her memory alive by continuing to live your life."

"You say that as if you have never had any heartache."

"I have lost loved ones; we all have," Melody said. "Although I can't know precisely what you are feeling, I can have an inkling of such."

Wesley's gaze locked with Melody's, his voice low but with barely controlled fury. "Someone took Dinah from me. I intend to find that person and make them pay," he said, the harshness of his words surprising even him. The anger was always there, lurking beneath the surface, waiting to boil over whenever Dinah's name came to mind.

"I believe you," Melody responded.

Some of the anger drained from him, replaced by a pang of guilt. He realized he had been unfair to Melody, taking his frustrations out on her when she had done nothing to deserve it. "Now, it is my turn to apologize—"

Melody put her hand up, silencing his words. "There is nothing to apologize for."

Wesley tipped his head in appreciation, though he retreated to his own thoughts. He didn't feel like talking anymore, not about Dinah and certainly not about the failure that haunted him. He had failed to protect her, and the weight of that failure was something he carried with him every day. It was no secret; everyone knew it, just as he did.

Melody reached for her book. "It is late. I should be going to bed." She stood, but she remained rooted in her spot. "How did your father die?"

Wesley's heart sank at that question. Botheration. The last thing he wanted was to delve into his father's death, especially after discussing Dinah. But as much as he hated discussing it, Wesley was tired of secrets. He realized at that moment that if he truly wanted Melody to trust him, he had to start trusting

A Shadowed Charade

her in return. He had to share the darker parts of his life, the parts he had locked away for so long.

He sighed heavily. "His heart supposedly gave out."

"But you don't believe that, do you?" Melody pressed, her eyes searching his.

The memories came rushing back and he fought back his emotions. "My father had gone ashore for an important meeting," he began slowly, carefully choosing his words. "The next morning, they found him dead in his bed. The coroner did a quick investigation and ruled it natural causes."

He paused. "But there were things that didn't add up. His death was sudden. Too sudden. And it mirrored Dinah's in a way that I can't ignore. The circumstances were too similar."

Melody's eyes softened, her voice filled with quiet compassion. "You have experienced so much death for your age."

Wesley let out a slight huff. "It is the natural order of our work, I suppose."

"It doesn't make it any easier."

"No, it does not," Wesley agreed.

Suddenly, a noise from outside the window broke the stillness of the room. Wesley raised a finger to his lips, signaling for Melody to remain silent. With practiced ease, he retrieved his pistol and rose from his chair, moving swiftly to place himself between her and whatever threat lurked beyond the wall.

Moments later, Jasper's unmistakable head poked up from the window, his breath coming in labored gasps. "Good gads, scaling that wall is no easy task," he muttered, pulling himself into the room.

Wesley lowered his pistol. "What, pray tell, are you doing here?"

"I could ask you the same question, my lord," Jasper said, brushing the dust off his clothes. "You made that look easy, by the way."

Returning his pistol to the waistband of his trousers, Wesley asked, "You saw me?"

"I did," Jasper said, still catching his breath. "I followed you, though at a far less graceful pace. I wanted to see for myself what you were doing in Lady Melody's room."

Melody stepped out from behind Wesley. "I can explain…" she started.

Jasper crossed his arms over his chest, his face stern. "I am listening."

With a glance at Wesley, Melody said, "Lord Emberly has started coming into my room to protect me."

"Protect you?" Jasper asked. "From what, exactly?"

Melody pressed her lips together. "Does it matter?"

Jasper scoffed. "Yes, it does matter," he replied. "Lord Winston instructed me to keep you safe while he was away, and I am sure he would be furious to know that Lord Emberly is visiting your bedchamber."

"It is my fault," Wesley interjected, stepping forward. "After Artemis was poisoned, I felt especially protective of Lady Melody."

"You think Artemis was poisoned intentionally?" Jasper asked.

"I do, and I believe that Lady Melody was the true target," Wesley replied.

Jasper's eyes flickered around the room, his mind clearly working through the implication. "And why do you believe this?"

Wesley's gaze hardened, unwilling to reveal the full extent of his suspicions. "I cannot say."

"You can't say or won't say?" Jasper pressed.

Wesley held Jasper's intense gaze without flinching. "I assure you that my intentions are entirely honorable," he said, his voice unwavering.

Jasper uncrossed his arms, his posture relaxing slightly, but his eyes were still sharp and distrustful. "Then we are at an impasse, my lord."

Melody spoke up. "You are not going to tell anyone about what you saw, especially not my brother."

Jasper's brow furrowed in skepticism. "And why is that?"

She took a step closer to Jasper. "Because nothing untoward is happening between Lord Emberly and me. There are strange things afoot at Brockhall Manor and I need his help to uncover the truth."

Jasper frowned. "You do realize the implications of being found with a gentleman in your bedchamber, don't you?"

"Of course, I am aware," Melody responded. "And I am willing to risk it."

Jasper shot a wary glance at Wesley before responding, "I don't trust him, but I trust you, my lady."

"Thank you, Jasper," Melody murmured, relief softening her tone.

"You need to be more careful," Jasper urged. "If I saw Lord Emberly sneaking into your bedchamber, others might have seen it as well."

Before anyone could respond, a soft knock echoed at the door, followed by the handle turning. "Melody? Are you in there?" came a familiar voice.

Panic flashed across Melody's face. "Quick, you must hide. It is my sister," she whispered urgently.

"Where?" Wesley asked, his eyes darting around the room.

"Under the bed," Melody replied, gesturing frantically towards it.

"Both of us?" Jasper asked.

Melody bobbed her head, her expression desperate. "Unless you have a better idea?"

Another knock came at the door, more insistent this time. "Melody? It is me, Elodie. Why is your door locked?"

Without wasting another moment, Wesley hurried over to

the bed and slid underneath it. Jasper followed quickly, squeezing in beside him, making the already tight space even more cramped.

He heard Melody's soft footsteps walk over to the door. As she unlocked and opened the door, she asked, "What are you doing awake?"

"I thought I heard voices," Elodie responded.

Melody let out a light, airy laugh. "Voices? You must be imagining things. I'm the only one here."

A terse silence followed. Finally, Elodie relented. "Perhaps I am more tired than I realized."

"You should go to bed, Sister," Melody encouraged. "Goodnight."

"Goodnight," Elodie replied, her footsteps retreating down the corridor.

The moment the door clicked shut, Melody hurried over to the bed, kneeling beside it and whispering, "That was entirely too close. You both need to leave, and quickly."

Wesley came out from under the bed, dusting himself off. "Make sure to keep that door locked and your pistol under your pillow."

"I will," Melody assured him.

As Wesley approached the window, Jasper asked, "Is it harder to climb down the wall than up?"

"Yes, very much so," Wesley said, giving him a wry smile. "Don't break anything."

Wesley carefully climbed out of the window, finding precarious footing on the jutting bricks that lined the manor. The cool night air brushed against his face as he descended with quiet precision, his hands gripping the rough stone. Once his boots touched the ground, he stepped back, scanning the area before turning to watch Jasper follow.

Jasper, breathing heavily, landed with a thud, muttering, "That wasn't so difficult."

Wesley took a step forward, his eyes narrowing slightly as he kept his voice low. "Why are you really here, Jasper?"

The Bow Street Runner straightened, meeting Wesley's gaze with a hardened look. "I could ask you the same thing, my lord."

"I am here to ensure no harm comes to Melody or her family," Wesley said, offering just enough truth to appease Jasper.

"Lord Winston hired me to do the same," Jasper said. "But at least my presence makes sense. Yours does not. You appear out of nowhere, claiming your intentions are honorable, yet your actions suggest there's more you are not telling me."

Wesley glanced up at Melody's window. "We don't trust each other, but we share a common goal. We both want to keep this family safe, and it would be foolish not to work together."

Jasper's jaw clenched, his suspicion palpable. "I don't like you, my lord. You are a man shrouded in secrets, and I have learned not to trust men like you."

A small, knowing smile tugged at the corner of Wesley's lips. "As are you. We are not so different in that regard."

Jasper considered him for a long moment. "Very well. But if I find out you are any kind of threat to this family's safety, I will deal with you swiftly. No hesitation."

"Agreed. And understand, if I find *you* to be a threat, I will handle it just the same."

The tension lingered in the cool night air, but Jasper gave a curt nod. "Then we are in agreement."

Wesley returned the nod. "Yes."

"Goodnight."

As Jasper turned and disappeared into the shadows of the nearby trees, Wesley remained rooted in his spot. Had he just made a dangerous pact with a man who could become his enemy at any moment? Or had he simply aligned himself with someone who might be crucial to protecting Melody and her family?

Only time would tell, but Wesley knew that Melody trusted Jasper. And he trusted Melody.

Chapter Twelve

Dressed in a pale yellow gown, Melody stepped out of her bedchamber and was surprised to find her sister waiting for her in the corridor. Elodie leaned casually against the wall, her expression unreadable.

Melody raised an eyebrow in question. "What are you doing loitering outside of my bedchamber?"

"I wished to speak to you," Elodie replied.

"You couldn't have knocked on my door?" Melody asked, amusement in her voice.

Elodie shrugged. "I could have, but I want this conversation to be private."

"And you thought the corridor was more private than my bedchamber?" Melody pressed, trying to grasp her sister's logic.

With a casual gesture down the hall, Elodie suggested, "Why don't we walk to the dining room together for breakfast? We can talk on the way."

"Very well," Melody conceded.

As they walked side by side down the corridor, Elodie glanced at Melody sideways. "I could have sworn I heard male voices in your bedchamber last night."

"Voices?" Melody echoed, forcing a tone of innocent confusion, though her heart quickened. "As in more than one male voice?"

"I know it sounds ridiculous, but—"

Melody quickly cut her off. "That is because it is ridiculous, Sister. Why would I entertain gentlemen in my bedchamber? I would be ruined if anyone even suspected such a thing."

Elodie lowered her voice as they walked. "Then what are you involved in?"

"Nothing," Melody answered quickly, perhaps too quickly. She hoped the urgency in her voice didn't betray her. But her sister wasn't easily swayed, and Melody could see the doubt deepening in her expression.

"You have always been the perfect daughter, the perfect sister, but now I wonder if it was all just an act," Elodie remarked.

Melody stopped at the top of the stairs, turning to face her sister. "I am the same sister that you have always known."

"Perhaps. But now, you are far more interesting. You have secrets, I can tell."

"I am not the least bit interesting," Melody attempted.

Elodie gave her a pointed look. "Then explain why Lord Emberly keeps swapping plates with you at meals."

"I cannot speak for him."

"And yet, you allow him to do so without even raising a complaint," Elodie said. "It is just odd."

Guilt washed over Melody as she struggled with the lies she was forced to keep. She longed to tell her sister the truth, but it was too risky to do so. No. This secret needed to stay hidden, especially from Elodie.

Placing a hand on her sister's sleeve, Melody remarked, "I assure you, nothing is amiss." But Elodie shook her head, her expression softening into one of concern. "You are keeping something from me. What is it?"

Melody sighed and dropped her hand. "You are reading too much into this."

The conversation was abruptly cut short by a knock at the main door. They both turned to see White crossing the entry hall to open it. The door swung open to reveal Mr. Bramwell standing on the threshold. His eyes immediately sought out Melody.

"Lady Melody," he greeted with a polite bow.

She tipped her head in response before turning back to Elodie. "Come, let me introduce you to Mr. Bramwell."

Together, the sisters descended the grand staircase, stopping before the vicar. Melody gestured towards Elodie. "Mr. Bramwell, allow me to introduce my sister, Lady Elodie."

Mr. Bramwell bowed again, his eyes flickering between them with mild curiosity. "You two are truly identical, are you not?"

Melody smiled playfully. "Only until you get to know us," she quipped, sharing a quick glance with Elodie, who wore a slight smirk of her own.

Mr. Bramwell chuckled. "I have something to look forward to, then."

Knowing what was expected of her, Melody extended her hand towards the drawing room. "Would you care for a cup of tea?"

Mr. Bramwell's next words came out in a rush. "No, actually. I was hoping, at least I thought, if you had the time, that perhaps you might take me on a tour of your gardens."

Melody decided to take pity on Mr. Bramwell. "I would be honored to."

A broad smile lit up Mr. Bramwell's face as he offered his arm. "Wonderful. Shall we?"

With a nod, Melody placed her hand lightly on his sleeve, and together, they walked towards the rear of the manor. A footman opened the door to the veranda, allowing them to step outside. The crisp morning air greeted them, and they began strolling down the garden path.

After a few moments, Melody slipped her hand off his arm, clasping her fingers together as she listened to the cheerful chirping of the birds in the trees. "It is a beautiful morning, is it not?"

"Yes, quite beautiful," Mr. Bramwell promptly agreed, though his gaze remained fixed on her.

Noticing his rigid posture, Melody decided to set him at ease by asking, "Have you settled into your cottage?"

"I have," Mr. Bramwell replied. "It is rather quaint."

Melody smiled. "I have many fond memories of that cottage. It is where my dear friend, Mattie, grew up."

"I understand she is now your sister-in-law," Mr. Bramwell remarked.

Melody's smile widened. "Yes, Mattie and Winston were perfect for one another. Everyone could see it—except for them, of course. But they eventually came around."

Mr. Bramwell clasped his hands behind his back as they walked. "You should know that Lord Wythburn speaks very highly of you."

"He is a kind man," Melody replied.

"That he is, but he is also an excellent judge of character," Mr. Bramwell added.

Melody pointed towards a shaded bench and asked, "Shall we sit?"

Mr. Bramwell glanced down the path ahead, his brow furrowing slightly. "If you have no objections, I would prefer to continue walking. I was hoping for some privacy."

She did have an objection. Trees shrouded the path ahead, and she did not doubt that her sister, likely watching from one of the windows, would lose sight of them. A slight twinge of unease crept into her thoughts.

"I think it might be best if we sat in view of the manor, for propriety's sake," Melody said.

"Of course," Mr. Bramwell responded with a smile. "My apologies. I have no wish to make you feel uncomfortable."

Melody gracefully sat on the bench, and Mr. Bramwell followed, ensuring he left a respectful distance between them. A brief silence settled over them until Mr. Bramwell cleared his throat, his nerves clearly resurfacing. "I must admit, I am truly awful at this," he confessed. "One would think Eton would offer a class on polite conversational skills with a young woman."

Melody grinned, amused by his honesty. "You are most fortunate, then. I happen to be quite skilled in the art of conversation."

Mr. Bramwell's expression lightened. "Are you, now?"

She shifted on the bench to face him more fully. "Indeed. Let us start with something simple. Where do you hail from?"

"Sussex," he replied, his tone still somewhat clipped.

"I understand that you are a grandson of a marquess," Melody continued.

Mr. Bramwell settled back onto the bench. "Yes, I am."

"Our conversation would go much more smoothly if you expanded on your answers," she teased.

He chuckled. "I'm sorry. I find that I am remarkably nervous around you."

"There is no reason to be nervous," Melody assured him.

Mr. Bramwell turned his attention towards the manor, his gaze lingering on one of the lower windows. Melody followed his gaze and wasn't surprised to see Elodie, peering at them from behind the curtain.

"Is your sister always so protective of you?" Mr. Bramwell asked, clearly bemused by the sight.

"She tends to have the unfortunate habit of eavesdropping on private conversations," Melody said. "But yes, we are very protective of one another. A plight of being a twin, I suppose."

"Are you two similar?" Mr. Bramwell asked, bringing his gaze back to meet hers.

Melody let out a soft laugh. "Heavens, no! We are as different as two sisters can be, but those differences keep us close."

"My sister and I are rather close," Mr. Bramwell admitted. "Our parents died when we were young, and we were sent to live with my grandfather. Given his responsibilities as a marquess, we had to rely on each other since he wasn't around very much."

"I am sorry to hear about your parents," Melody acknowledged.

"It was the fever," Mr. Bramwell explained, his voice growing more dejected. "It took them both within days of each other." He paused. "But that is not what I wish to discuss with you."

Just as he was about to continue, Melody noticed movement on the veranda. She turned her head and saw Wesley stepping out, his eyes meeting hers with a steady gaze. He gave her a nod before leaning against the wall, adopting a less formal posture. His presence seemed to shift the air between her and Mr. Bramwell.

Mr. Bramwell must have noticed, too, as his expression grew tight. "Do you have an understanding with Lord Emberly?"

"An understanding? With Lord Emberly?" she repeated. "Good heavens, no. We are merely friends."

Furrowing his brow, Mr. Bramwell remarked, "Lord Emberly seems rather protective of you, more so than your sister."

"He can be rather intense at times. But I assure you that he means no harm."

Abruptly, Mr. Bramwell rose from the bench. "I should be heading back to my parish," he said, his voice suddenly distant.

"Didn't you wish to speak to me about something?" Melody asked, rising.

Glancing at Lord Emberly, he replied, "It can wait." He extended his arm. "I do apologize for calling upon you at such an early hour."

"I found it to be a most enjoyable way to start the day," Melody said, accepting his arm. Her words seemed to puff Mr. Bramwell's chest with pride.

"You know how to flatter a gentleman, my lady."

"It was merely the truth," Melody stated.

After a moment of silence, Mr. Bramwell asked, "May I call upon you again?" He seemed to hold his breath as he waited for her reply.

Melody bobbed her head. "You may."

While Mr. Bramwell led her back to the manor, he inquired, "I understand that you are quite the linguist?"

"You could say that, sir," she responded, a bit surprised by the change in topic.

"That is an impressive feat," Mr. Bramwell said. "Not everyone can read and understand Russian."

At his words, Melody's back stiffened. She halted mid-step, turning to look at him fully. "How did you know I speak Russian?"

Mr. Bramwell shrugged. "Lord Wythburn mentioned it to me. I hope that is not an issue."

"It is not common knowledge, especially since my father would not be pleased if he found out," Melody shared.

"Forgive me," Mr. Bramwell said. "I shall not speak of it again."

As they approached the veranda, Melody's thoughts were clouded with confusion. She found it odd that Mr. Bramwell knew such a specific detail about her—something she had only shared with a select few. Mattie knew she spoke Russian, but why had she passed that information along to her father? Russian was not a common language for young women of the *ton*, considering it was primarily regarded as an uncouth language.

Once they reached the veranda, she discreetly withdrew her arm from his and took a small step back, putting more distance between them.

Wesley straightened and stepped forward. "Good morning, my lady," he said with a bow. "Mr. Bramwell."

Mr. Bramwell's lips pressed into a thin line. "Lord Emberly," he responded.

Turning his attention towards Melody, Wesley asked, "Shall we adjourn for breakfast?"

"I think that is a grand idea," Melody said.

Wesley sat in the drawing room, a book in hand, watching Melody quietly absorbed in her needlework. Across the room, Elodie played the pianoforte, her fingers gliding effortlessly over the keys, filling the air with soft music.

Despite the calm atmosphere, Wesley's body remained tense, his mind burdened by the weight of his assignment. His duty was to protect Melody, and the frustration of his failure to uncover the identity of her would-be assassin gnawed at him. Days had passed, and he was no closer to finding the person who sought to harm her than when he had first arrived.

What if he failed her?

The thought threatened to consume him, but he clenched his jaw, pushing it away. No. He wouldn't allow that to happen. He refused to fail anyone else. He already carried too many regrets.

Lady Dallington swept into the room and her eyes settled on Melody. "Child, why don't you sing something for our guests?" she suggested, though her tone made it clear it was more of a command than a request.

Melody looked up from her needlework, her expression reluctant. "I believe we are all rather content listening to Elodie's performance."

"Nonsense," Lady Dallington replied. "You two perform so nicely together. Go on."

At that, Elodie stopped playing and rested her hands on the keys, glancing at her sister with an amused glint in her eyes. "What do you want to sing, Monkey?"

"I am not a monkey," Melody asserted.

Elodie's grin widened as she teased, "Are we not just performing monkeys for Mother's enjoyment?"

Lady Dallington did not look amused by Elodie's antics. "Dear heavens, I think I shall turn you over to the circus and let them deal with you."

Elodie perked up in her seat. "Do you promise?"

Melody rose from her chair, moving towards her sister with a whisper Wesley couldn't catch. Then, turning to face the room, she smiled faintly, though Wesley could sense her hesitation. "This is a song that I wrote myself," she announced.

Wesley leaned back in his seat. He had heard Melody had a lovely voice, but he didn't realize she wrote her own music.

As the music began, the melody was soft and gentle at first, matching the lightness of Elodie's touch on the keys. Then Melody's voice filled the room. The first few notes took Wesley by surprise—her voice was rich, captivating and undeniably beautiful. He found himself staring at her, entranced, wondering how she had ever managed to keep such a gift hidden. Each note seemed to reveal something deeper, more intimate, about her, and the longer she sang, the more Wesley found himself lost in the sound.

There was something about her voice, something about her presence, that made everything else—the dangers, the uncertainties—fade away. And in that moment, he silently hoped she would never stop singing.

But all good things must come to an end.

Melody stopped singing as the music came to a close. Wesley jumped up from his seat and applauded. "Well done!" he praised.

Across the room, Lord Belview also stood, joining in. "Bravo!" he called out.

Elodie came to stand next to Melody and joked, "Why didn't I get this reaction for my playing?"

Wesley made his way towards Melody. "You have the most extraordinary voice," he praised.

Melody ducked her head, a hint of pink rising to her cheeks. "Thank you," she murmured.

A maid entered the room carrying a tray and Elodie's eyes lit up. "Biscuits!" she said with excitement, excusing herself quickly to investigate the treats.

Wesley leaned in closer, lowering his voice. "Why do you not sing more often?"

She brought her gaze up. "I do not enjoy the attention my voice commands. It makes me stand out."

"For a good reason," Wesley replied.

In a quieter, more serious tone, Melody added, "I prefer anonymity. It makes accomplishing what I need to easier without drawing unnecessary attention."

Wesley understood her point, but he couldn't help feeling it was a shame to keep such a gift hidden. Her voice had moved him in a way he hadn't expected, and he found himself wishing to hear it again, despite her reluctance. Just as he was about to say more, Jasper stepped into the room, meeting his gaze.

"Please excuse me," Wesley said to the ladies before turning and walking over to the Bow Street Runner.

Rather than remain where she was, Melody followed him and asked, "What is it, Jasper?"

A Shadowed Charade

Jasper tipped his head. "May I speak to you both for a moment?"

"Follow me," Melody said, gesturing for them to follow her out of the drawing room. She led them through the manor and onto the veranda.

Jasper had a solemn look on his face. "A traveler was discovered in the woodlands," he began. "He was found unconscious, beaten badly, and his clothes were missing. The innkeeper called for a doctor, but the man didn't wake for two days. When he finally did, he kept repeating the same words: 'Brockhall Manor.'"

"He said nothing else?" Melody asked.

"No, but that is not the worst of it," Jasper said. "In an effort to identify the man, the doctor spread the word around, hoping someone would come forward with information."

Wesley let out a groan, sensing where this was going. "Tell me that the man is still alive."

Jasper shook his head. "I'm afraid not. The coroner investigated and ruled it was natural causes. His heart supposedly gave out."

Wesley's fists clenched at his sides, a familiar anger simmering beneath the surface. "Were the windows shut and the door locked?" he asked, already suspecting the answer.

"They were," Jasper responded, eyeing Wesley with curiosity. "How did you know that?"

"Because he was murdered," Wesley declared.

Jasper crossed his arms over his chest. "There were no signs of a struggle or marks of asphyxiation."

"There never are," Wesley said. "But I have seen this before, multiple times, in fact. It is the perfect murder. The coroners dismiss the possibility of foul play too easily."

"I could speak to the coroner about reopening the case," Jasper offered.

Wesley exhaled heavily. "It won't matter. He will reach the same conclusion unless we can produce solid evidence."

"And do you have any evidence of what you are saying?" Jasper asked.

"No," Wesley admitted, running a hand through his hair.

Melody gently placed a hand on Wesley's sleeve, her touch comforting. "This is not your fault."

Wesley turned to face her. "Then whose fault is it? I was supposed to stop this person, and now they have claimed another life. I have failed again."

"You are doing your best…" she insisted.

Wesley huffed. "My best is not good enough. You are at risk as long as this person is out there."

Jasper cleared his throat, his gaze shifting between the two of them. "Do you want to explain what you two are involved in?"

"It is not important," Wesley replied dismissively. "What did the man who was murdered look like?"

It was evident that Jasper had more to say on the topic, but thankfully, he let it drop. "The man was short, thin and spoke with a French accent."

"He was French?" Wesley asked.

Jasper nodded. "Yes, the doctor confirmed it."

Wesley walked over to the railing, his gaze drifting over the grounds of Brockhall Manor. His mind raced with questions. Why would a Frenchman be involved with Brockhall Manor? What connection did he have to the danger surrounding Melody?

Melody stepped up beside him. "What are you thinking?"

"I have to stop him," Wesley replied.

She offered a small smile. "You will."

"And what if I can't?" he asked, feeling the doubt creep in. "How many more people will die because I am incompetent at my job?"

Melody reached out, placing a firm hand on his sleeve, turning him to face her. "Do not speak like that. We will figure this out, and we will do so together."

Wesley winced, guilt gnawing at him. "You are in danger because of me, Melody. This is my fault."

She gave him a stern look. "Are you quite done feeling sorry for yourself? I only ask because we have work that we need to do."

"Melody..." he began.

Melody's expression grew thoughtful. "I think we should talk to Artemis," she said. "Someone poisoned him, but he didn't die. Why?"

"Maybe they gave him the wrong dose?" Wesley suggested. "Or perhaps it was just a warning—to you?"

Before Melody could respond, Jasper stepped closer to them. "I am sorry to interrupt, but I am still here."

Melody barely spared Jasper a glance as she continued with her thoughts. "This person has killed before, so why would he have administered the wrong dose? It makes me wonder if this person used poison to kill others."

"But no drink or food is ever found beside the bed," Wesley pointed out.

Melody's eyes grew wide. "What if they inhaled it?" she asked, her voice quickening with excitement. "There would be no trace of it after the fact."

A slow smile spread across Wesley's face. "That is precisely what is happening. We need to speak to Artemis and see what plants could be fatal from inhaling them."

Jasper rocked back on the balls of his feet. "I am a Bow Street Runner, in case anyone needed to be reminded," he said dryly.

Wesley chuckled despite the gravity of the situation. "We are well aware," he said. "Come, let us go inside before anyone misses us." He offered his arm to Melody before he led her inside.

As they stepped back into the manor, Wesley felt a flicker of hope he hadn't experienced in days. The pieces of the puzzle were finally starting to fall into place, and for the first time, they had a direction—a tangible lead that might reveal the truth. And it was all because of Melody.

His Melody.

The thought hit him out of nowhere, catching him off guard. No. She was not his. Where had that thought even come from? No matter how deeply he admired her, she was not his to claim. His job was simple: track down the killer, ensure Melody was safe, and then walk away.

He repeated the thought in his head. *Walk away.*

It was what was best—for both of them.

Chapter Thirteen

Melody quietly slipped out the back door of Brockhall Manor, her footsteps quick as she hurried down the garden path. She needed to reach her Aunt Sarah's cottage without being noticed, especially without Wesley's watchful eyes following her every move. She wanted to speak to her aunt privately, free from prying ears.

Her thoughts were a tangled mess, her mind swirling with too many questions and too few answers. And much to her frustration, her thoughts kept drifting back to Wesley. It was infuriating. He was supposed to be her partner, nothing more. Yet, her heart betrayed her with its racing beats.

Drats. She couldn't afford to be distracted by such nonsense. Wesley was just a man—a handsome man, yes, but still just a man. She shook her head, hoping to clear her mind of him. Right now, she needed clarity, and there was only one person she could trust to provide it—Aunt Sarah.

Melody's eyes darted across the fields, making sure no one was giving her any heed. She knew Wesley would be furious if he found out she had left the safety of the manor without him. But she had to do this.

As she neared the cottage, the rhythmic sound of chopping wood reached her ears. She circled to the back and found Jasper, mid-swing, splitting logs with practiced precision. She waited until he set the ax aside before approaching, lifting her hand in greeting.

"Good afternoon," she called out.

Jasper glanced up, a smirk already forming on his lips. "Where is your shadow?"

"My shadow?" Melody asked, feigning ignorance.

His smirk deepened. "Lord Emberly," he said with a knowing tilt of his head.

She pressed her lips together before saying, "Lord Emberly is not my shadow. He is…"

"Your friend," Jasper interrupted, amusement dancing in his eyes. "An unusually close friend, I'd say."

Melody was not in the mood for this line of conversation. Eager to change the topic, she said, "I have come to invite you and Sarah to dine with us this evening."

Jasper raised an eyebrow as he bent to gather the chopped wood. "Truly? Your father wishes to dine with a Bow Street Runner?"

"I haven't spoken to him about it, but it won't be an issue," Melody replied.

"I will pass."

Melody had expected as much but wasn't ready to give up. "It could be fun," she insisted.

Jasper gave her a pointed look as he cradled the chopped wood in his arms. "Fun?" he huffed. "I don't even have anything to wear."

"You can come as you are," Melody said.

He chuckled. "That would be a sight to behold," he remarked. "Your family in their finest, and I stroll in wearing this?" He gestured to his work-worn clothes.

Melody crossed her arms over her chest. "My father may be a stickler for propriety, but I am not. Neither is Elodie. You are welcome as you are."

Jasper's expression softened, but he shook his head again. "Thank you, but I must decline your invitation. It is best for everyone if I stay here."

"Including Sarah?" Melody pressed.

He paused. "What does Lady Sarah have to say about this?"

Melody shrugged. "I haven't asked her."

"I'm sure she would think it is utter nonsense," Jasper said. "A Bow Street Runner has no right dining at the same table as a marquess."

"Shall we ask her?"

Jasper shook his head, exasperation creeping into his voice. "Why are you being so insistent about this?"

Melody stepped closer to Jasper, lowering her voice so only he could hear. "Artemis will be at dinner tonight. Do you not want to be there when Lord Emberly and I speak to him?"

Indecision flickered across Jasper's face as he weighed the situation. "I do," he admitted.

Before he could say more, the cottage's back door creaked open, and Aunt Sarah stepped out, wiping her hands on her apron. "Melody, what a lovely surprise," she said. "What brings you by my home?"

Jasper spoke up. "She has come to invite us both to dine at Brockhall Manor this evening."

Sarah smiled, but it looked forced. "What wonderful news," she said, her voice a little too cheery.

Jasper raised an eyebrow, his disbelief evident. "Is it, though?"

"Yes, I will ask Mrs. Warren to watch Matthew this evening," Sarah said.

Jasper exhaled in resignation, shaking his head slightly. "I shall go, but only because you wish it."

Sarah's smile softened into something more genuine as her gaze met Jasper's. "You will get a glimpse into the life I once belonged to."

Jasper shifted the pile of wood in his arms. "I should put these down," he said, gesturing towards the woodpile. "I will come back later to escort you to dinner."

"Thank you, Jasper," Sarah acknowledged as she watched him walk away.

Melody couldn't help but notice the unspoken tension between them, the way they looked at each other with emotions neither seemed willing to admit fully. There was something deeper between Sarah and Jasper. She was sure of it. Now, how did she go about having them recognize it for themselves?

Sarah turned to Melody and gestured towards the door. "Come inside. I need to speak with you in private."

Melody followed her aunt into the cottage, watching Sarah pacing the small space, her brows knitted in concern. "What is wrong?" she asked.

Her aunt stopped and threw her hands in the air in frustration. "Why did you have to invite Jasper?"

"Is that a problem?"

With a sigh, Sarah slumped into a chair, rubbing her temples. "I no longer belong in that world, Melody. What if Jasper starts thinking it is the life I deserve?"

"It *is* what you deserve."

Sarah shook her head. "You are kind, but we both know I am an outcast amongst Society. I made my choices and now I must live with them."

Melody took a step closer to her aunt. "You are family, and we love you dearly." After a pause, she added gently, "And I suspect Jasper cares deeply for you as well."

Her aunt's eyes drifted towards the window, her expression distant. "I care for him," she admitted quietly. "But even if my feelings were reciprocated, it cannot be."

"Why not?" Melody asked, sensing there was more to her aunt's hesitation than she was letting on.

Sarah's gaze grew heavy with sorrow. "I want Matthew to

grow up surrounded by family, especially now that your father has agreed to oversee his education."

"I fail to see the problem," Melody said.

Turning to face her, Sarah replied, "If I did marry Jasper, he would have to give up his work as a Bow Street Runner. He would have to stay here. With me. I cannot ask him to give up something he loves."

"Have you discussed it with him?"

Sarah huffed. "Heavens, no," she declared. "Jasper is a kind, considerate man. I won't trap him in a life he doesn't want."

"But what if it is a life he *does* want?" Melody pressed.

Her aunt looked at her, clearly torn. "Who would want this life?" she asked. "I have seen the way he speaks about his work, the passion in his eyes when he talks about being a Bow Street Runner. I won't be the reason that light fades."

Melody sighed softly, realizing the depth of her aunt's struggle. Sarah wasn't just worried about herself—she was trying to protect Jasper from a decision he hadn't even made. But what if she was wrong to take away Jasper's right to choose?

Sarah rose from her chair, smoothing her skirts as she did. "I suppose I should find something suitable to wear for tonight."

"Would you like me to help?"

Her aunt laughed. "It is not too difficult. Fortunately, your mother sent over a few gowns for just this sort of occasion. I only need to make a few adjustments to ensure they fit properly."

Melody smiled. "I am quite proficient in needlework if you need a hand with those modifications."

Sarah's gaze drifted towards the window, her eyes lingering outside. "It would appear that Lord Emberly has come to escort you back to the manor."

"He has?" Melody asked, moving to stand beside her aunt.

Her eyes followed Sarah's gaze, landing on Wesley, who was in a conversation with Jasper near the woodpile.

"Do you have an understanding with Lord Emberly?" Sarah asked.

Melody shook her head vehemently. "No, absolutely not. We are merely friends."

Sarah eyed her curiously. "Does he know that?"

"Yes, we have discussed marriage—" Melody began, but her words were cut off as Sarah's expression shifted to surprise.

"You have discussed marriage?"

Realizing the implication of her own words, Melody hurried to correct herself. "It was not like that. It was a passing conversation, truly! He mentioned a marriage of convenience, and I told him I wanted more than that."

"As well you should," Sarah said approvingly. "But it is evident that you care for him."

Melody pressed her lips together, feeling the warmth rise in her cheeks. "I may have developed the tiniest of feelings for Lord Emberly, but that doesn't mean I intend to act upon them."

Sarah shifted to face her, her expression thoughtful. "Whyever not?"

"It is complicated," Melody replied, hoping to end this line of questioning.

An understanding look came to Sarah's expression. "It always is."

Melody glanced back at the window, watching Wesley as he stood in the yard, still conversing with Jasper. His presence was commanding, and for a brief moment, she imagined what it would be like to be married to him. He was a good, honorable man. Life with him would be safe—perhaps even content. But would she ever capture his heart?

Did she want to?

The answer came to her before she could stop it. Yes.

A Shadowed Charade

As she watched him, her heart betrayed her with a sudden, undeniable truth. She cared for Wesley far more than she had allowed herself to admit. The realization tightened her chest, knowing she was falling for the most infuriating man she had ever known.

Sarah placed a gentle hand on her sleeve. "It is all right to feel confused, especially regarding matters of the heart."

Melody took a step back, overwhelmed by the moment. "I should go," she said, the words coming out a bit too quick. "I do not wish to keep Lord Emberly waiting."

"I shall see you tonight."

Spinning on her heel, Melody made her way to the cottage's back door. She stepped outside and immediately met Wesley's eyes, sensing his annoyance even from a distance. Not that she had expected anything different.

"Lady Melody," Wesley greeted her, his tone formal despite the tension in his voice. "I have come to escort you back to Brockhall Manor."

Melody forced a smile. "Wonderful."

Wesley stepped closer, his voice lowering to a hushed but curt tone. "Are you mad? How could you leave Brockhall Manor without me?"

"It is good to see you, too," Melody said dryly as she brushed past him.

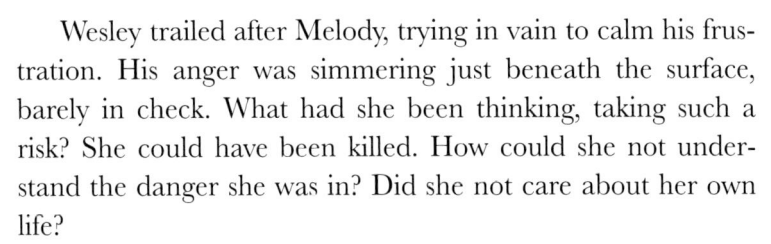

Wesley trailed after Melody, trying in vain to calm his frustration. His anger was simmering just beneath the surface, barely in check. What had she been thinking, taking such a risk? She could have been killed. How could she not understand the danger she was in? Did she not care about her own life?

Or worse, did she not care for him?

The thought brought him to a halt, rooting him in place. What would have happened if Melody had been hurt, or worse—killed? Could he live with himself knowing he had failed again, failed to protect someone who mattered to him? And more troubling than that, could he live without her? She had started as just another assignment, a duty, but she had become much more than that somewhere along the way.

Blazes.

Wesley rubbed a hand across his face. He couldn't afford to let these pesky feelings distract him. Melody had made it clear she had no interest in marriage, especially to him. But it would have been the perfect solution to all their problems. If they were married, he would take her to his estate and hire as many guards as it took to keep her safe.

As his gaze swept across the woodlands, his instincts remained on high alert, scanning for any sign of danger, any lurking threat. But the woods were still, offering no sign of a hidden enemy. He shook off his unease and hurried to catch up with Melody, who was walking briskly ahead, her chin lifted high, and her back rigid. She was angry with him, but she had to understand that he would do anything to keep her safe, even if she resented him for it.

After a long stretch of silence, Wesley decided it was time to speak. "I know you are angry at me—"

She spoke over him, her tone clipped. "Why would you think that, my lord?"

Wesley sighed, recognizing the trap in her words. His mother had once warned him about questions like these. There were no right answers. Still, he decided to be frank. "What were you thinking?"

"I was thinking I wanted to invite my Aunt Sarah and Jasper to dine with us this evening," Melody said, barely sparing him a glance.

Wesley frowned. "Why didn't you ask me to accompany you?"

"Because I am perfectly capable of walking down a path to my aunt's cottage," Melody replied, her words sharp with defiance.

He stopped in front of her, gently taking her hand and turning her to face him. "Your thoughtless actions could have gotten you killed," he said, his voice lower but no less intense.

Melody refused to meet his gaze. "I needed a moment alone, considering you are always underfoot."

"You know why I have to stay close. It is because I need to protect you."

"Yes, I am *your* responsibility," Melody stated flatly.

Wesley dropped his hand from her arm and placed a finger under her chin, forcing her to look at him. "You are more than just a responsibility to me, Melody."

Her eyes searched his as if trying to decipher his meaning. "What am I, then?" she asked, her voice quiet, uncertain.

"I don't know," he admitted honestly, surprising himself. "But I care for you. You must know that."

She nodded. "I do."

"Then please, do not do something so foolish again," Wesley said. "I can't bear the thought of losing you."

A flicker of annoyance crossed her face. "It was not foolish. I can take care of myself."

Wesley dropped his hand. "Not this argument again," he muttered.

Melody's expression grew guarded. "You seem to think I am some weak, simpering miss, but I am anything but."

"Why do you insist on being so obstinate about this?" Wesley demanded. "I am trying to keep you safe."

Before she could respond, a voice called from behind them. "Mother has requested we begin our dancing lesson soon," Elodie said, smiling innocently as she approached.

Melody turned towards her sister, her frustration still evident. "Good, because I have reached my stupidity limit for today."

Elodie giggled. "You have a stupidity limit? I think that is brilliant."

"Lady Melody..." Wesley started, but she raised her hand, stopping him.

"I'm sorry, but I am needed in the music room. I wouldn't want to disobey my mother, now, would I?" Melody asked, her tone sharp as she turned towards the manor.

"You are welcome to join us, my lord," Elodie offered cheerfully, clearly enjoying the tension.

Melody shot her sister a withering look. "I'm afraid Lord Emberly is much too busy to attend a dancing lesson."

Wesley considered pressing the matter but decided it was best to give her space. "I will leave you to it," he said, bowing slightly. Just because he gave her space didn't mean he wouldn't be watching over her. He would always watch over her.

Elodie looped her arm through Melody's, and the two sisters began their walk back to the manor. Wesley trailed a few steps behind, his sharp eyes scanning their surroundings, ever alert for any sign of danger.

A footman opened the door, and they stepped inside. The ladies continued towards the music room while Wesley paused outside the doorway. He had no intention of joining the dancing lesson, and it wasn't because he disliked dancing. No, it had to do more with the eccentric Mr. Durand. The last lesson had been memorable, to say the least.

Lord Belview strolled down the corridor and caught his eye. "What are you doing loitering outside the music room?" he asked. "I would make a run for it if I were you, or else you might be drawn into the lesson. Surely, you remember the last time?"

Gesturing towards the parlor, Wesley asked, "Care for a drink?"

Lord Belview's face brightened. "I was hoping you would ask."

They made their way into the parlor and Wesley moved to the drink cart, his fingers lightly brushing over the decanter of brandy. "What has been occupying your time?" he asked, pouring two glasses.

"Elodie," Lord Belview replied without a hint of shame, his tone casual, though there was something more behind his words.

"Are you interested in pursuing her?" Wesley asked as he handed one of the glasses to his friend.

Lord Belview took a sip, leaning back with a thoughtful expression. "I don't rightly know. She despises me, I think." He looked over at Wesley. "Do you know why that is?"

Wesley shrugged. "I don't. Lady Elodie is a mystery to me as well."

Lord Belview chuckled. "It is odd. The more she dislikes me, the more fascinated I am by her. And I can't quite figure out why I care so much."

"What do you intend to do about it?" Wesley asked as he sat down on a chair.

Lord Belview sighed. "I don't know if anything can be done. Everything out of my mouth seems to irritate Elodie. She is impossible to figure out."

"I feel your pain, considering I have the same effect on Melody. No matter what I do, I somehow manage to vex her," Wesley shared.

Lord Belview gave him a knowing glance. "You two appear rather… close."

"Appearances can be deceiving, I'm afraid."

Lord Belview dropped into a chair next to him. "What happened to us?" he mused, staring into his glass. "We used to be carefree, with women flocking to us at every turn. Now, it seems we can't say anything right."

"It matters little to me. I have no desire to fall prey to the parson's mousetrap at this time," Wesley responded.

"My mother wants me to marry, and quickly," Lord

Belview said, his tone more serious now. "She is convinced it will bring me happiness."

Wesley noted the pain in his friend's words and asked, "Are you happy?"

Lord Belview grew silent. "I thought I was," he responded, his voice trailing off. "But now… I don't rightly know anymore."

Swirling his drink, Wesley admitted, "I stopped being happy long ago. It is much easier to live with disappointment."

"That was rather morbid," Lord Belview said, a wry smile tugging at his lips.

Wesley's fingers tightened around the glass. "It is the truth."

Lord Belview tossed back his drink and placed the empty glass on the table before him. He sat back, a gleam of mischief in his eyes. "We should do something fun tomorrow. What will it be—angling, shooting, pall-mall?"

"Shooting?" Wesley asked. "You have always been a terrible shot, Belview."

"I have gotten better," Lord Belview defended, adopting a mock air of wounded pride.

Wesley smirked. "I doubt that."

With an exaggerated grin, Lord Belview puffed out his chest. "I can now hit the target… on occasion," he said, smiling broadly.

"Whatever you do, never challenge anyone to a duel. You would be dead before you even raised your pistol," Wesley joked.

Lord Belview waved his hand dismissively. "Duels are pointless and immature. Besides, I do believe I have learned from my brother's idiotic mistakes."

Wesley's smile dimmed. "He was lucky he wasn't thrown into jail for his part in the duel. It could have ruined him and your family."

"I have no doubt my father paid off the magistrate. But

Stephen? He will never take responsibility. Not for that, nor anything else," Lord Belview said.

"Some people never do," Wesley mused.

Lord Belview picked up his glass and said, "I could use another one." He rose and moved towards the drink cart, refilling his glass with deliberate slowness. "I wonder how we turned out so well. Especially considering the families we come from."

Wesley grinned. "Luck, perhaps. Or sheer stubbornness."

Lord Belview raised his glass in a mock toast. "To sheer stubbornness, then." He took a sip, his smile fading slightly as his thoughts drifted elsewhere.

Lady Dallington entered the room, causing Wesley to rise. "Wonderful, you both are here. The dancing master has requested your presence in the music room."

Wesley resisted the urge to groan. "Who are we to turn down such a request?" He hoped the faint smile he wore seemed cordial enough despite his inner reluctance. He doubted Melody would be pleased with him joining the lesson, but he wasn't about to defy Lady Dallington.

"I expect nothing less from gentlemen such as yourselves," Lady Dallington said, turning on her heel, leaving them no choice but to follow.

As Lady Dallington led the way, Wesley exchanged a glance with Lord Belview, who sighed dramatically before tipping his glass towards him in a final, silent toast.

Chapter Fourteen

Dressed in an elegant green gown with an intricate lace net overlay, Melody descended the grand staircase. Just as she reached the bottom step, a knock echoed through the entry hall. She paused as White crossed the marble floor to open the door.

As the door swung open, it revealed her Aunt Sarah and Jasper standing in the doorway. Melody blinked in surprise, her gaze landing on Jasper, who looked almost unrecognizable. He wore a finely tailored jacket and trousers, his usually unkempt hair neatly combed to the side. Despite the transformation, he stood stiffly, clearly uncomfortable in his new attire.

"Jasper, you look…" Melody began.

Tugging down on the lapels of his jacket, Jasper interrupted with a grimace. "Like a dressed-up cretin."

Sarah smiled gently, stepping in to explain. "You will have to excuse Jasper. He is not accustomed to such fine clothes."

"They are deucedly uncomfortable," Jasper muttered under his breath. "I much prefer my usual clothing, but Lord Emberly was insistent I wear what he sent over."

Melody couldn't help but feel a flicker of warmth at the mention of Wesley's name. It was thoughtful of him to ensure

Jasper was properly dressed for dinner. A small, secret smile tugged at her lips, but her sister's voice cut through her thoughts before she could respond.

"So, the rumors were true. We do have a real Bow Street Runner joining us for dinner this evening," Elodie said, appearing at Melody's side.

Jasper bowed. "Lady Elodie," he greeted. "The pleasure is mine."

Elodie's eyes sparkled with curiosity. "Does Father know?"

"I informed Mother that I invited Sarah and Jasper to dine with us," Melody replied, though she knew her father's reaction might be less than welcoming.

Elodie smiled. "This should be fun. Our dinners have been far too dull as of late."

Gesturing towards a door off the entry hall, Melody asked, "Shall we wait for the others in the drawing room?"

Jasper nodded, offering his arm to Sarah. "I think that is a splendid idea."

Once inside the drawing room, the warm light of the fireplace cast a soft glow over the room's furnishings. Melody turned to her aunt. "You look lovely this evening, Aunt Sarah."

Sarah ran a hand down the fabric of her gown. "You are most kind, Dear. I am fortunate that your mother and I are of a similar size. I only had to do a few alterations."

Melody noticed Jasper's gaze fixed on Sarah, approval shining in his eyes. "You are being far too modest, my lady," he said softly.

Sarah let out a light laugh, her cheeks flushing faintly. "What a pair we make," she remarked, glancing at Jasper. "I feel like we are both playing dress up."

Elodie walked over to the settee and gracefully sat. "If you are in need of more gowns, I will be happy to give you some. The dressmaker and I had a bit of a disagreement on some of the styles Mother insisted on commissioning."

"Thank you for the offer, but I prefer the more simple gowns, especially lately," Sarah said.

As the conversation flowed, the door opened again, and Wesley entered the room. Melody's breath caught as his eyes immediately sought her out, his gaze as intense as it always seemed when he looked at her. "Lady Melody," he greeted, tipping his head in a formal nod.

Unwanted warmth spread across her cheeks, and she cursed the blush that seemed to rise whenever Wesley was near. "Lord Emberly," she replied, her voice steadier than she felt. Why did she always act like this around him? The man was maddening, yet her heart refused to listen to reason.

As more guests began to fill the room, Melody drifted towards the settee where Elodie sat. She sank into the seat beside her sister, but her mind remained far from the conversation happening around her. She couldn't shake her thoughts of Wesley. Earlier, he had told her he cared for her, but what did he mean by that? Did his feelings run deep, or was she simply a friend to him?

Her mind was filled with uncertainty as she replayed the memory. She had always told herself she wasn't interested in Wesley that way, but how her emotions twisted at the mere idea of him feeling something for her—or not—betrayed her true feelings. With a mix of reluctance and hope, she was beginning to realize that maybe, just maybe, her heart had been his far longer than she was willing to admit.

Elodie nudged her shoulder with hers. "Melody, did you hear me?"

"Sorry, I was woolgathering," Melody replied.

In a conspiratorial voice, Elodie said, "Artemis has just arrived. A botanist and a Bow Street Runner at the same table. I think I am going to rather like this dinner."

Melody couldn't suppress a grin. "You would be happy with a clown at supper."

Elodie's eyes lit up. "Do you think Mother would let us see Grimaldi's performance when we are in London?"

"I doubt it," Melody replied. "I have heard his shows can oftentimes be immoral."

Her mother stepped into the room as if on cue and announced, "White has just informed me that dinner is ready. Shall we adjourn to the dining room?"

Wesley appeared at Melody's side, offering his hand with a smile. "May I escort you, my lady?"

Melody hesitated for the briefest moment before accepting his hand, rising to her feet. "Thank you."

Wesley kept hold of her hand and moved it to rest in the crook of his arm. His presence beside her was steady and comforting, though it unsettled her in ways she wasn't quite ready to acknowledge.

Leaning slightly, she whispered, "It was thoughtful of you to send Jasper proper clothing for this evening."

He brushed off the compliment. "It was the least I could do. I didn't want him to feel uncomfortable this evening."

Melody glanced at Wesley. "I hope my father behaves."

"He will."

"I wish I shared your confidence," Melody murmured, falling quiet as they reached the dining room.

Melody was pleased when Wesley sat beside her as they took their seats. His subtle scent of orange drifted towards her, and for a fleeting moment, she felt the almost irresistible urge to lean closer.

Her parents, seated at the head of the long, grand table, welcomed the guests with their usual formality. Most of the seats were filled, save for one conspicuously empty chair beside Lord Belview. Elodie, who stood hovering near the door, seemed reluctant to take it.

"Elodie, take your seat," her mother encouraged, though her tone had an unmistakable edge.

Elodie cast a sideways glance at Lord Belview before speaking. "That particular seat is notoriously drafty. Perhaps I should fetch my shawl, or better yet, move the chair to sit by Melody? By doing so, there is less chance of catching a cold and dying."

"I am sure you will be fine," her mother said.

"But there is a perfectly good spot next to Melody and a footman only needs to move the plate setting..." Elodie began to protest, only to be cut off by their father's stern voice.

"Sit, Elodie."

With a resigned frown, Elodie slid into the seat beside Lord Belview, her movements stiff and reluctant.

Their mother's face brightened with an exaggerated smile as she addressed their guests. "We are delighted to have Mr. and Mrs. Nelson, and their son, Artemis, joining us for dinner once more."

Melody, who was seated next to Artemis, turned towards him. "I am glad to see you are feeling much better."

Artemis reached for his glass, not bothering to hide his disinterest. "Yes, bravo," he muttered before taking a long sip.

Melody smiled tightly, forcing herself to remain civil. She had made the effort; no one could say she hadn't. Artemis, however, seemed intent on being as ungracious as ever.

The footmen stepped forward, placing bowls of soup in front of each person at the table. Melody reached for her spoon, but her father's voice cut through the quiet clinking of silverware. He turned his attention towards Jasper, who sat somewhat stiffly in his borrowed finery.

"It is not every day that one has a Bow Street Runner seated at their table," Lord Dallington remarked.

Elodie bobbed her head enthusiastically. "No, it certainly is not. Perhaps he could regale us with tales of criminals he has arrested?"

Jasper opened his mouth to respond, but Lord Dallington

waved a hand dismissively before he could speak. "That is hardly an appropriate conversation for dinner, Elodie."

Undeterred, Elodie flashed a mischievous grin. "But it would make dinner so much more interesting."

Jasper cleared his throat. "I would rather not discuss my cases, if you don't mind."

Elodie's shoulders slumped slightly. "Well, how will I ever learn how to commit the perfect murder?"

Lord Belview chuckled. "First, poison, and now murder? You really should find better hobbies, my lady."

With a gleam in her eyes, Elodie leaned forward. "I don't intend to kill anyone, but I was thinking about trying my hand at writing a book."

Her father's spoon clattered into his bowl and his expression hardened with disapproval. "Absolutely not! No daughter of mine will write a book. It is unseemly."

Elodie gave a half-shrug. "'A Lady' wrote two books, which are all the rage right now."

"I am well aware of this unfortunate *reading mania,*" Lord Dallington said, his brow furrowing, "but that doesn't make it right."

In response to his disdain, Elodie just smiled. "Father, I need something to occupy my time besides endless hours at the pianoforte."

Lady Dallington interjected, "You will have plenty to do when we arrive in Town for the Season."

"I suppose so," Elodie murmured, not appearing entirely convinced.

Lord Belview shifted in his seat to face Elodie. "If it pleases you, I would be honored to take you for a carriage ride through Hyde Park when we are in Town."

Before Elodie could reply, Lady Dallington said, "She would be honored."

Elodie lifted her gaze to meet Lord Belview's. Her voice

was flat, her words lacking any genuine enthusiasm. "Yes, nothing would give me greater joy."

Lord Belview's lips twitched, clearly amused by her lukewarm response. "I shall plan on it, then."

At the other end of the table, Jasper, who had been listening quietly, placed his spoon down and dabbed the sides of his mouth with his napkin. "As to Elodie's earlier comment about committing the perfect murder, I would say it is becoming increasingly difficult," he remarked. "A good coroner conducts a thorough investigation, and poisons almost always leave some trace."

The light returned to Elodie's eyes. "Interesting," she said, almost to herself.

Artemis raised his hand slightly to draw the table's attention. "I do not mean to contradict you," he began, though his tone carried no real hint of apology, "but it depends on how the poison is administered."

Elodie leaned forward in her seat. "Please, do continue."

Lord Dallington shot Artemis a stern look. "Please refrain from indulging my daughter's curiosity any further."

Artemis gave a slight, almost dismissive nod. "Very well."

Melody exchanged a glance with Wesley, her gaze lingering on his tense expression. His jaw was clenched, his thoughts clearly troubled by the talk of poison and perfect murders. Her heart ached for him, and she wished she could do something to ease his burden. But it was not her place to do so.

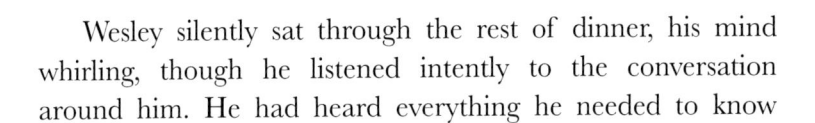

Wesley silently sat through the rest of dinner, his mind whirling, though he listened intently to the conversation around him. He had heard everything he needed to know about Artemis's discussion about the perfect murder. The way he had spoken, so calculated and self-assured, sent a shiver down Wesley's spine. This wasn't the first time Wesley had suspected Artemis of being far more dangerous than he appeared.

Artemis was a botanist. His knowledge of poisons was extensive. Wesley couldn't shake the unsettling thought that Artemis might have poisoned himself deliberately to divert suspicion. He had to find out the truth.

Melody cast him worried glances throughout the meal, but Wesley's focus remained on Artemis. He needed answers and he wasn't about to let this opportunity slip away.

At long last, Lord Dallington pushed back his chair, signaling the end of the meal. "I do believe it is time for a glass of port. Gentlemen, shall we?"

Wesley rose, as did the other men. Just as he was about to follow Lord Dallington to the study, Melody gently touched his sleeve, leaning in close. "Be careful," she whispered, her eyes filled with concern.

"I will," he replied. Her quiet show of worry touched him, but this was something that had to be done.

The men made their way into the study, the heavy door closing behind them with a quiet thud. Wesley stood back, biding his time, waiting for the right moment to speak to Artemis.

Lord Dallington poured glasses of port and handed them out. "Enjoy, gentlemen."

As Wesley took a sip, Lord Belview approached him, his eyebrows raised in curiosity. "Why are you staring daggers at Artemis?"

Wesley didn't bother denying it. "Am I?"

"You are," Lord Belview said with a knowing look. "And you've been doing it since the soup was served. What is the matter?"

Wesley tried to keep the emotions off his face. "It is nothing."

"Doesn't seem like nothing to me," Lord Belview countered.

Jasper placed his nearly full glass onto the drink cart and turned towards Artemis. "Our conversation earlier got me thinking. What poisons could be undetectable if administered correctly?"

Artemis's face grew solemn. "There are several poisons that mimic natural illnesses—arsenic, nightshade, and oleander, to name a few. But I am sure you already know that."

"I do," Jasper said. "Is there not oleander in the gardens of Brockhall Manor?"

The shift in Artemis's demeanor was subtle, but Wesley noticed it. His posture stiffened ever so slightly, and his eyes narrowed. "That is true. What about it?"

Wesley interjected, "Could someone administer oleander in a way that would leave no trace of poison?"

Artemis's voice grew lower, more guarded. "It is possible, but only if the person was not discovered for several hours after death. If ingested, oleander causes nausea, vomiting, and increased heart rate."

"Yes, we know all of that," Wesley said impatiently. "But what if it were inhaled?"

Leaning forward, Artemis placed his glass down on the table. "If oleander were burned and inhaled, it is possible a person could fall asleep and never wake up."

Jasper crossed his arms over his chest, his gaze steady. "Surely, there would be some signs."

"Perhaps," Artemis admitted. "Foaming at the mouth is a common symptom, but it would fade within an hour, leaving little trace of the poison."

Wesley frowned. "How much oleander would need to be burned to cause death?"

Artemis shrugged. "I can't say for certain. But it is more

than a theory. Our gardener died by burning oleander bushes at our country estate. We found him hours later by the remains of the fire."

Lord Dallington clasped his hands together, breaking the tension. "What a dismal topic for after dinner. Why don't we join the ladies in the drawing room for some card games?"

Lord Belview spoke up. "That sounds like a grand idea."

After the two men departed from the room, Artemis cleared his throat and turned his attention to Wesley. "I was hoping to ask you a question, Lord Emberly."

Wesley raised an eyebrow. "I had a question for you as well. But go ahead."

With a sigh, Artemis asked, "Do you have an understanding with Lady Melody?"

Wesley stared at Artemis for a moment, caught off guard by the unexpected turn in the conversation. "No, I do not."

Artemis nodded, his lips twitching into a brief smile of approval. "Good. I intend to ask her to marry me."

"You... *what!?*" Wesley managed, his voice edged with disbelief.

Walking over to the settee, Artemis dropped down onto it. "My parents are forcing me to marry, and I have decided that Melody is agreeable enough."

Wesley's temper flared. "Agreeable enough?" His hands clenched into fists at his sides. "That is your reasoning?"

"She likes flowers and is pleasant to look at."

Wesley pursed his lips together. "She is so much more than that," he growled. "She is beautiful, inside and out."

"That is what I said," Artemis remarked.

"No," Wesley said, "you said the opposite."

Artemis waved a dismissive hand in front of him. "Do you think she will agree to a marriage between us?"

Wesley already knew the answer and saw no reason not to tell him the truth. "No, she won't."

Artemis gave him a bemused look. "Whyever not?"

"She wants a love match," Wesley replied. "She will never agree to a marriage of convenience."

Artemis turned his attention to Jasper with an air of arrogance. "What say you, Runner?"

Jasper grew visibly tense. "What did you call me?" His voice held a dangerous edge, but Artemis was too self-absorbed to notice the shift in tone.

"A Runner," Artemis repeated. "I thought that is what you preferred to be called."

Jasper's lips twisted into a grimace. "No, you are quite mistaken."

Artemis didn't appear too upset by his mistake. "Casper, was it?"

The tension in the room thickened as Jasper's eyes locked on to Artemis, his expression hardening. "It is *Jasper*."

"Ah, yes, Jasper," Artemis repeated. "Unusual name, is it not?"

Ignoring Artemis's question, Jasper shifted his focus to Wesley. "I will leave you to it," he muttered before turning on his heel and exiting the study.

Artemis stared after him, looking genuinely perplexed. "What is the matter with him?"

Wesley shook his head, torn between disbelief and suspicion. How could Artemis be so blind to the tension in the room? But then again, perhaps this was all an act. No one could truly be that stupid, could they?

"Didn't you have a question for me?" Artemis asked.

"I do." Wesley sat down across from Artemis. "Do you truly intend to offer for Lady Melody?" It wasn't the question he had initially planned to ask, but it seemed far more urgent right now.

Artemis leaned back, smoothing down his already slicked-back hair. "I don't know what else to do. My parents are pressing me to marry, and I am tired of their incessant pestering."

"That is not a good enough reason to marry."

Artemis shifted in his seat, looking uncomfortable for the first time that evening. "I know plants, but women…" His voice trailed off. "They are a mystery to me. It was much easier when I lived in France."

Wesley's brow shot up. "You lived in France?"

"Yes, for many years while I studied botany. I traveled all over Europe, documenting my findings."

Before he could respond, Melody stepped into the room and met Wesley's gaze. "My mother was wondering if you intended to join us for games."

Wesley rose. "I do, assuming I can be on your team."

Melody laughed, the sound easing some of the tension in his chest. "I play to win, my lord," she joked. "I hope you can keep up."

Reluctantly, Wesley tore his gaze from her to address Artemis. "Will you be joining us?"

"No," Artemis replied. "I am tired and intend to retire for the evening."

"Very well," Wesley said, offering his arm to Melody.

As they left the study and made their way down the corridor, Melody leaned closer to Wesley, her voice dropping to a whisper. "Did you discover anything of importance?"

"You were right. It is entirely probable to kill someone with oleander just by burning it and having them inhale it," Wesley revealed.

"Which means the killer could just drop branches of oleander into the hearth, depart, and no one would be the wiser," Melody said.

Wesley stopped just outside of the drawing room, his face serious. "We both need to be extra vigilant. We are dealing with someone who has killed multiple times and knows how to cover their tracks."

"Do you think Artemis could be involved?"

"I don't know, but he let it slip that he lived in France for an extended time," Wesley replied. "That is a coincidence that we cannot ignore."

"No, we cannot," Melody agreed as she slipped her hand off of his and turned to face him. "I spoke to White about the staff and recent hires. He informed me that he already spoke to your valet about this."

"That is true."

"I thought we were going to work together," Melody remarked. "Why have I not seen or heard of this list before?"

"My valet has been speaking to each of the recent hires and has started to eliminate suspects, one by one."

Melody placed a hand on her hip, determination flashing in her eyes. "I can help with that."

"Do you truly think it won't raise suspicion if you are seen questioning the household staff? It would draw unwanted attention," Wesley pointed out.

She stood her ground, her voice steady. "I can be discreet. Besides, they are more likely to open up to me than to your valet."

Wesley studied her for a long moment, weighing her words. He couldn't deny how capable she was. But the thought of her putting herself in any sort of danger left him uneasy. He decided to be honest with her. "My valet is not just a servant but also an agent. He is experienced with getting people to trust him and drawing out information without raising alarms."

Melody's posture relaxed slightly, her hand dropping from her hip. "I hadn't realized."

"I don't tell very many people that piece of information," Wesley said. "It is much safer that way for him and me."

A shadow passed over Melody's expression. "It must be nice to have someone to confide in about all of this. I have no one."

Her words tugged at his heart, causing him to take a step forward. "You have me, Melody."

Melody lowered her gaze to the lapels of his jacket. "Yes, but once this is over, you will go home and I will remain here. Alone. Unable to talk to anyone about what I do."

He tilted his head, trying to catch her gaze. "Melody," he murmured gently, "look at me."

Slowly, she lifted her eyes to meet his. The moment their gazes locked, his next words escaped him before he could fully think them through. "Marry me," he said, the intensity in his voice surprising even him. "And I promise you will never feel alone again."

A flicker of sadness darkened her eyes. "You know why I can't."

Reaching for her hand, he brought it up to his lips. "What you are asking is not impossible," he admitted, his lips brushing her gloved fingers. "But right now, is it not enough that I care for you?"

For a moment, her eyes stayed on him, her expression unreadable. He desperately wanted to know what was happening behind those eyes, what she was thinking at that precise moment. But she remained silent, and the silence felt heavier than any words she could have spoken.

Finally, she withdrew her hand, clasping them in front of her. "We should join the others."

"Melody..." Wesley began, his voice low, almost pleading.

She spoke over him. "I know your heart still belongs to Dinah, which is all right. I hope to find a love so dear one day."

"You are right. I do still love Dinah, and a part of me always will. But that doesn't mean I can't learn to love another."

She winced. "I don't want you to *learn* to love me. Love isn't something you can teach yourself to feel. It is something that happens unexpectedly, when you least expect it. It is not a skill."

"Perhaps I misspoke," he attempted.

Melody's voice dropped to a whisper. "No, I think you said it perfectly."

Wesley watched her go, realizing that for all his logic, all his carefully measured words, he had no idea how to fix this. He wanted to marry Melody. More than anything else in his life. But how could he convince her of such a thing?

Chapter Fifteen

Dressed in a pale yellow gown, Melody descended the stairs and headed towards the dining room. As she approached the door, she came to an abrupt halt when she saw Wesley seated at the table, looking as composed as ever. The memory of his words from the previous night weighed heavily on her mind, and suddenly, she wasn't ready to face him.

Not after what he had said.

After a long, restless night, she had made a decision. She wanted to marry him, but not like this, not out of practicality or duty. She wanted Wesley to fall in love with her, the way she was already halfway there with him. He made her feel safe, protected and cherished, but she longed for more. She wanted to feel loved. Truly loved. She wanted everything—or nothing at all.

Her eyes darted towards the doorway behind her, plotting her escape. Wesley hadn't acknowledged her yet, so perhaps she could slip away unnoticed. But just as she picked up her foot to retreat, he turned, his eyes meeting hers with a knowing smirk at the corners of his lips.

"I thought we were past this childish behavior," Wesley teased.

Melody stiffened, knowing she had been caught. She raised her chin, determined to maintain her composure. "I don't know what you are referring to," she replied, walking towards the table with as much grace as she could muster.

Wesley stood, pulling out a chair for her as if nothing had changed between them.

With a polite nod, Melody sat, trying not to let his proximity affect her. But it did. She reached for her napkin and placed it on her lap to distract herself.

"Good morning, Melody," Wesley greeted as he returned to his seat.

She briefly spared him a glance, but she could feel his eyes on her. "Good morning."

"I trust that you slept well," he remarked.

No.

She had hardly slept at all, her mind haunted by thoughts of him. But she didn't dare admit that to him. "I slept well," she lied.

Wesley leaned in, his voice dropping just for her. "You look lovely this morning."

She let out a sigh as a footman placed a plate of food before her, and she hurriedly reached for her fork and knife, needing something—anything—to occupy her trembling hands. The last thing she wanted was to fall into a conversation with Wesley where she might say something foolish, like confessing how deeply she cared for him.

"Would you like me to switch plates with you?" Wesley asked, remaining close.

Melody shook her head. "I do not think that is necessary. We have been switching plates intermittently for the past few days, and neither of us has been poisoned."

Wesley leaned back in his seat. "Will you tell me about yourself?"

She hesitated, taken off guard by the sudden shift in

conversation. "That is a long, convoluted answer," she replied. "Can you be more specific?"

He grinned. "Let's start with an easy question. What were you like as a child?"

Placing the fork and knife down, she shifted towards him. "I was an inquisitive child," she began. "I always wanted to know how things worked, constantly taking things apart to figure them out. Sometimes I succeeded, other times… well, not so much." She laughed softly. "It drove my parents mad."

"I think I would have liked to have seen you as a child," Wesley said.

Melody returned his smile. "I may not say—or do—outlandish things like my sister, but I do have my moments of humor."

Wesley's expression grew more serious, his voice gentler. "Why do you insist on comparing yourself with your sister?"

Her smile faltered slightly. "We are twins," she said simply. "I do believe that goes with the territory. I will always be the boring one compared to her."

Wesley leaned forward, their faces now just inches apart, and his eyes locked on to hers with a fierce intensity. "You, my dear, are nothing short of extraordinary. In my eyes, there is no comparison."

Melody could feel her heart pounding in her chest, and she hoped that Wesley couldn't hear it. "That is because you are biased," she managed, her voice barely above a whisper.

"There are very few women in the world who can do what you do," Wesley said. "You are kind, compassionate and strong. Do not forget that."

She felt her throat tighten as his words sank in. She always felt overshadowed by Elodie, but not in Wesley's eyes. He made her feel seen. And important.

Elodie's overly cheerful voice rang out from the doorway. "Dear heavens, what am I interrupting?"

Wesley immediately leaned back, clearing his throat

awkwardly as Melody forced a smile to her lips. "Nothing," she attempted.

"It definitely looked like something," Elodie responded, her words holding mirth. "Good thing it was me who walked in and not Father."

Elodie made her way around the table and sat down, studying both Melody and Wesley with a curious glint in her eyes. "I wonder what you two are hiding." She paused. "Last night, you two barely exchanged a word while playing cards, and now, suddenly, you are back to being thick as thieves."

Melody's attention dropped to her plate. She was afraid of what Elodie might see in her expression. "Can we just eat and forget about what you saw?"

A terse moment followed before Elodie relented. "I suppose we can, but I am in need of a favor."

Wesley spoke up. "What kind of favor?"

Elodie waved a dismissive hand in front of her as though it were the simplest of matters. "Mother has decided that we are to play pall-mall after breakfast. But I refuse to partner with Anthony." She looked pointedly at Melody. "Will you do it?"

"I have never quite understood your aversion to Anthony," Melody said.

"He is most insufferable," Elodie declared. "He had the nerve to compliment me on my dancing yesterday."

Melody suppressed a laugh. "Why did you take issue with that?"

Elodie huffed. "We both know I am a terrible dancer. He only said it to be polite."

"I do not see what the problem is," Melody responded.

Elodie shot her an exasperated look before turning towards Wesley. "Do you see the issue, my lord?"

Wesley tipped his head thoughtfully. "I believe I do. You want someone to be genuine in their words and actions."

"Precisely," Elodie remarked.

As if summoned by the conversation, Lord Belview

entered the room, a smile on his face. "Good morning," he greeted.

Melody looked over at him. "Good morning, Anthony."

Lord Belview came around the table and sat down beside Elodie. "Lady Dallington just informed me that we are to play pall-mall after breakfast."

"Yes, we were just discussing that," Melody said. "I should warn you that playing pall-mall with our family is not for the faint of heart."

Elodie bobbed her head. "We take winning very seriously here."

Lord Belview leaned back in his chair. "Then I will do my best not to embarrass myself."

As Elodie placed her napkin on her lap, she remarked, "You must do better than just 'try.' If your performance at whist is any indication of your skills, you are in trouble."

Lord Belview grinned, clearly amused. "I seem to recall besting you at whist a time or two."

Elodie reached for a knife and began to butter her bread with slow, exaggerated precision. "Only because I let you win."

"You *let* me win?" Lord Belview repeated. "That doesn't sound like you."

"I merely felt bad for you," Elodie said.

A smirk tugged at Lord Belview's lips. "Why, Elodie, it almost sounds like you hold me in high regard."

Elodie tightened her grip on the knife, her eyes narrowing playfully. "You would be wrong, my lord. The word you are looking for is *pity*. I pitied you."

Lord Belview's smile broadened. "I don't think that is it at all," he said, leaning forward slightly. "I think you fancy me, at least a little."

Elodie's mouth dropped open. "Heavens, no! You would be undoubtedly wrong to think such a thing."

Undeterred, Lord Belview had a smug look on his face. "I

don't know. You obviously think about me, despite your insistence that you do not."

"No, my lord, I assure you that you are the farthest thing from my mind," Elodie contended as she jutted her chin in the air.

Melody found the exchange between her sister and Lord Belview to be rather amusing. But as they continued their sparring match, her thoughts kept drifting back to Wesley—who, despite his calm exterior, seemed to have just as much on his mind.

A short, light-haired man stepped into the room and met Wesley's eye. "May I have a word with you, my lord?"

Wesley nodded and set the napkin from his lap onto the table. "You may." Then, turning to Melody, he extended his hand. "Lady Melody, would you care to accompany me?"

Melody quickly realized that this man was Wesley's valet—the agent he had mentioned earlier. "I would like that very much."

As they left the dining room, she was touched that Wesley had taken her words to heart. He was including her, valuing her input. For the first time in a long while, Melody felt seen. Heard. Respected. It was impossible not to care for this man, who seemed to understand her in ways she hadn't expected.

Once they reached the corridor, the short man bowed before introducing himself. "I am Watkins. Lord Emberly's most trusted confidant."

"It is a pleasure to meet you, Watkins," Melody responded.

Wesley, however, was quick to get to the point. "What is it?"

Watkins's face grew solemn, the lightness in his earlier tone disappearing. "I have discovered that one of the footmen was caught sneaking out late last night. It might be nothing, but it is equally possible that it could be something more significant. He may have been meeting with someone."

Wesley considered this for a moment. "That is certainly a possibility," he said slowly. "Although I didn't encounter this footman last night. I was keeping watch over Lady Melody's window from a distance."

Melody turned towards Wesley, her eyes wide with surprise. "You were watching my window last night. Is that why you didn't come inside?"

Wesley nodded. "I thought it was for the best. Lady Elodie nearly caught us the night before, and I couldn't risk putting you in that kind of position again. But I couldn't simply do nothing. I needed to make sure you were safe."

Melody felt deeply moved by Wesley's words. Even though she would have never admitted it out loud, she had been slightly disappointed when Wesley had not come to her bedchamber the night before. But knowing that he had still been there, watching over her from afar, filled her heart with an unexpected sense of comfort.

Watkins cleared his throat, returning the conversation to the matter at hand. "What would you like me to do, my lord?"

Wesley's eyes flickered to Melody for a brief moment before answering. "Keep an eye on the footman, but don't raise suspicion. We can't afford to alert anyone that we are onto them."

"And me?" Melody asked. She wasn't about to sit idly by while danger lurked in the shadows.

Wesley's expression softened as he looked at her. "Stay close to me. Together, we will get to the bottom of this."

Melody knew that Wesley wasn't giving her empty reassurances. He was promising to face the danger with her. And with him by her side, she felt ready to confront whatever came her way.

With Melody on his arm, Wesley led her out of Brockhall Manor and onto the expansive lawn where the pall-mall course had been carefully arranged. His alert eyes swept over the landscape, scanning for any signs of danger, though everything appeared calm. He inwardly cursed himself for indulging in such frivolousness. Playing games at a time like this seemed foolish, but maintaining appearances was crucial. The other guests needed to believe all was well.

Still, he couldn't shake the satisfaction that came with finally having a lead in their investigation. Perhaps they would soon uncover who was after Melody, a thought that both relieved and troubled him. The sooner they caught the culprit, the sooner his time with Melody would come to an end. A time that had been far more enjoyable than he had anticipated.

Wesley found himself falling for her despite the constant reminders that he shouldn't. He had vowed never to entangle himself with another agent. But Melody was not just any agent—she was becoming everything to him.

Melody slipped her arm off his and picked up a mallet. "Have you prepared yourself, my lord?"

Wesley quirked an eyebrow. "For what?"

She tsked, shaking her head with mock exasperation. "Dear heavens, you are not ready. Our family takes this game very seriously and you must be prepared for mockery. It is, after all, inevitable."

Wesley picked up a mallet. "You do not need to worry about me. I am rather proficient at pall-mall."

"We shall see," Melody said.

At that moment, Elodie appeared by his side. "It has been decided that I will partner with Lord Emberly and Melody will team up with Anthony."

Lord Belview moved to stand by Melody. "I have no objections."

Wesley glanced at the manor. "What of Artemis?"

Elodie shrugged. "Last I saw him, he was wandering towards the gardens. No doubt he will be distracted by plants for the better part of the day." Her eyes shifted to Wesley's mallet, and she frowned. "Is that the mallet you have chosen?"

He held it up for her inspection. "Is there something wrong with it?"

Elodie crossed her arms, her expression serious. "Yes. That is not a lucky mallet. Pick another one."

Wesley shot a glance at Melody, half-expecting her to laugh at its absurdity, but she merely smiled. "I would do as Elodie says, my lord," she advised.

Suppressing a sigh, Wesley placed the mallet down and selected another, feeling somewhat ridiculous but knowing it wasn't worth the debate. "Will this one do?"

Elodie shook her head. "I do hope you play better than your lackluster effort at choosing a mallet."

Before Wesley could respond, Lord Belview picked up the mallet Wesley had just discarded. "I shall use this one," he declared, testing its weight. "It feels rather lucky to me."

"You would be wrong," Elodie remarked. "Now, we shall discuss our strategies. The game will commence once we are all prepared."

Wesley turned to face Elodie. "I thought our strategy was to win. What more should we discuss?"

Elodie stared at him as if disappointed in his lack of understanding. "Just follow my lead."

He wasn't quite sure what to say to make this situation better. It was just a game—not a matter of life or death. But Elodie was treating it as such.

Before he could question her further, Elodie leaned in closer, her voice dropping to a whisper. "I know you were in Melody's room two nights ago."

Wesley opened his mouth to object, but she put a hand up to stop him. "Do not even try to insult me by denying it. But do not worry. Your secret is safe with me. I would never betray my sister."

Wesley remained silent, unsure of how to respond. He hadn't anticipated Elodie to be so perceptive. Or direct, for that matter.

Raising an eyebrow, Elodie continued. "What are your intentions towards my sister?"

He straightened, meeting her gaze with a calm resolve. "We are friends," he replied, hoping the statement would put an end to her questioning.

Elodie looked unimpressed. "Do you expect me to believe that, my lord?"

Wesley held her gaze. "I do, because it is the truth."

Turning her attention towards the mallet in her hand, Elodie's voice grew softer, more reflective. "You seem to think that your actions are going unnoticed. But you are mistaken. I notice everything. And I have noticed my sister's behavior, too. You two are keeping secrets."

Wesley's mind raced, wondering how much Elodie truly knew and whether it was wise to continue this conversation. Hoping to steer away from the uncomfortable topic, he asked, "Shall we play the game now?"

Elodie smirked, clearly not fooled by his attempt to change the subject. "Oh, we will play," she said, her voice light again. "But I am not done questioning you. There is much more we need to discuss."

"Is there?"

Elodie cocked her head. "Why did you come here in the first place, my lord? And this time, I would prefer the truth."

Wesley forced a smile, hoping to ease the tension. "I came to speak with Lady Melody, and your mother kindly invited me to stay."

Elodie didn't look convinced. "And you just happened to have your trunks and valet with you?"

He hesitated, realizing he had indeed underestimated her.

Fortunately, before he could respond, Melody appeared by his side, her presence easing the tension. "Have you two properly discussed your strategy?" she asked, glancing between him and Elodie.

"You could say that," Elodie murmured with a wry smile.

A bright smile spread across Melody's face. "Then let us play," she declared. "Elodie, why don't you go first?"

Elodie raised the mallet in her hand. "I will show you how it is done."

Melody's smile faded as Elodie strode over to the first arch. She turned to Wesley, her brow furrowing with concern. "What is wrong?"

Wesley gave her a bemused look. "Why do you suppose something is wrong?"

"Just tell me," Melody said. "We don't have time to waste with foolish questions."

With a glance at Elodie, who was busy lining up her shot, he lowered his voice. "Your sister is quite perceptive."

"I do believe people dismiss Elodie as thoughtless, but she can be very observant when she wants to be," Melody said.

Wesley nodded, leaning closer. "She knows I was in your bedchamber," he revealed. "But she says our secret is safe with her."

"We need to be more discreet. If Elodie suspects something, who else might?"

Wesley gave her a knowing look. "There is an obvious solution."

Melody's lips tightened into a flat, white line. "If you even *mention* marriage, I will hit you with this mallet."

"It is the perfect solution," Wesley defended.

"For you, perhaps, but not for me."

Elodie's voice rang out from across the lawn. "Melody, it is your turn. Hurry up, or we will be here all day!"

Wesley raised his hand, gesturing towards the game. "You heard the lady."

Melody gave him a quick, playful glare before moving to take her shot. As she lined up her ball, Lord Belview appeared beside Wesley, leaning casually on his mallet.

"I must admit," Lord Belview began, a slight smile playing on his lips, "a part of me is rather intimidated by how seriously Elodie takes this game."

Wesley chuckled. "It is still just a game."

"To us, perhaps. But to Elodie…" Lord Belview's words trailed off. "It is a shame that I will undoubtedly beat you both, but I will take no pleasure in it."

"I wouldn't discount us so easily."

Lord Belview adjusted the mallet in his hands, his expression turning thoughtful. "Do you intend to visit Town for the Season?"

"I haven't quite decided yet, but I do need to take up my seat in Parliament," Wesley responded.

"And what of Lady Melody?" Lord Belview asked, eyeing him closely.

Wesley schooled his features. "What about her?"

"Anyone with eyes can see that you hold her in high regard."

"I do," Wesley said evenly. "But we are just friends."

"Ah, denial, then."

Wesley turned his attention back towards the lawn, not wanting to engage in this line of questioning. "As I said before, I have no intention of getting married now."

"It changes when you find the right woman," Lord Belview said. "You must accept your fate."

His jaw tightened slightly. "I prefer to chart my own course."

Placing a hand on Wesley's shoulder, Lord Belview gave him a sympathetic look. "If only it were that easy, my friend. But I wish you luck in your endeavors, whatever they may be."

As Wesley watched Melody take her shot, her ball gliding smoothly past Elodie's and through the arc, a surge of pride welled up within him. Melody let out an excited laugh, jumping slightly in triumph, and for a moment, the rest of the world fell away. Her joy and beauty were captivating, and it was impossible to look away.

His friend leaned closer and said, "You are staring."

"Am I?" Wesley asked, tearing his gaze from Melody.

"You were, and it was very telling."

Wesley tried to brush it off, but the truth was his heart was betraying him in ways he hadn't expected.

Melody met his gaze, her lips curving into a smile as she gestured towards his ball. "Your turn, my lord."

With a slight nod, Wesley approached his ball and carefully lined up his shot. As he drew his mallet back to strike, Elodie's voice pierced the air.

"STOP!"

Wesley froze mid-swing. "What is it now?"

Elodie strode over to him. "That is a terrible shot," she declared. "You must try again. This time, imagine you *are* the ball."

"I beg your pardon?" Wesley asked.

Elodie crouched down next to his ball, her tone serious. "You need to see the ball as an extension of yourself. Feel its weight, its purpose. Embrace the ball, my lord."

Wesley couldn't tell if Elodie was joking, but he suspected she wasn't. "It is just a game, my lady."

Elodie's eyes grew wide. "*Just* a game," she sputtered. "And Napoleon is *just* a general!"

Melody laughed. "Let him play, Elodie."

Rising, Elodie said, "But I want to win."

With practiced ease, Wesley swung the mallet and hit the ball, rolling past Elodie's. He straightened, watching its path with a faint smirk. "I would say that was a fairly decent shot."

"It wasn't as good as Melody's, but I suppose it will do," Elodie remarked indifferently. "You are full of surprises, aren't you, Lord Emberly?"

His smile grew. "I like to think I can hold my own."

Elodie tapped her chin thoughtfully. "Perhaps," she mused. "But we will see if you can maintain that confidence when we reach the final arch."

Lord Belview stepped up with a grin of his own. "I do believe it is my turn," he announced. With one solid strike, his ball shot forward, knocking Elodie's ball out of the way. He turned towards her. "Better luck next time, my lady."

Elodie narrowed her eyes, though her lips twitched. "I wouldn't get too comfortable, my lord."

Lord Belview held up his mallet. "I daresay that this is indeed a lucky mallet. I do hope that *you* can keep up, Elodie."

Chapter Sixteen

Melody sat beside Wesley in the drawing room, their knees nearly touching. His closeness distracted her. She wondered how easy it would be to reach out and take his hand. Would he welcome her touch? No. She needed to banish these wayward thoughts. She was supposed to be focused on her needlework, but her stitches were uneven, the thread tangling as she tried to concentrate.

With a sigh, Melody placed the needlework in her lap, surrendering to the fact that she was making a mess of it. She glanced across the room at Elodie, who was energetically debating with Lord Belview about the merits of women wearing trousers.

White entered the room with a silver tray in his hand. "Two letters have arrived for Lady Melody," he announced, stepping towards her.

Melody retrieved the neatly folded letters with a smile. "They are both from Josephine," she announced. But her relief was short-lived when she opened the first letter.

Elodie's head snapped up. "Josephine sent you two letters?"

"Isn't that what I just said?" Melody replied absently, her

brow furrowing as she scanned the letter. The handwriting was unfamiliar, and to her surprise, it was a coded message—using the same cipher she had deciphered just days ago.

Wesley leaned closer, his voice low and concerned. "I did not send that particular letter."

Melody's breath caught in her throat. "Then who did?"

Before Wesley could reply, Elodie's voice broke through their conversation. "What did Josephine say?"

Thinking quickly, Melody folded the letter and slipped it into the folds of her gown. "She apologizes for not writing sooner, but her family went on a trip. I shall read the other letter later."

"Where did Josephine vacation to?" Elodie pressed.

"Bath," Melody replied quickly.

Elodie scrunched her nose. "At this time of year? That seems like an odd choice. Surely, there are better places to visit than Bath right now."

Melody retrieved her needlework, trying to focus on the task at hand. However, her mind was still on the coded message. "I cannot speak as to why her family chose now to go, merely that they did go."

Lord Belview interjected, "Why does it matter to you where her family went?"

Elodie gave him a sideways glance. "It is just… convenient. Josephine was going on a trip right when we have guests."

Leaning back in his chair, Lord Belview's eyes twinkled with mischief. "That is quite the leap of logic. Perhaps your time would be better spent on more womanly pursuits."

Melody watched her sister's eyes widen, barely suppressing the smile threatening to break free. Lord Belview was clearly baiting Elodie, and she was walking right into it.

Her mother entered the room and announced, "It is time for Elodie's lesson with the dancing master."

Elodie groaned theatrically. "Again? Surely, there is a better use of my time."

"I can't think of one," her mother responded.

"Truly? Not even *one*?" Elodie pressed.

Her mother smiled. "It is not my fault you dance like a drunken hippopotamus."

Elodie clutched her chest as if mortally wounded. "You raised me! If you had put me in lessons sooner, I might have been more graceful."

"I don't think that would have helped," her mother retorted.

Rising, Elodie said, "I could have become the most famous dancer in all the world. Ballads would have been written about my elegance and beauty. But, no, alas, it is too late now."

Their mother turned to Melody with a sigh. "Your sister is utterly delusional."

Melody couldn't hold back her giggle. "I am well aware."

As Elodie continued to argue her point with their mother, Melody's thoughts drifted back to the coded letter hidden in her gown. She needed to slip away and find a quiet moment to decipher the message. But what excuse could she give that wouldn't raise suspicion?

Elodie gave a dramatic bow, pulling Melody back to the present. "And that is why I will never master the art of dance."

"It is one dance lesson," her mother said, a note of exasperation creeping into her voice. "I am not asking you to fight in the war."

Elodie pointed at Melody. "Why doesn't Melody require this torture?"

Their mother gave Elodie a sharp look. "Because, my dear, Melody has learned how to dance."

Elodie shook her head. "Only someone who truly loved me would be so brutally honest."

Lord Belview stepped forward. "I would be happy to accompany you to your lesson."

Raising her chin defiantly, Elodie said, "I think I would rather brave this ordeal alone, thank you." She headed for the door, pausing in the frame. "Wish me luck. If I die in the music room, all my possessions will go to Melody."

Their mother frowned. "You are not going to die."

"I might die from dancing," Elodie quipped with a swipe of her hand.

Once Elodie had departed from the room, her mother looked heavenward. "Give me patience with that one."

Taking advantage of the moment, Melody stood and turned to Wesley. "Would you like to see our library?"

"I would," Wesley replied, offering his arm.

Just as they began to leave, her mother's voice stopped them. "I believe Lord Belview would also like to see the library."

Melody stifled her disappointment and turned with a polite smile. "Of course. How thoughtless of me. Lord Belview, would you care to join us?"

Lord Belview inclined his head. "I would be honored."

They made their way down the hall, and Melody's mind raced as she tried to devise a plan to be alone with Wesley. But every excuse felt too obvious, and Lord Belview's presence complicated things. She would have to be careful.

Once they arrived in the library, Melody moved towards the writing desk, retrieving the folded letter from her gown. She picked up the quill and quickly began deciphering the code.

Her breath caught as the message revealed itself:

Your life or your sister's

Melody gasped, the quill slipping from her hand and clattering onto the desk. Wesley was at her side in an instant. "What is it?" he asked, concern darkening his features.

She showed him the message, her hands trembling. His eyes hardened, a silent understanding passing between them. Without a word, Melody quickly folded the letter and tucked it away before Lord Belview, still browsing through the shelves, could see.

Wesley leaned in, his voice low and controlled. "We need to find out who sent this, and quickly."

Melody nodded, her mind spinning. She shoved back her chair and rose. "I need to see to Elodie."

Lord Belview raised an eyebrow, watching her closely. "Is something wrong, Melody?"

"No," Melody replied too quickly, trying to mask the panic building inside of her. "I just miss my sister."

"Weren't you just with her?" Lord Belview asked, confusion evident in his voice.

Melody crossed the room swiftly, not meeting his eyes. "Excuse me. I will be back shortly."

As she hurried down the corridor, dread curled in her stomach. The coded letter's warning echoed in her mind. *Your life or your sister's.* What if something had happened to Elodie already? The thought made her quicken her pace.

Wesley caught up to her, falling into stride beside her. "Elodie is fine," he assured her, though his voice had a hint of tension.

She barely spared him a glance. "How can you be so sure?"

"I'm not," Wesley admitted. "But it is important that you don't panic. We need to stay calm and think clearly."

But Melody was far past calm. Panic gnawed at her, quickening her breath. If anything had happened to Elodie, if someone had taken her, she didn't know how she would survive it.

They burst into the music room, startling Mr. Durand,

who threw his hands into the air. "Finally, Lady Elodie!" he exclaimed, clearly irritated. "I have been waiting."

Melody came to an abrupt halt, her eyes scanning the room. "Where is my sister?" she demanded, her voice tight with fear.

Mr. Durand blinked at her in confusion. "Why would I know where your sister is?" he asked. "Would you care to begin the lesson?"

"I am *not* Elodie. I am Melody," she replied.

"Then where is your sister?" Mr. Durand asked.

Melody felt her heart drop. "I… I don't know."

"Well," Mr. Durand snapped impatiently, "inform her that she is late when you find her. I don't have time to wait around for her whims."

Wesley stepped closer, placing a comforting hand on her shoulder. "We will find her. She may have just gone up to her room for a moment."

Melody looked up at him. "Do you honestly believe that?"

He hesitated, his jaw tightening. "I don't know what to believe yet, but if someone has taken her, she couldn't have gone far."

Tears welled in her eyes, threatening to spill over, but she blinked them back, willing herself to stay composed. Now was not the time for tears. "What do we do?"

"First, we need to check the manor," Wesley replied calmly. "She might still be somewhere inside."

"I will go speak to White."

Wesley gave a nod of approval. "Good. I will fetch Watkins and meet you back in the library."

A single tear slipped down her cheek despite her efforts to remain composed. Wesley reached up gently, brushing it away with his thumb. "I promise you, we will find her. Everything will be all right."

Melody took a step back, shaking her head. "Remember what I said about making promises you can't keep."

"Melody..." he began.

She spoke over him. "I need to go speak to White."

As she moved past him, Wesley caught her arm, stilling her. "You need to think like an agent, not just a sister. Be vigilant."

Melody swallowed hard. "I will be."

"Good," he said, holding her gaze, his hand lingering on her arm. "I swear to you, I will do everything in my power to ensure Elodie is safe."

Her gaze searched his face, and she saw a fierce determination in the depths of his eyes. His promise wasn't empty, and for a brief moment, she found a sliver of calm. "I shall hold you to that."

Wesley's expression softened, and his touch provided her with a strange sense of comfort. "We are a team, you and I."

"Yes," she agreed softly. "A team."

It had been hours since Elodie had gone missing, and Wesley sat in the drawing room, a drink forgotten in his hand. Melody was nearby, doing her best to console her distraught parents. From the steady tone of her voice, anyone might have thought she was in control, but Wesley could see the truth in her eyes. Fear.

No word had come yet from Elodie's abductor, but that didn't unsettle Wesley. He knew the target wasn't Elodie—it was Melody. Whoever was behind this wanted her, and they would make their move when the time was right. Until then, they had to keep calm and prepare.

Lady Dallington, her face pale and streaked with tears, wiped at her eyes with a trembling hand. "Where is the constable?" she asked, her voice shaking with barely controlled emotions. "He should have been here by now."

Melody placed a hand on her mother's arm. "I am sure he is on his way. Why don't you rest for a bit until he arrives?"

Lady Dallington shook her head. "And do what? How can I lie down when my daughter is out there, all alone?"

Lord Dallington slipped an arm around his wife's shoulders. "Melody is right. You are exhausted. You should lie down, if only for a little while."

At her husband's urging, Lady Dallington relented, leaning heavily into his side for support. "Very well. Will you remain with me?"

"There is nowhere else I would rather be," Lord Dallington assured her, offering a small, strained smile.

As Lord Dallington escorted his wife from the room, Melody came and sat down next to Wesley on the settee. She exhaled slowly, her fingers twisting together in her lap. "My poor mother," she murmured.

Wesley leaned forward and placed his drink on the table before facing Melody. "How are you faring?"

Her composure shattered for a brief moment, her frown deepening. "How do you think I am faring?" she asked, her voice rising with frustration. "Elodie has been taken and it is all my fault."

"We will get her back," Wesley assured her.

Melody's eyes flickered to the windows. "Where is the constable? He should have been here by now."

"It hardly matters. The constable will likely be of little help to us anyways."

At that moment, Watkins entered the room, quietly shutting the door behind him. His expression was grim. "I have spoken to most of the household staff. No one saw anything that could be useful."

"No one saw anything?" Wesley repeated in disbelief. "Someone must have witnessed Lady Elodie being taken. She couldn't have just disappeared on her way to the music room."

"I'm afraid not," Watkins said. "However, there is more.

The footman caught sneaking out last night is nowhere to be found."

"How is that possible?" Wesley demanded.

Watkins shrugged. "He vanished. But I do believe it is safe to assume he was involved in Lady Elodie's abduction."

Wesley shot to his feet. "If this footman was sent here with ill intentions towards Melody, it would explain how the poison made its way into Artemis's food. Footmen often go unnoticed, blending into the background. No one would question his movements."

"Who *is* this footman?" Melody asked.

Watkins hesitated before answering. "Not much is known about him. He arrived two weeks ago with what appeared to be solid references from a large manor up north. According to White, he worked hard and kept to himself—until a few days ago."

Wesley's mind raced, piecing together the puzzle. "He was planted here. Whoever sent him wanted Melody. This abduction of Elodie is just a tactic to draw her out."

"You think this footman is working with someone else?" Watkins asked.

"It would only make sense to assume so," Wesley replied.

At that moment, a sharp knock came at the door. Jasper entered, his expression solemn. "I have just spoken to the constable," he informed them. "He is making some inquiries but is not quite convinced that Lady Elodie was abducted."

"And why not? What are his reasons?" Wesley inquired.

Jasper pressed his lips into a thin line. "He is entertaining the notion that she may have left voluntarily... possibly eloping to Gretna Green."

Melody's face went pale. "Eloping? With *whom*?" she demanded.

Jasper's gaze softened with sympathy. "In his experience, ladies of noble rank, especially daughters of marquesses, don't tend to be abducted. He believes she might have run off with someone."

Rising abruptly, Melody moved to the window, staring into the distance as though she might find answers. "I can't just sit here and do nothing. I need to search for her. I *have* to do something."

Wesley stepped forward, his voice firm but measured. "You will do no such thing. You will remain here, where it is safe."

Melody spun around, her eyes flashing with defiance. "You have no right to order me about, my lord."

Jasper interrupted, his tone calm. "Lord Emberly is right. No good would come from you leaving the manor. We need to think rationally."

Watkins tipped his head, drawing back Wesley's attention. "I will continue to gather information and report back as soon as I find anything useful."

As his valet departed from the room, Melody clenched her fists, her frustration palpable. "I feel so helpless," she muttered, more to herself than anyone else.

Wesley approached her. "You are not helpless. We will find her. But you need to trust us to handle this the right way."

"And how is that?" Melody asked. "Other than the footman, we have no leads. No real answers. We are grasping at straws."

Wesley reached for her hand. "You are not wrong, but whoever is behind this has finally tipped their hand. Now, it is our turn to make our move. It is time to find out who is truly after you."

Melody glanced down at their entwined hands. "I should have been the one taken, not Elodie. This is all my fault."

His grip tightened slightly. "You mustn't think that way. None of this is your fault."

Tears welled up in her eyes, but she blinked them away. "I can't lose my sister, Wesley. I won't."

A Shadowed Charade

"I know. We won't let that happen," he assured her, his gaze unwavering.

Jasper took a step closer to them. "It would help if I knew what we are up against."

Melody's eyes implored Wesley's. "Jasper is right. He deserves to know the truth."

Wesley paused. It was a difficult decision. Melody trusted Jasper, and Wesley respected the man's skills. However, by revealing their lives as agents, the very nature of their work could change everything. "I am not sure if that is wise."

"It is the only way," Melody responded.

Wesley knew that Melody was right. With a heavy nod, he let her take the lead.

Melody turned fully towards Jasper, squaring her shoulders. "I am an agent of the Crown," she confessed, her voice steady despite the weight of her admission.

Jasper's eyes widened slightly, but he held his composure. "An agent? You?"

"Yes," Melody confirmed. "I decipher enemy codes and have been doing so for over a year."

Shifting his gaze to Wesley, Jasper remarked, "And you, Lord Emberly, I presume, are also an agent. Assigned to protect Lady Melody, no doubt?"

Wesley nodded. "It is true."

Jasper let out a long sigh. "This certainly does explain a few things. But why do you think it is your fault that Lady Elodie was abducted?"

Wesley cleared his throat. "There was a leak within the agency. We believe that our enemies learned of Lady Melody's true identity."

"And recently, I deciphered a message taunting me about how someone is coming for me," Melody added.

Jasper grew silent for a long moment. "I had my suspicions, especially after seeing how capable Lady Melody is with a pistol," he admitted. "But why didn't you tell me sooner?"

Wesley met his gaze. "Until now, I wasn't sure I could trust you."

"That is fair," Jasper said with a curt nod. "This explains why you thought Artemis was poisoned as a part of a plot to reach Lady Melody."

Melody clasped her hands in front of her, her voice softer now. "Now that you know the truth, will you help us retrieve Elodie?"

Jasper bobbed his head. "I promised Lord Winston I would keep your family safe, and I keep my promises."

"Thank you," Melody murmured.

Crossing his arms over his chest, Jasper asked, "Have you considered that Artemis might be behind this? He is a botanist, knowledgeable about poisons, and he was conveniently in the gardens when Lady Elodie disappeared."

"I have thought about that. But I have not yet decided whether Artemis is a criminal genius or simply a fool," Wesley replied.

"I shall speak to him," Jasper asserted.

Melody shook her head, saying, "I will speak to him."

"With all due respect, my lady—" Jasper began, but Melody cut him off.

"Your presence would only raise suspicion," she argued. "But Artemis and I have known each other since we were children. I can approach him without arousing any suspicion."

"I will go with you," Wesley said.

"No, you won't," Melody responded. "I can do this on my own."

"And if he tries to abduct you?" Wesley pressed, his voice tight with concern.

With quiet resolve, Melody reached into the folds of her gown and pulled out her muff pistol, the cold metal gleaming faintly. "I will be prepared for anything."

Wesley's chest tightened. He did not like this, nor did he like the idea of her walking into danger alone. Every instinct screamed at him to stop her, to protect her. But he knew better. Melody was capable. She was not some simpering miss in need of constant protection. Yet, that knowledge did not lessen the knot of anxiety twisting in his gut.

He exhaled slowly, forcing himself to let go of his fear. "I want you to promise me one thing," he said.

"What is it?"

"If anything feels wrong—if something does not seem right—you get out of there. You get yourself to safety, understand?"

"I promise," Melody said.

It wasn't much, but it was enough. For now.

Chapter Seventeen

As Melody entered the gardens of Brockhall Manor, she took a deep breath, steeling herself for the most difficult conversation ahead. She wasn't entirely convinced that Artemis was behind Elodie's abduction, but she needed to be sure. Quite frankly, she didn't think he was clever enough to be involved in espionage.

She found Artemis sitting near a bed of crops, meticulously sketching plants in his journal. When he noticed her approach, he glanced up briefly. "Lady Melody," he greeted.

"Artemis," she responded, her tone more serious. "I need to—"

He put his hand up, cutting her off. "Give me a moment," he said, his attention returning to the plants as he added a few more lines to his sketch. Only after what felt like an unnecessarily long pause did he finally set the book aside and stand. "What can I do for you, my lady?"

Melody frowned, not in the mood for pleasantries. "Have you been out here all day?"

"I have," Artemis replied proudly. "I have been cataloging all the plants in your gardens."

"For what purpose?"

Artemis sputtered as if the answer should have been obvious. "For your own knowledge, of course! You would not want to be unaware of your gardens' flora."

Melody sighed. That was the least of her concerns. She decided to say what needed to be said and be done with it. "Did you hear that Elodie has been abducted?"

His eyes widened. "I did not hear that. How dreadful."

"Have you seen or heard anything unusual while you have been out here?"

"No, but I was rather preoccupied with these fascinating plants," Artemis replied, gently stroking the petals of a nearby flower.

Melody had to admit that Artemis was rather convincing, but she wasn't done with her questions. "And you have been alone this entire time?"

"Yes, why would you…" Artemis's voice trailed off and his expression darkened as realization dawned. "You think I had something to do with Lady Elodie's abduction, don't you?"

"I don't know what to think," she admitted, her frustration creeping into her voice.

Artemis narrowed his eyes, clearly insulted. "What reason would I have to abduct Lady Elodie? And if I had, why would I remain in plain sight?"

"All I know," Melody said, meeting his gaze steadily, "is that my sister is missing, and I would do anything to find her."

He scoffed. "You are barking up the wrong tree. I am tired of these accusations from you and your suitor."

"I have no suitor," Melody responded.

Artemis tilted his head towards the manor. "I believe Lord Emberly would disagree," he said, gesturing towards the veranda where Wesley stood, his sharp eyes searching the gardens.

"Whatever you may think is between Lord Emberly and me, you are mistaken."

"Are you sure about that?" Artemis challenged, raising an eyebrow. "Because it looks inevitable from where I stand."

Melody stepped closer, her irritation growing. "I assure you, you are wrong."

Artemis looked her over thoughtfully. "Well then, if that is the case, would you consider marrying me?"

Melody reared back. "I beg your pardon?"

"It would make perfect sense for us to wed," Artemis said as if they were discussing nothing more significant than the weather. "You need a husband, and I need a wife. Simple."

"That is your reasoning for us to wed?"

Artemis shrugged. "I want to focus on my research, and you can go about doing… whatever it is that women do."

Melody's disbelief turned into anger. "My answer is no."

"Very well," Artemis said, utterly unfazed by her rejection. "Will there be anything else? I have work to do."

She gaped at him, unable to believe his indifference. "You are not upset?"

"Why would I be?" Artemis asked, looking genuinely confused.

"I just turned down your offer of marriage."

Artemis merely blinked. "I will find a wife eventually. No need to make a fuss over it." Then with a dismissive wave, he returned to his plants, leaving Melody stunned.

She stared at Artemis for a long moment before spinning on her heel. There was no question in her mind—Artemis had nothing to do with Elodie's abduction. His devotion to plants eclipsed all other interests. He cared for nothing but his precious flowers and research.

As Melody approached Wesley, he straightened from the wall, his expression solemn. "Well, what did you discover?"

"Artemis is a muttonhead," she muttered.

He smiled. "I won't disagree with you there."

"After I questioned him about Elodie, he had the audacity to ask me to marry him."

Wesley's smile vanished, his posture growing rigid. "I take it that you turned him down."

Melody tossed her hands up in the air. "Of course I turned him down. I could never be married to that man. He cares more for plants than anything else."

A faint wince crossed Wesley's features. "Artemis mentioned that he intended to offer for you, but I didn't think he would be so bold as to do it under these circumstances."

Melody pressed her lips together. "You knew and didn't warn me?"

"I should have," he admitted, his voice tinged with regret. "Forgive me."

She sighed, realizing she wasn't truly angry with Wesley. It was herself she was frustrated with. She felt helpless in her inability to find her sister. All she wanted was to bring Elodie home and end this nightmare. "I forgive you."

Wesley stepped closer, the warmth of his presence drawing her in as she tilted her head to meet his gaze. His eyes held a quiet intensity that made her feel seen. "We will find Elodie."

"How?" she asked. "The only suspect we had is a dolt."

"Jasper is out right now looking for the footman."

"And what if he doesn't find him?"

Wesley placed a comforting hand on her sleeve. "The worst part about an investigation is waiting."

Melody gave him a weak smile. "Patience is not exactly my strong suit."

"There is nothing wrong with that," he said, his tone encouraging. "But you are strong."

"I don't feel strong."

His eyes remained on her, unwavering. "Being strong does not happen overnight. You became strong by overcoming everything that was meant to destroy you."

Melody lowered her gaze to the lapels of his jacket. His words cut through her fear, offering a flicker of hope, but all she could think about was Elodie. "You are kind, but all I want to do is find my sister."

"And we will," he stated. "I made a promise to you, and I intend to keep it."

In that quiet moment, Melody felt vulnerable, more so than she had ever allowed herself to be in front of anyone. But with Wesley, she didn't feel judged or weak—just safe enough to admit the truth. "I am scared," she whispered.

"You? Scared?" Wesley teased.

She brought her gaze back up. "I am being serious."

Wesley's eyes softened with understanding, the kind of look that made her want to stay in that moment, lingering in his gaze. "Aren't you the same person who told me you didn't need my help?" he asked. "Where is that fire, that fierceness?"

"It is gone."

"No," Wesley assured her. "It is not gone. It is still there, in your heart. You just have to believe it."

As Melody stared into Wesley's eyes, searching for the strength to continue, she realized she loved this man. That thought sent a wave of emotions coursing through her. She had always valued her independence and her ability to handle things on her own. But this feeling? It was different, more profound than anything she had experienced. And yet, with her sister missing, there was no time to dwell on these emotions.

She took a small step back and his hand dropped to the side. "I should go inside."

Wesley's gaze lingered on her as though he wanted to say more, but instead, he simply tipped his head. "Allow me to escort you inside."

No.

The word echoed in her mind, though she couldn't say it aloud. She wanted—no, *needed*—to be alone. She didn't trust herself around Wesley, not after realizing the depth of her feelings.

Melody put her hand up. "I need a moment alone."

Wesley's disappointment was palpable, but he didn't fight her request. "Very well. I shall inform you at once if I discover anything of importance."

"Thank you."

Without waiting for a response, Melody brushed past him. She could practically feel his gaze on her back as she hurried inside the manor, desperate for a moment to collect herself, to push away the whirlwind of emotions that had come crashing over her.

Melody stepped into the manor and saw her mother at the far end of the corridor, deep in conversation with Mr. Bramwell.

"There you are, Child," her mother said, her voice fraught with worry. "I have been looking everywhere for you."

"I was out in the gardens with Artemis and Lord Emberly," Melody explained.

As she approached, Mr. Bramwell's eyes settled on her, filled with a pity that made her stomach tighten. "You poor, brave thing," he said. "I can't imagine what your family must be going through at the moment, what with Elodie being abducted and all."

Melody's steps faltered. "How did you know about that?" she asked, her voice holding a slight edge.

Her mother interjected. "Mr. Bramwell was gracious enough to call upon us, and we shared the devastating news with him."

Mr. Bramwell reached for Melody's gloved hand. "Please, let me know if there is anything I can do for you. Rest assured, I will keep this between us."

Though his touch felt intrusive, Melody fought the urge to pull her hand away, not wanting to appear rude or ungrateful. "Thank you, Mr. Bramwell."

"I shall be praying for your family during this most difficult time," Mr. Bramwell continued as he held her hand.

"Well, I do thank you," Melody replied, taking a small step back to create distance as she gently freed her hand.

Her mother's gaze shifted back to Melody, the red-rimmed eyes betraying the deep exhaustion and worry she carried. "Your father and I do not want you to leave this manor. Not for any reason. Not until Elodie is back home, safe."

"I understand."

Reaching up, her mother cupped her right cheek. "I couldn't bear it if something happened to you, too," she whispered. "I am already struggling with the thought that Elodie has been taken. My heart can't take much more."

Melody placed her hand over her mother's, trying to offer what little comfort she could. "We will get Elodie back."

Her mother's eyes flickered with doubt as she pulled away. "The constable believes that Elodie has run away. Is that what you believe?"

"Heavens, no. Elodie wouldn't have left on her own."

Her mother offered her a grateful look. "I always feared that Elodie would bring trouble to our doorstep, but I never imagined this." Her words were soft, resigned.

Melody knew she had to be brave, for both of their sakes. "Elodie is many things, but she is not reckless with her safety. She will find a way back to us."

"Let us hope you are right," her mother said, turning slightly. "Just promise me that you will stay indoors."

Melody mustered up a smile on her lips. "I promise." There. It was what her mother needed to hear, not the truth.

As her mother turned and walked away, Melody's heart ached. She had made the promise, but she knew full well she would not keep it. There was too much at stake, and Elodie needed her. She could not just sit and wait. Not now. Not ever.

Her thoughts were interrupted by the sound of Mr. Bramwell clearing his throat. "I suppose I should take my leave. Unless, of course, you would prefer to continue our conversation in the gardens?"

"No, thank you," she replied. "My mother has requested I remain inside for the time being, and I shall respect her wishes."

The vicar stood rooted in his spot for a long moment before he bowed. "Then I shall leave you to it, my lady."

Melody watched him walk away, his figure disappearing down the corridor with measured, deliberate steps. Something about his visit unsettled her. Why had he come today, of all days? She couldn't help but wonder if there was more to his visit than he let on.

Wesley sat in the study, swirling the port in his glass as he watched Lord Dallington pace the length of the room, his forehead creased with worry. He understood the marquess's frustration. Elodie had been missing for hours, and they were no closer to finding her or identifying her abductor. The entire household was on edge, and dinner was a silent, tense affair.

Lord Belview, seated across from him, sighed deeply as he set his half-full glass on the table. "I should retire. I am leaving at first light to ride out to my estate. I will bring back every available man to help with the search for Elodie. I refuse to sit back and do nothing."

"We could use all the help we can get," Wesley responded.

His friend stood, running a hand through his hair. "I just keep replaying the last conversation I had with Elodie. We were arguing about pickles, of all things."

"Pickles?" Wesley echoed.

"Yes, and at the time, it seemed so important," Lord Belview admitted with a shake of his head. "Now, I just wish I had not wasted that moment on something so trivial."

Wesley met his friend's gaze. "We will get her back," he responded, his words steady, even if doubt gnawed at him.

Lord Belview's expression grew determined. "We will, even if it is the last thing that I do."

"It won't come to that," Wesley said. He understood how Lord Belview felt. Elodie had disappeared, and every moment that passed without a word made her rescue feel increasingly impossible.

Lord Belview clenched his fists as he spoke. "Let's hope not, but I will do whatever it takes to get her back." His voice cracked slightly. "I can't lose her… not now."

Wesley remained silent for a moment, watching his friend struggle. He knew that Lord Belview harbored deeper feelings for Elodie than he was willing to admit. It was clear now more than ever how deeply her abduction had shaken him. "We will find her," he assured Belview, hoping he wasn't making a promise he couldn't keep.

Lord Belview's eyes grew moist. "I hope so," he said before he departed from the room.

The silence that followed felt suffocating, but it was broken by Lord Dallington's sharp, demanding voice. "Why haven't we heard anything? If it is a ransom they want, where is the demand? Why the silence?"

Wesley fought the urge to reveal what he knew. The abduction wasn't about money; it was about Melody. The enemy wanted her, but he could not bring himself to say it out loud. "I don't rightly know," he said instead.

A shadow crossed Lord Dallington's features. "I would give everything I have for Elodie's safe return."

"I know," Wesley said, rising. "We will get her back."

Lord Dallington frowned. "You keep saying that, but how can you be so sure? The constable believes she ran off, and I have no idea where that blasted Bow Street Runner is."

"Jasper is chasing down leads," Wesley remarked.

Lord Dallington scoffed. "Not fast enough, if you ask me."

Wesley couldn't help but smile faintly. The man sounded

remarkably like his daughter, Melody. It seemed that impatience was a family trait.

With a glance at the darkened window, Wesley suggested, "It is late. Why don't you go to Lady Dallington?"

Lord Dallington's shoulders sagged slightly. "I don't know if I can sleep, but you are right. I should be with Catherine."

"Go to her, my lord," Wesley encouraged. "I will send word if anything new arises."

"Thank you," Lord Dallington said before departing the room.

Wesley sank back into his chair, picking up his glass of port and staring into the liquid. His mind drifted to Melody. She had retired earlier, but his concern for her safety gnawed at him. He debated whether to check on her when the door creaked open, and White, the butler, appeared.

"My lord, your sister, Lady Rosella—"

Before White could finish, Rosella, tall and dark-haired, swept into the room, cutting him off. "Brother, you look awful," she declared with a half-smile.

Wesley stood to greet her, his tone dry. "Charming as ever, Rosella."

Rosella's sharp eyes scanned his face. "What is wrong?"

"Where to start?" Wesley gestured towards a chair. "Lady Elodie has been abducted and we are no closer to finding her than we were this morning."

His sister's expression grew serious as she took a seat. "It is a good thing I am here, then. The spymaster sent me. He was concerned that you might be distracted."

Wesley frowned. "Distracted? By what?"

She gave him a knowing look. "This case bears an eerie resemblance to what happened with Dinah."

His jaw tightened. "I do not want to talk about Dinah."

"You never do," Rosella responded, "but that doesn't change the fact that we need to focus on finding Elodie."

"I can handle it," Wesley insisted.

She leaned forward, her gaze softening for a moment. "I do not doubt that, but I care about Lady Melody, too. She is my friend, and I won't sit idly by if there is something I can do to help."

Wesley knew he had a choice. He could turn her away, but knowing Rosella, she wouldn't go anywhere. She was as stubborn as he was—and just as skilled. It seemed pointless to argue.

With a resigned sigh, he nodded. "All right. What do you wish to know?"

"Start from the beginning," Rosella said, leaning back in her seat, her sharp eyes focused on him.

Wesley glanced at the long clock in the corner, noting the late hour. "Lady Elodie was abducted to lure Lady Melody out. We haven't received any demands yet, but I am certain we will."

Rosella's expression didn't change as she listened intently. "And who are your suspects?"

Wesley winced slightly, rubbing the back of his neck. "I initially suspected Mr. Artemis Nelson. His knowledge of plants, especially poisons, made him the perfect candidate for a French spy. But after speaking with him, I am beginning to think he is just an imbecile. Not the kind of man capable of orchestrating something like this. However, we do believe a footman is involved in Elodie's abduction. Watkins is currently looking into that."

Rosella nodded thoughtfully. "How is Watkins? I haven't seen him in some time."

"He is well," Wesley replied, grateful for the shift in conversation.

His sister smiled faintly. "It is nice that you have someone to confide in. I do not have the same luxury with my servants."

Wesley lifted his brow. "You could come home anytime, you know. Mother would be thrilled."

"Mother and I have a complicated past," Rosella said with a swipe of her hand. "She wants me to behave like a proper lady and I am not interested in that life."

He studied his sister. "You would rather be a spinster?"

Rosella clasped her hands in front of her. "Being a spinster gives me the freedom I so desperately crave. I don't have to answer to anyone. More importantly, it allows me to continue my work as an agent without constraints."

"Don't you want more?" Wesley asked, leaning forward. "A family? Children?"

For a brief moment, Rosella's eyes flickered with something resembling regret as she glanced down at her hands. "I have made peace with my choices. It is best if you did as well."

Wesley moved to sit on the edge of his seat. "You are my sister, and I support you in whatever you want to do with your life. I just want to make sure you are happy."

"Happy?" she repeated, a touch of bitterness creeping into her voice. "Is anyone truly happy?"

An image of Melody flashed in Wesley's mind. How could she smile and laugh, even amidst the chaos around her? She seemed to find joy in the smallest things.

"You are smiling," Rosella remarked.

He wiped the smile from his lips. "I was thinking…"

"About Melody," she finished for him, a smirk on her lips. "Don't even bother denying it. From the moment I met her, I knew she was perfect for you. The way she sees the world is extraordinary. She has not been tainted by the darkness of our work, by what we do and who we have become."

Wesley knew he couldn't deny the truth in his sister's words. Melody was different. She always had been. She had not been hardened by their world of secrets, lies and danger. And that was precisely why he found himself drawn to her. She was everything he did not realize he needed. But loving her, or admitting to it, felt like inviting a storm into both of their lives.

Rosella's eyes softened. "Do not let her slip away, Wesley. She is the kind of woman who can make you happy, even if you do not think it is possible."

Wesley hesitated before sharing, "I told her about Dinah."

Her eyes widened slightly. "You did? And what did she say?"

Wesley settled back into his chair, exhaling slowly. "She told me that Dinah's death wasn't my fault."

"It wasn't. Dinah knew the risks. We all do, being in this line of work."

"I was supposed to protect her," he said, his voice tightening with the weight of his old guilt.

Rosella leaned forward and placed her hand on his sleeve. "You did the best you could with what you knew then."

Wesley knew she meant to comfort him, but the words didn't lift the burden from his heart. Instead, they reminded him of his failures. But this time had to be different. He couldn't fail Melody. He wouldn't.

In a steady voice, Wesley revealed, "We believe the same French spy who killed Dinah has been murdering others by placing oleander in their fires."

"And by others, you mean Father?"

"I do, and we believe that same spy is after Lady Melody now."

Rosella withdrew her hand, her eyes darkening with a mix of grief and anger. "I haven't thought of Father in some time now," she admitted. "I can't do what I do, believing that one day I will end up like him."

"Rosella..." he began.

Abruptly, she rose from her seat and crossed to the window, staring into the night. "When Father was murdered, I realized that no one—no matter how skilled or careful—is invincible. We all die when it is our time." Her voice wavered with unspoken pain.

Rising, he moved to her side. "We will catch Father's killer. I promise you that."

Rosella turned to face him, her eyes filled with unshed tears. "Will that change anything? He is still dead. Nothing we do will bring him back."

"No, but it will give us some answers."

Tears slipped down Rosella's cheeks, and her voice broke. "I want to be the one who catches Father's killer."

"Then stay. Help us," Wesley said.

Without warning, Rosella wrapped her arms around him, her body shaking with sobs. Wesley was taken aback. His sister was not one to show her emotions so openly. He held her close. It was rare to see her so vulnerable, and it hit him just how much she had been carrying on her own.

After a long moment, Rosella stepped out of his arms, wiping at her tear-streaked cheeks. "I am sorry."

"You have nothing to apologize for," he assured her. "You are allowed to feel this."

She took a deep, steadying breath. "I am ready to get to work," she said, determination hardening her voice again. "Let us catch Father's killer."

Chapter Eighteen

Melody sat by the window, her heart heavy with guilt. She couldn't shake the thought that she had failed her sister. Elodie had no part in the dangerous life Melody led as a spy, yet she was suffering because of it. It wasn't fair, and that realization gnawed at her. Somewhere out there, her sister was alone and in danger, and all Melody wanted was to find her and bring her home.

A soft knock at the door interrupted her thoughts. It creaked open to reveal her lady's maid, Lydia, holding a candle. "Are you ready to dress for bed, my lady?" she asked gently.

"Not yet."

Lydia's face softened, her eyes full of pity. "Worrying yourself sick about Elodie won't help. You need rest."

Melody turned from the window, a frown pulling at her lips. "This is all my fault."

Lydia furrowed her brow. "How could it be your fault? Did you abduct her?"

"No, but—"

Before Melody could finish, Lydia cut her off, her tone kind but firm. "It is natural to blame yourself when something bad happens, but that doesn't make it true. This isn't your fault, my lady."

Melody fell silent. Lydia didn't understand. No one did. She couldn't reveal the truth—that Elodie was caught in the crossfire of her life as a spy. It was a secret she had to bear alone.

Suddenly, a faint sound came from beneath the door. Lydia noticed it first, bending down to retrieve the paper that had been slipped inside. She examined it for a moment before handing it to Melody. "It is addressed to you."

A sense of dread filled Melody as she took the letter. Slowly, she unfolded the paper and read the ominous words:

Meet in the gardens. Come alone. Tell anyone and your sister dies.

Melody crumpled the note in her hand. She had no choice in the matter. She had to go down and meet with whoever sent this letter.

Lydia gave her a curious look. "Who is that letter from?"

"No one of importance."

"Is it from Lord Emberly?" Lydia pressed.

Melody shook her head. "No. It is not from him."

Lydia eyed her, unconvinced. "The servants say he is smitten with you."

Reaching into the folds of her gown, Melody's fingers brushed the hidden pistol. "He is not smitten. Now, I need to handle something before bed."

Moving towards the door, Lydia remarked, "I don't think you should meet with Lord Emberly at this hour. It is not proper."

"As I have told you, I am not meeting with Lord Emberly," Melody repeated, growing impatient.

"Then what is so important that it can't wait until morning?"

Melody gave Lydia a tight smile, knowing she was only trying to help. But this was something that she had to do on her own. It was her fight, no one else's. "I will only be a moment. Do not wait up for me."

Lydia hesitated, her concern evident. "Please don't go. Stay here, where it is safe."

"I am just going to the gardens for a breath of air. I shall return shortly," Melody insisted. "I know what I am doing."

Reluctantly, Lydia stepped aside. "Very well, my lady."

Melody made her way towards the back of the manor, slipping through the corridors. If Lydia had known why she was truly going into the gardens, she would have tried to stop her. And she couldn't let that happen. Melody had to face whoever was behind this, knowing she could handle it herself.

As she passed by the study, she saw Wesley embracing his sister. A part of her wanted to greet them, but she couldn't afford to waste time explaining her actions. Wesley would never allow her to go through with her plan. Right now, she needed to do just that.

She exited the manor and didn't stop until she reached the bench Matilda so often occupied. Melody's eyes scanned the darkened area, knowing she wasn't alone. A tall, blond man emerged from the cover of the trees, his face shadowed but his demeanor smug. He gave her a mocking bow. "My lady."

Melody didn't have time for pleasantries. Her hand tightened around the pistol hidden in her gown. "Where is my sister?"

The man smiled, clearly amused by her demand. "Patience, Lady Melody," he said, his words thick with a French accent.

"I'm afraid I don't have any," Melody snapped, pulling out her pistol and aiming it at him. "You have taken someone important to me. I won't ask again—where is she?"

"You won't shoot me," he said.

"Yes, I will," Melody replied. "For Elodie's sake, I will."

The man's smirk didn't falter. "If you kill me, you will never know where she is. And that would be a shame, would it not?"

Melody's grip tightened on the pistol, but she didn't lower it. "How do I know she is still alive?"

"Because we don't want Lady Elodie. She is just leverage. You are the one we want."

Melody's stomach twisted. "Who is *we*?"

The man stepped closer, his voice low and taunting. "You did not think I would come alone to confront a spy, did you?"

"All I do is decipher codes, nothing more."

He chuckled. "You have done much more than that, my lady. You have written a code that no one has been able to break. And that makes you very valuable."

"So this is about the code?"

The man held his hands out wide. "If you willingly come with us, we will release Lady Elodie."

"Where do you want to take me?"

"To France, of course."

Melody's resolve hardened. She had no intention of going to France or letting this man control the situation. She cocked the pistol, her voice sharp and deadly. "Tell me where my sister is, or I will kill you."

The man's smile faltered for the first time. "You are no killer, my lady."

"Given the right circumstances, I can be," Melody responded.

"Put the pistol down and I will take you to your sister," the man said smoothly, his eyes never leaving hers.

"Why should I trust you?" she demanded.

The man bowed again. "Forgive me. I am Pierre. I was posing as a footman in your grand manor."

Melody's heart skipped a beat. The footman. She had found him. "And who is your partner?"

Pierre tsked, wagging a finger. "I cannot reveal that just yet."

"Yet you expect me to trust you?" Melody shot back, keeping her stance firm.

Glancing at the manor, Pierre asked, "Where is your shadow, my lady? Isn't that what your friend, Jasper, called him?"

"I have no shadow."

Pierre's lips curled into a sly smile as he took a deliberate step closer. "I am referring to Lord Emberly. You two seem awfully close. Not that I blame him. You are quite beautiful."

"We are merely friends," Melody said, training the pistol on him.

"Do not insult me by implying there is not anything more going on between you," Pierre stated. "Lord Emberly is a spy, just like us."

Melody's arm was beginning to tire, but she had no intention of lowering the pistol. She refused to give Pierre the advantage. "Do not come any closer, or I will shoot."

Instead of backing away, Pierre walked over to the bench and sat down as if the threat of being shot didn't faze him in the least. "I want you to come work for us."

Her eyes narrowed. "You want me to work for the French?" she repeated in disbelief.

Pierre nodded, his smile returning. "You are on the losing side."

Melody huffed. "Not from where I am standing."

"Napoleon will eventually conquer England, and you could be on the right side of history," Pierre said confidently.

"I am quite content where I am," Melody responded.

Pierre settled back into his seat, studying her with a calculating gaze. "I have watched you for some time. Your family doesn't know your true brilliance. They don't see what you are capable of."

"Yet you think they would be proud of me for betraying them? For working with the French?" Melody asked, incredulous.

"You think of us as the enemy," Pierre said.

"You *are* the enemy."

"And yet we are conversing as old friends."

"No, the only reason why we are speaking is because you have my sister," Melody declared. "Tell me where she is."

Pierre stood, his expression still calm but his eyes cold. "Come work for us."

"No."

"Think of your sister."

Melody tilted her chin in defiance. "I am. Elodie would never forgive me for working with the French."

"But she would be safe," Pierre countered.

Taking a commanding step towards Pierre, Melody said, "This ends now."

Pierre chuckled. "You are so young, so naïve. You can't possibly believe that."

"I just want my sister back," Melody said, her voice trembling ever so slightly as she tried to maintain control.

A flicker of something unreadable passed Pierre's face. "And I want to finish my mission. We both can't have everything we want, can we?"

The snap of a twig echoed from the nearby trees, drawing Melody's attention for the briefest of moments.

"Time's up," Pierre said. "What is your decision?"

Melody met his gaze. "I already told you my decision. I would rather die than betray my country."

Pierre's face darkened, his playful demeanor vanishing. "That can easily be arranged, my dear. Don't say that I didn't warn you."

The tension hung thick in the air as they stared each other

down. Melody's heart pounded in her chest, but her grip on the pistol never wavered. The very idea that she would work for the French was absurd. She would die before betraying her country or her family.

Suddenly, the sound of footsteps approached from behind her. Before Melody could turn to see who it was, something hard struck the back of her head. Pain radiated through her skull, and the pistol slipped from her fingers as she crumpled to the ground, her vision diminishing.

As she rolled onto her back, she caught a glimpse of a familiar face before everything went black.

Wesley was jolted awake by the crash of his bedchamber door swinging open. Startled, he blinked against the morning light. Standing in the doorway, Watkins had an urgent look in his eyes.

"Wake up, my lord. Lady Melody is missing," Watkins announced with uncharacteristic tension in his voice.

Wesley shot up in bed. "*Missing?!*"

As Watkins moved efficiently to the wardrobe, pulling out a fresh set of clothes, he continued, "Yes, her lady's maid noticed that she didn't return from the gardens last night."

Wesley's mind raced as he threw off his bedcovers. "What in the blazes was Melody doing in the gardens last night?"

Still busy collecting garments, Watkins paused briefly to meet his master's gaze. "Apparently, her lady's maid thought she was meeting with you."

Wesley cursed under his breath. "Fetch that lady's maid. I want to speak with her now."

Holding a pair of trousers, Watkins said, "She is already waiting for you in Lady Melody's bedchamber. Shall you dress first, or would you like to cause a scandal in the household?"

Wesley hastily threw on his clothes, barely bothering with his cravat, before making his way briskly down the hall. His mind was a storm of questions and concerns. Upon reaching Lady Melody's chamber, he pushed the door open to find a young woman inside, her face streaked with tears. This had to be the maid.

Not one for pleasantries, Wesley asked, "When did you see Lady Melody last?"

The lady's maid, clearly distraught, tried to compose herself. "It was late—"

"I need specifics, Woman!" Wesley interrupted, his voice harsher than he intended.

Watkins, who had followed him silently, cleared his throat in disapproval. "This is Lydia, and she has been Lady Melody's lady's maid for many years now."

Wesley forced himself to soften his tone, though the urgency remained. "I am sorry, Lydia, but I need to know precisely how long Lady Melody has been missing."

Lydia swiped at the tears and stammered, "She went to the gardens before midnight."

He scrutinized her, searching for any hint of doubt. "You are certain of that?"

"I am, my lord."

Running a hand through his hair, Wesley asked the next question that gnawed at him. "Why did you believe she was meeting with me?"

Lydia hesitated before responding, "A note was slipped under the door. I didn't read it, but I assumed it was from you."

"And you let her go?" Wesley exclaimed.

Before he could press further, Rosella's voice came from the doorway. "Wesley, you are being rather rude," she chided lightly. "She did nothing wrong here."

Wesley shot his sister a frustrated look. "What do you want, Sister?"

Ignoring his irritation, Rosella walked over to Lydia, sitting beside her on the bed. "It is all right. My brother is just concerned. Can you tell us exactly what happened?"

Lydia sniffled. "Lady Melody was upset about her sister. Then the letter arrived. I tried to dissuade her from going, I swear, but she insisted."

Rosella gave her a sympathetic look. "Why didn't you tell anyone about her plans to go to the gardens?"

Lydia sighed heavily, guilt evident in her voice. "I didn't want her to get into trouble."

"So you were protecting her?" Rosella pressed.

Lydia nodded, her voice cracking. "Yes, I thought I was, but I should have gone with her…"

Rosella squeezed Lydia's hand. "If you had, something terrible might have also befallen you."

Lydia sobbed. "I am so sorry."

Rising, Rosella gave Wesley a pointed look. "I do not think Lydia did anything wrong. Do you?"

Wesley was a smart enough man to know when to let a matter drop. Lydia didn't know anything more than what she had already shared. "No, she did not."

Rosella gave him a brief smile. "Was that so hard to admit?"

"It was, actually," he responded with a grimace.

Lowering her voice, Rosella walked over to her brother and spoke softly. "We need to talk privately."

Wesley followed her down the corridor to the parlor. Once inside, Watkins closed the door behind them. Wesley wasted no time. "What do we know?"

Watkins crossed his arms over his chest. "There are signs of a struggle in the gardens, near a bench."

Wesley's hands balled into fists as the anger surged again. "Why would Melody go out alone? It is madness."

Leaning against the wall, Rosella answered quietly, "It

must have been about Elodie. That is the only reason she would take such a risk."

"Regardless, she should have come to me," Wesley declared. "I would have kept her safe."

Rosella gave him a knowing look. "Would you have let her go?"

"Of course not!" Wesley shouted, his voice shaking. "She is under my protection, and I take that duty very seriously."

His sister's expression softened. "Melody is capable. I do not doubt that she thought she could handle this on her own."

"She was careless!" Wesley's voice cracked with emotion. "Now she is gone, just like her sister. I failed her…"

He turned to the window, his failure pressing down on him like a suffocating fog. The thought that he might never see Melody again gripped his heart, refusing to let go.

His sister's voice came from behind him. "Wesley, we will get Lady Melody back," she assured him.

Wesley whirled around to face her. "How?" he demanded. "We don't even know who took her."

Before Rosella could answer, the door creaked open. Jasper stepped into the room, his expression grim. "I know who took her," he announced.

Now, Jasper had Wesley's attention. "Who?" he asked, his words coming out like a growl.

Jasper's gaze flickered briefly to Rosella. "I do not believe we have met," he said, offering a slight bow. "I am Jasper."

Rosella returned the gesture with a curtsy. "Lady Rosella," she introduced herself. "I am this stubborn mule's sister. You can speak freely in front of me. Wesley has filled me in on the situation and I am here to help."

If Jasper was taken back by her forwardness, he didn't show it. Instead, he nodded, his tone pragmatic. "That will save us some time, then," he remarked. "A woman arrived in the village yesterday, searching for her husband—Mr. Durand."

Wesley raised an eyebrow. "The dancing master?"

"Yes," Jasper confirmed. "But when she described him, something felt off. So, I described the Mr. Durand that we know and she met me with a blank look. That is when I realized the truth. The man who was murdered recently was the real Mr. Durand."

Wesley stared at Jasper. "You are saying the man we have been dealing with—the one we thought was Mr. Durand—was an imposter? A spy?"

"It would appear so," Jasper said, holding up his hand. "A French spy was right under our noses this entire time."

Wesley felt the room close in on him, his mind racing as the implications sank in. "And you are sure about this?"

"As sure as I can be," Jasper replied. "The man posing as Mr. Durand disappeared last night around the same time Lady Melody went missing."

Wesley's fist clenched as he turned towards Watkins. "How in the blazes did we miss that?" he barked.

Watkins's expression remained impassive, but his eyes betrayed his regret. "He just seemed eccentric, like many dancing masters. And he came with impeccable references."

"Yes," Jasper cut in, his tone sharper now. "References he stole from the real Mr. Durand, along with his identity."

Turning back towards the window, Wesley couldn't quite believe that he had been so blinded by Artemis that he had failed to see what was right in front of him the entire time. Now, Melody was gone because of it. He gritted his teeth, fighting against the sense of failure that gnawed at him.

Rosella placed a hand on his sleeve. "You couldn't have known."

"You don't know that," he responded. "For all we know, Lady Melody and her sister might already be dead."

"If that were the case, we would have found her body in the gardens," Rosella pointed out. "No, this spy needs her alive—for now."

Wesley squeezed his eyes shut for a moment, trying to steady his breathing. "How do we find her?" he asked, his voice quieter but still edged with desperation.

Rosella placed a hand on her hip. "Why don't you stop being a naysayer and start getting to work?" she asked, a challenge in her tone.

In a voice so low it was almost a whisper, Wesley replied, "I can't lose her."

"You won't, Brother," Rosella encouraged. "But wallowing in your self-pity won't help anyone—not Lady Melody, and certainly not you. We need to be smart. We need to act. You are stronger than this."

Wesley looked at his sister, her words sinking in. She was right. Feeling sorry for himself wouldn't save Melody. "You are right," he said, his voice now steadier, more resolute. "We will find her. And we will bring her back."

Jasper stepped forward. "I think I can help with that," he began. "Earlier, I saw smoke rising from a chimney deep in the woodlands. It caught my attention because White told me the place had been abandoned for years. That might be the best lead we have."

"How did you manage to see such a thing?" Wesley asked.

"I have been staying at the old gamekeeper's cottage," Jasper explained. "Lord Winston ordered me to remain close, and from there, I have kept watch over the estate."

Wesley's gaze sharpened as he considered the information. "If that is where Lady Melody and her sister are being held, then we only have one chance to do this right." His lips curved into a smile as a plan began to form in his mind. "And I think I know exactly how to pull it off."

Chapter Nineteen

Melody awoke to a pounding headache, her temples throbbing as if they were being hammered from the inside. She groaned softly, bringing a shaky hand to her head, but kept her eyes closed, the weight of sleep still clinging to her.

"Melody!" a familiar voice called, sharp with worry.

She recognized that voice. It was Elodie. Her sister's voice cut through the haze, and fragments of her memory began to return with it. The gardens... the figure approaching... the sudden pain as she was struck. Before she could piece it all together, Elodie spoke again, more urgently, "Wake up, Melody."

But Melody didn't want to wake up. She tried to sink back into the comforting darkness, where the pain was distant, and the confusion didn't matter. Just a few more moments of rest...

This time, Elodie shook her firmly. "Melody! I need your help."

The desperation in Elodie's voice jolted Melody awake. She forced her eyes open, blinking against the dim light. The first thing she saw was Elodie's face, pale and tense with worry.

"Where are we?" Melody asked, her voice hoarse as she slowly pushed herself into a sitting position.

"We are in a cottage," Elodie replied. "Somewhere in the woodlands, I think. It looks like it used to be the old gamekeeper's cottage, but it has been abandoned for years." She paused, biting her lip. "How are we going to escape?"

Melody's mind was still reeling from the blow to her head. "Escape?"

Elodie nodded, her eyes darting to the small, grimy window across the room. "The windows are nailed shut, and the only door is locked from the outside. We need to figure something out, and quickly."

Melody's gaze swept over the room. It was bare and small, with only the straw mattress she had been lying on and little else. The papered walls were stained with years of neglect, and the air was thick with dust. She felt her stomach churn with dread.

Holding up a rusty, bent nail, Elodie said, "I found this. It might help us—somehow."

Melody instinctively reached into the folds of her gown, searching for her pistol. Her heart sank when her fingers found nothing. She must have dropped it when she had been struck in the gardens. Drats. How was she supposed to protect them now?

"I tried to remove the nails in the window, but they won't budge," Elodie continued, a trace of frustration in her voice. "If we can't get out that way, we will have to fight our way through whoever comes for us next."

Melody groaned softly as she swung her legs over the side of the mattress, trying to gather her thoughts. But the pounding in her head made it difficult to think clearly. Each pulse of pain reminded her of the mistake she had made—the reckless decision to meet Elodie's abductor in the gardens alone. She had walked straight into a trap.

"Are you all right, Melody?" Elodie asked, her voice softer now.

No.

She was not all right. She had made a mistake. She should have known better than to trust the cryptic note luring her into the night. Now, they were both prisoners, and it was all her fault.

Elodie gently placed a hand on her shoulder. "Perhaps you should rest a little longer."

"I am fine," Melody insisted. "I just need a moment."

Sitting back, Elodie offered her a sympathetic look. "I understand. I have had plenty of time to think since I have been here. I knew something was wrong with Mr. Durand from the moment I met him."

"Why do you say that?"

Elodie waved her hand dramatically as though it were the most obvious thing in the world. "Why else would he abduct me? The man is clearly up to something nefarious."

Melody stifled a sigh. What should she tell her sister? Could she trust her with the truth? Would Elodie even believe her?

As Elodie started pacing the small room, she said, "Ever since I was taken, I have been left alone in this room. No one has told me anything until you arrived. What do you suppose Mr. Durand wants with us?"

Melody bit her lip, knowing it was time. She had no choice but to tell Elodie the truth. She gestured for her sister to sit beside her on the mattress. "Come sit."

Elodie stopped pacing and sat beside her, her expression expectant and curious. "What is it?"

Melody took a deep breath, gathering the courage to say what needed to be said. "I know why Mr. Durand abducted us. It was never about you. It is all about me."

"Why would you say that?" Elodie asked.

Melody exhaled softly, steeling herself for her sister's reaction. "I am a spy."

For a moment, Elodie just stared at her. Then, she burst into laughter. "You? A spy? That is impossible!"

Melody should have anticipated her sister's reaction, but she pressed on. "I am being earnest. I am an agent of the Crown. Mr. Durand—well, the man we thought was Mr. Durand—is a French spy. That is why he took us."

Elodie's laughter died in her throat, her eyes widening in shock. "You… are being serious," she said, her voice suddenly soft.

Melody nodded, feeling the weight of her confession settle heavily between them. "Yes. And now, because of me, we are both in danger."

Her sister's brow furrowed. "How is it possible that you are a spy?" she asked, her voice incredulous. "None of this makes sense. You are perfect."

Melody let out a small laugh. "I am far from perfect, Elodie. I was recruited when we were at boarding school. I am not the cloak-and-dagger type of spy, but rather one that deciphers codes."

Elodie rose from the bed and walked to the small, grimy window, her footsteps heavy on the wooden floor. The silence between them grew louder, and Melody wondered if her sister would ever truly believe her. It was, after all, a near-impossible truth to swallow.

After a long moment, Elodie turned back to face her. "Is Lord Emberly your partner?"

"He sends me the codes to decipher under the guise of 'Josephine.' It is all done in secrecy," Melody replied.

Elodie bobbed her head slowly as if digesting the information. "I believe you," she finally said.

Melody's brow shot up in surprise. "You do?"

Crossing the room, Elodie came to stand beside her. "Yes, because I know you. You wouldn't lie to me about something like this. Besides, I am a little frustrated that I wasn't recruited as a spy. I would have been brilliant at it."

Melody couldn't help but smile, despite the gravity of the situation. "You would have been," she agreed.

A bright smile came to Elodie's lips. "I can't believe you are a spy. Father would be furious if he ever found out."

Melody's expression grew serious. "You must never tell him or anyone. No one can know."

Elodie nodded her understanding. "Your secret is safe with me. But I want to know everything."

Before Melody could answer, the sound of a key turning in the lock echoed through the room. The door swung open, and there stood the man they had known as Mr. Durand. His sharp eyes swept over the sisters as he stepped inside.

"Good, you are awake," Mr. Durand said, stepping into the room.

Elodie moved swiftly to place herself between Melody and the man. "Let us go," she demanded.

"Sit down, my lady," Mr. Durand ordered. "I am here to speak to Lady Melody, not you."

Melody stood, gently placing a hand on Elodie's shoulder. "It will be all right," she said, hoping it was not an empty promise.

Mr. Durand advanced further into the room, his movements deliberate. He produced a folded piece of paper from his jacket and held it up. "This code," he said. "You created it. I need you to tell me how to read it."

Melody's stomach dropped as she recognized her handwriting. It was a crucial cipher meant for Wellington's troops. If she revealed the key, it could cost thousands of lives.

"No," she replied, her voice steady despite the fear twisting inside her.

A cruel smile came to Mr. Durand's face. "I'm afraid you don't have much of a choice. If you refuse, I will kill Lady Elodie."

Elodie gasped softly but held her ground, standing silent beside her sister.

Melody's heart raced. She had no doubt that Mr. Durand meant what he said. Slowly, she held out her hand for the paper. Her eyes scanned the familiar code, dread sinking deeper into her bones. Giving him the solution could alter the course of the war, but refusing might cost her sister's life.

"I can't do as you ask," Melody said, forcing the words out.

Without hesitation, Mr. Durand pulled a pistol from the waistband of his trousers and aimed it directly at Elodie. "This isn't a negotiation," he said, coldly. "You will tell me how to crack the code, or your sister dies—slowly and painfully."

Melody moved to stand protectively in front of Elodie. "This is between you and me. My sister is innocent in all of this."

Mr. Durand chuckled, but the sound held no warmth. "Innocent?" he sneered. "Your code has led to the slaughter of many French soldiers. Our best minds have tried to decipher it and failed. You will tell me, or I will make sure Lady Elodie suffers."

Melody's mind raced as she tried to buy some time. Could she even bargain with this man? "If I give you what you want, you will let my sister go?"

Mr. Durand smirked, and for a moment, a flicker of something dark passed through his eyes. "Oh, I promise," he said, his voice dripping with false sincerity. "But you are not going anywhere. Napoleon has plans for you in France."

A shiver ran through Melody as she squared her shoulders. "I am not going anywhere with you, least of all to France."

Mr. Durand's smirk twisted into a mocking grin. "I'm afraid you don't have a choice."

Elodie touched Melody's arm and whispered urgently, "Don't tell him anything. He is going to kill me anyway."

"You don't know that," Melody whispered back, though in her heart, she feared Elodie might be right. Mr. Durand was not a man who seemed capable of mercy.

Mr. Durand scoffed. "I tire of this. Perhaps I should just kill Lady Elodie now and be done with it."

"No!" Melody put a hand up to stop him. "I won't tell you anything unless I have your word that Elodie will be unharmed."

Mr. Durand took a step closer, his voice low and threatening. "You are in no position to be making demands, my lady."

Melody held her ground, meeting his gaze with steely determination. "I will not let my sister die because of me. This is my fight, not hers."

Mr. Durand's amusement grew. "You truly are naïve. As a spy, your friends and family are nothing more than liabilities. Surely, your dear Lord Emberly warned you of this."

"He did, but why should they suffer for my mistakes?" Melody shot back.

His expression shifted to one of false pity. "You truly have no idea what you are involved in. Your codes have killed innocent French soldiers. And now, you will face the consequences."

Melody stared down the barrel of his pistol, knowing full well she would rather die than betray her country. But the thought of Elodie being killed because of her made her stomach churn. She couldn't let that happen—not to her sister. But how could she protect both Elodie and the lives of thousands depending on that code?

"Time is up, my lady," Mr. Durand growled. "What did you decide?"

Elodie spoke up. "Melody isn't going to tell you anything," she declared, her voice unwavering. "I won't allow it."

A sneer came to Mr. Durand's lips. "You won't allow it?" he repeated, cocking his pistol. "I do believe I am going to enjoy killing you."

Melody's heart pounded in her chest as the moment stretched out, the air thick with dread. She tried to think of something—anything—to stop him. But just as Mr. Durand's finger hovered over the trigger, a sharp knock echoed through the small cottage, shattering the tense silence.

Mr. Durand's head snapped towards the door, his sneer faltering. "Stay here," he hissed, lowering the pistol slightly as he moved towards the door. He threw a warning glance over his shoulder at them. "We shall see who else came to die today."

Wesley raised his hand and slammed his fist against the weathered cottage door. This plan was reckless, but time was running out, and it was his only chance. Melody's and Elodie's lives depended on it.

The door swung open, revealing a blond man with a hardened face, a pistol aimed directly at Wesley's chest. "What do you want?" the man barked, his voice rough with suspicion.

Wesley inclined his head slightly. "You must be the footman that we have been searching for."

The man's eyes narrowed as he went to shut the door. "Go away."

Putting his hand out, Wesley held the door open. "I have come to barter."

The man snorted, a derisive laugh escaping him. "Barter? You have come to die, then." He cocked the pistol. "Why should I not shoot you right where you stand?"

Wesley didn't flinch, his eyes locked on the man's. "Because, as I said, I am here to barter."

A voice came from inside of the cottage. "Who is it, Pierre?"

A Shadowed Charade

The man—Pierre, apparently—didn't lower the pistol as he called back. "Lord Emberly."

Another figure emerged from the shadows, stepping beside Pierre. Wesley immediately recognized the sharp, calculating features of Mr. Durand. "Shoot Lord Emberly and be done with it," he ordered.

Wesley shook his head. "I promise you will want to hear what I have to say."

Pierre hesitated, his gaze flickering to Mr. Durand. "What do you think, Marceau?"

"Let him in," Mr. Durand—no, Marceau, as Wesley had learned—ordered coldly.

Taking a step back, Pierre opened the door wide but kept the pistol trained at Wesley. "Come in, my lord," he sneered, his voice thick with contempt.

The room Wesley entered was stark and empty, save for the thick tension that clung in the air. Marceau moved to the center, his posture exuding authority. "What do you want?" he demanded.

"I have come to barter for Lady Melody and her sister," Wesley replied.

Marceau's lip curled. "Save your breath. Lady Melody is coming to France with me, whether you like it or not."

Wesley clenched his jaw but kept his voice calm. "That is not something I can allow."

"You have little choice in the matter, considering you are a dead man." Marceau removed the pistol from the waistband of his trousers and aimed it at him. "You have saved me the trouble of hunting you down."

"Hear me out first," Wesley said.

Marceau let out a dismissive huff. "You have one minute. Not that it will change anything."

Wesley leaned forward slightly, his voice low but clear. "If you release Lady Melody and Lady Elodie, I will pay you a hundred thousand pounds."

Pierre's mouth fell open in shock. "That is… a fortune."

"It is," Wesley agreed, his eyes never leaving Marceau. "In exchange, you will walk away and leave us in peace."

"That will not happen," Marceau said. "Napoleon has plans for Lady Melody."

Pierre's eyes lit up with greed. "Think of what we can do with that money. We would be rich."

"You are forgetting our mission," Marceau said firmly. "We are loyal to Napoleon."

Lowering his pistol, Pierre's tone turned defiant. "I am tired of scraping by. I want to be rich, and now we have the opportunity to be so."

Marceau's face twisted with anger. "You are a fool if you think Lord Emberly will keep his word. The moment we lower our weapons, he will kill us."

Wesley kept his voice steady. "I am a man of my word. All I want is to ensure Lady Melody's and Lady Elodie's safety."

Pierre glanced back at Marceau, uncertainty in his eyes. "We could disappear. No one would control us."

Marceau's hand tightened around his pistol. "You are being insubordinate. You are forgetting who you are."

"How can you not be tempted by this? We could escape this life, free and rich," Pierre said, his jaw set stubbornly.

"I am loyal to France. Loyal to Napoleon. That is more important than money," Marceau replied.

Pierre's lips pressed into a thin line. "You are a bigger fool than I thought."

Turning towards Pierre, Marceau pointed his pistol at him, his eyes cold and calculating. "If you take that money, you are a traitor and will be hunted down and killed."

Pierre matched him, raising his pistol as well. "No one would know if you died here tonight."

Marceau's gaze shifted briefly to Wesley, suspicion etched across his features. "This is what he wanted all along. To turn us against each other."

"When can I get the money?" Pierre asked, ignoring Marceau's warnings.

Wesley allowed himself a small smile. "As soon as my man of business arranges it. It might be a few days, but I give you my word."

Marceau spat. "His word? He is a spy, a liar. How can you trust him?"

Pierre looked uncertain. "And you won't turn me in for my crimes?"

"As I have said," Wesley responded, "I have come to barter. I have no interest in your past."

Marceau's expression was one of steely resolve. "Think of your family. They will be branded as traitors, too."

Pierre's face hardened with determination. "Then I will take them with me. We will live like kings."

"You are a fool, Pierre," Marceau shouted, his voice rising with disbelief. "You would betray your country, betray Napoleon, for money?"

Pierre didn't hesitate. "I would."

Marceau pointed his pistol at Wesley. "The plan was always to kill Lord Emberly. We were to leave no witnesses."

"The plan can change," Pierre responded.

"And what will you tell Coralie?" Marceau snapped. "Do you think she will look kindly upon you betraying your country?"

"Leave Coralie out of this," Pierre snapped.

Marceau took a step towards Wesley. "You would never get the money, Pierre. He is lying to you."

With a shake of his head, Wesley replied, "I am not lying."

"All Englishmen are liars!" Marceau exclaimed.

Wesley huffed a bitter laugh. "And all Frenchmen are murderers, I suppose. You have killed people I loved."

Marceau gave a careless shrug as though it meant nothing. "I do what I must to survive."

Despite having a pistol pointed at him, Wesley took a step

closer to Marceau, his voice sharp with purpose. "Do you remember Dinah?"

"No," Marceau replied.

"She was one of your victims," Wesley continued, his anger simmering beneath the surface. "You murdered her by dropping oleander in her fire."

A smirk crept across Marceau's face. "You will have to be more specific. I have killed many people with that method."

Wesley's fury boiled over, his voice thick with emotion. "Dinah was special. She never wronged you, yet you killed her."

Marceau's smirk grew, his indifference palpable. "Her death brought me no joy, I assure you. It was just another assignment."

Wesley clenched his fists, fighting his composure. "I have loved two women in my life. One you took from me, and the other I kept at arm's length while trying to protect her. But I would rather die than lose Melody."

"I will gladly oblige you, my lord," Marceau declared.

Before Marceau could act, Wesley spoke again, his voice calm despite the storm inside him. "One last question before you kill me—did you murder my father, the late Lord Emberly?"

Amusement flickered in Marceau's eyes. "Ah, yes, I almost felt bad about him. A miniature portrait of a woman was on the table next to his bed. He loved her deeply; that much was clear."

Wesley's voice dropped, barely a whisper. "That was my mother."

"Well, we both know how that ended," Marceau mocked.

Wesley turned his gaze to Pierre, his voice low but commanding. "This is your last chance, Pierre. Side with me, and you will be a rich man."

Pierre's brow furrowed in doubt. "Marceau is right. You

would never give me the money." He straightened. "I side with Marceau."

Wesley let out a sigh. "That is a shame because you have already lost."

Marceau threw his head back and laughed, the sound harsh and triumphant. "No, Lord Emberly, it is *you* who have lost."

Wesley's eyes shifted to the staircase just as Melody appeared, her delicate hand clutching a pistol aimed directly at Marceau. Her once pristine gown was rumpled, her hair had come loose from her chignon, and her face was smudged with dirt. Yet, despite her disheveled state, she had never looked more beautiful to him.

Taking advantage of the distraction, Wesley swiftly pulled the pistol from behind his back and aimed it at Marceau. "As I said, you have lost."

Marceau grinned, undeterred. "And what exactly is Lady Melody going to do with that pistol? Intimidate me?"

Wesley's expression didn't waver. "Oh, did I forget to mention? Lady Melody has a marksman's aim." He paused. "But she is not the only one."

A moment later, Rosella emerged silently from the second level, positioning herself beside Melody, a pistol drawn and ready.

Wesley met Marceau's gaze. "My job was to distract you long enough for my associates to rescue Lady Melody and Lady Elodie."

Rosella interjected, "Actually, Lady Melody insisted on speaking to Marceau. And she made her wishes very clear."

Lady Melody's eyes narrowed slightly. "I wanted to personally thank you, Marceau, for how you treated my sister and me."

Marceau's smirk faded as he lowered his pistol. "What is your plan, exactly? Shoot us? That won't solve anything. There will be many others who will come for Lady Melody."

"I will protect her, no matter what," Wesley declared.

"You are a fool if you think that," Marceau snapped. "As long as she is alive, she will have a target on her back."

Lady Melody tilted her chin. "Let them come. I will be ready."

Marceau's gaze grew thunderous, his hand tightening around his pistol. He raised it suddenly, violently, aiming directly at Melody. "Or I could kill you right now."

Without hesitation, Wesley hurled himself at Marceau. A gunshot rang out, the sound deafening in the enclosed space. Pain laced through Wesley's arm as he slammed into Marceau, knocking him to the ground. Ignoring the burning sensation in his left arm, Wesley drew back his fist and delivered a powerful blow to Marceau's face, knocking him unconscious in one brutal strike.

Breathing heavily, Wesley stood and turned to Pierre, who was being subdued and led away by Rosella. "You made the wrong choice," he informed the spy.

Pierre groaned. "I always do," he muttered.

Melody hurried over to Wesley, her eyes filled with concern. "I'm sorry I shot you," she said, pointing at the blood seeping from his left arm.

Wesley glanced down. "It is nothing," he said, offering her a weak smile. "I have had much worse."

"You should have a doctor look at it," Melody suggested.

"Doctors are useless," Wesley replied dismissively. "Watkins will stitch me up just fine."

She came closer, stopping right in front of him. Her voice softened, her eyes holding his transfixed. "Thank you for coming to save me."

Wesley's smile grew. "I made you a promise, did I not?"

"You did," Melody whispered, biting her lower lip as she looked up at him.

The door swung open and Elodie ran into the room. "Is it over?" Her gaze darted to Marceau's limp form. "Is he dead?"

"No," Wesley replied, shaking his head. "Just unconscious."

A mischievous glint appeared in Elodie's eyes as she marched over to Marceau's body and delivered a swift kick to his side. "That is for taking Melody and me hostage."

Wesley chuckled. "You two should go home at once. I have no doubt that your parents are worried sick."

In a low voice, Elodie leaned in and said, "Just so you know, my lord, now that I learned you are a spy, I like you even more."

Melody laughed. "Let's go home, Elodie."

With a final glance at Wesley, the two sisters turned and made their way towards the door. He watched them go, his heart swelling with relief and something deeper—something he finally was ready to put into words.

Love.

He loved Melody. And now he needed to do something about that.

Chapter Twenty

Melody sat in the coach as it rumbled along the short road to Brockhall Manor, her thoughts swirling as the landscape passed by. The silence in the carriage was comforting since no one seemed to be in a talkative mood, which suited her just fine. Her mind was on Wesley, who had risked everything to rescue her. How could she not love him? He had come for her, just as he had promised he would.

Next to her, Elodie broke the quiet, her voice filled with dry humor. "Well, that was eventful," she muttered. "I have never had to climb out of a window before."

"You did remarkably well," Rosella praised from across the coach.

With a thoughtful look, Elodie said, "I think I could be a spy."

Rosella laughed. "You would make an awful spy."

Elodie's brow furrowed. "Why do you say that?"

"You lack seriousness, for one. Furthermore, a spy needs to blend into their surroundings, not stand out," Rosella explained.

"I shall take that as a compliment," Elodie stated.

Rosella leaned forward and smiled. "You should. You are delightful, but espionage is best left to others."

Elodie glanced at Melody. "Like my sister." She paused. "And you."

Settling back in her seat, Rosella responded, "I may dabble in espionage, yes."

Melody kept her silence, careful not to reveal that Rosella had, in fact, along with her brother, recruited her into the world of spying. It wasn't her secret to tell.

The coach came to a stop in front of Brockhall Manor. Elodie exited first, but as Melody prepared to follow, Rosella placed a gentle hand on her sleeve, halting her.

"You care about my brother, don't you?" Rosella asked quietly, her tone serious.

"I do," Melody admitted, seeing no reason to deny it.

Rosella's gaze was steady, searching. "Do you love him?"

Melody hesitated. How could she answer that? Did she dare reveal the truth? The answer was simple—she loved Wesley deeply, with all her heart. But the words refused to come.

With a knowing look, Rosella said, "You don't have to say anything."

After a long pause, Melody decided to confide in her. "It doesn't matter how I feel. Wesley is still in love with Dinah."

Rosella shook her head gently. "He did love Dinah, yes. But I believe his heart has found someone new to claim it."

Melody was appreciative of what Rosella was attempting to do, but she felt she owed her the truth. "I know Wesley cares for me, but I deserve someone who loves without restraint."

"You do deserve that," Rosella agreed, releasing her grip and leaning back. "Now that you are safely home, I am returning to help my brother secure the prisoners."

"I wish you luck, then," Melody said before stepping out of the coach.

Elodie was waiting for her outside, her expression bright. "I am rooting for Lord Emberly," she whispered.

"You only say that because he is a spy," Melody teased, linking arms with her sister.

Elodie placed a hand to her chest, feigning sincerity. "I daresay I liked him before. He is dark. Mysterious. And he can do the impossible and tell us apart."

Melody laughed as they began walking towards the manor. "Lord Emberly is a good man, but now that his assignment is over, he will return home."

"And is that what you want?" Elodie asked, her voice more serious.

Melody's smile faltered. "No, but it is what will happen."

Elodie held up the rusty, bent nail she had found in the cottage. "I could force him to stay."

"With a nail?"

Her sister waved the nail playfully through the air. "I can be very persuasive."

"Thank you, but this is not your fight."

Elodie stopped and turned to face her, her expression firm. "Your fight is *my* fight. We are sisters, and we look out for one another."

Before Melody could respond, the door to the manor swung open, and their parents rushed towards them, relief flooding their faces. Both girls were immediately wrapped in their parents' warm embrace.

Their mother pulled back, eyes filled with emotion. "I am so relieved that you both are home. Unharmed."

Their father nodded in agreement. "We have been terribly worried."

"How did you escape?" their mother asked.

Elodie glanced at Melody, silently deferring to her for the answer. Melody understood that whatever she said, Elodie would support her.

"Lord Emberly discovered where we were being held and

secured our release," Melody said carefully, hoping the explanation would satisfy them without too many details.

Their mother's eyes narrowed slightly in curiosity, but thankfully, she didn't press for more information. "We will have to thank Lord Emberly for his efforts," she said, glancing behind them. "Where is he?"

"He shall be along shortly," Melody assured her.

"Come now," their mother said, leading them inside. "You need a bath and a long rest. You must be exhausted."

Elodie tipped her head. "It has been a long few days. I think I will just hurkle-durkle today."

As they entered the manor, their mother leaned closer to Melody and whispered, "Do you plan on telling me the full truth someday?"

"Perhaps, but not today," Melody replied.

Her mother's gaze softened with understanding. "I hope that one day, you will trust me with the truth."

White approached them and said, "The baths are being prepared for Lady Melody and Lady Elodie."

"Thank you, White," Melody acknowledged with a grateful nod.

Their mother paused in the entry hall, her eyes scanning Melody and Elodie with a discerning gaze. "These gowns will have to be thrown out," she declared, noting the dirt and grime that clung to every inch of their attire.

The main door opened, and Sarah rushed into the entry hall. "Melody! Elodie! You are back!" she exclaimed, hurrying over.

Melody embraced Sarah tightly before pulling back. "Jasper is all right, just so you know."

Sarah let out a visible sigh of relief. "Thank you for telling me," she said before throwing her arms around Elodie.

In a low voice, Elodie shared, "Jasper taught me how to climb out a window."

Sarah's eyes sparkled with amusement. "A useful skill for any genteel woman to have."

Elodie giggled. "Much safer than lessons from a dancing master, I daresay."

Their mother interjected, "We received word from the constable that the real Mr. Durand was murdered and that an imposter was in our home."

"It is true," Melody confirmed.

Their father stepped forward, wrapping an arm around his wife's waist. "But we must set that aside for now. Most importantly, our daughters are home, safe and sound."

Their mother leaned into him, her eyes glistening. "It is wonderful, is it not?"

White cleared his throat from the doorway. "The baths are ready, my lady."

"You both should go clean up," their mother encouraged. "You must be eager to wash away all the dirt from your ordeal."

Melody didn't need to be told twice. She couldn't wait to rid herself of the dirt and grime that clung to her. She began walking towards the stairs, and Elodie quickly fell into step beside her.

Elodie glanced around to ensure no one was listening before whispering, "Is it just me, or does Aunt Sarah love Jasper?"

"It is not just you," Melody said. "I have suspected it for quite some time."

"So," Elodie said, grinning, "what is the plan?"

"The plan?" Melody asked.

Elodie gave her an amused look. "You are a spy. I assume you always have a plan, especially in matters like this."

Melody glanced over her shoulder at Sarah, who was chatting with her parents. "We can't let Jasper leave without them confessing their feelings to one another."

Holding up the nail, Elodie said, "I could persuade Jasper to stay."

Melody laughed. "Will you stop trying to threaten people with that rusty nail?"

"It can be rather convincing," Elodie replied. "I might use it to stop Bennett and Winston from stealing food off my plate."

"I would stick to knives," Melody quipped.

They reached Elodie's door, where her sister paused. "Love is a risk. Opening yourself up to another person and being vulnerable… it is terrifying. But it is worth it."

Melody lifted her brow. "I thought you didn't believe in love. That it is elusive."

Elodie grew quiet. "I will admit that my thoughts are changing on that notion."

"Regardless, I hope Aunt Sarah recognizes that love is a risk worth taking."

"Do you believe that?" Elodie asked pointedly.

"Elodie…" Melody began, unsure where this was going.

Elodie put her hand up, stilling her words. "I saw the way Lord Emberly was looking at you when you walked out of the cottage. He loves you."

Melody placed a hand on her sister's sleeve. "Wesley is the best of men, but his duty is to protect me. Nothing more."

"It may have started that way, but I think it is more than that now," Elodie attempted. "You can't let him leave without telling him how you feel."

"And how do I feel?" Melody asked, afraid of what her sister might see in her.

Elodie's face softened into a smile. "You love him. With your whole heart. I can see it in your eyes. They light up whenever you mention him."

Melody was speechless. Had she been so obvious?

Elodie opened the door to her room and stepped inside. "Just think about what I said while I hurkle-durkle today."

"You just like saying that word," Melody quipped.

"It is true. The Scottish have the best expressions," Elodie admitted before closing the door behind her.

Melody walked down the corridor to her bedchamber. She opened the door and entered, finding her lady's maid waiting by the bath. At the sight of Melody, Lydia gasped.

"My lady, you look awful," she exclaimed.

Melody's lips twitched. "Thank you for being honest with me."

Lydia rushed over to her. "How did you escape?"

"Lord Emberly bartered for us," Melody explained as she began to peel off her soiled clothing.

"It is a good thing for Lord Emberly, then," Lydia declared. "I should have never let you go into the gardens last night."

"You must not blame yourself. I do not regret what I did because I was able to ensure Elodie's safe return."

Lydia frowned as she gathered Melody's discarded clothes. "Surely, there could have been a safer way."

"It was the only way," Melody replied, though she could see Lydia remained unconvinced.

"Well," Lydia sighed, "we should get you into the bath."

Once Melody had slipped into the warm water, she closed her eyes and felt herself relax. These quiet moments were rare, and she was grateful for the reprieve.

"I am most grateful that you are home, my lady," Lydia said.

"As am I," Melody murmured.

Melody let herself sink deeper into the water when she was finally alone. She was safe, back home where she belonged. Yet, her heart yearned for something more. It was Wesley. She wanted to be in his arms, to confess how she truly felt. But did she have the courage to do so?

What if he didn't feel the same?

The thought gnawed at her. Being a spy seemed easy compared to following one's own heart.

Wesley had just secured Marceau in the back of the wagon when his coach pulled up behind him. The creak of the door opening caught his attention, and he turned to see his sister stepping out and walking towards him.

"I came to see if you needed any assistance with the prisoners," Rosella said.

"We have it under control," Wesley informed her, facing her fully. "Jasper contacted the constable, and they are waiting for the prisoners in the village. Watkins will escort Marceau and Pierre to Newgate to ensure they are dealt with properly."

Rosella nodded in approval as the wagon started driving away. "That is good to hear. But now that it is settled, you really should have a doctor look at your wound."

Wesley winced as he glanced down at his left arm. "No need. Watkins stitched me up before you arrived."

"Watkins is not a doctor."

"No, but doctors ask too many questions. Questions I would rather not answer," Wesley replied.

"Fair enough," she conceded. "However, if you die from an infection, I will be sure to have 'I told you so' carved into your gravestone."

Wesley chuckled. "Duly noted."

Her playful expression faded, replaced by a more serious one. "You should go to her."

His smile dimmed. "I want to, but I don't even know where to begin."

"Start at the beginning," Rosella advised gently.

Running a hand through his hair, Wesley sighed deeply. "I have made a muck of things."

"I know, but fixing it is not too late."

Wesley appreciated what his sister was attempting to do, but he needed to do it on his own. In his own way. "Rosella, I am grateful for your concern, but—"

Rosella stepped closer, cutting him off. "I know you do not think I speak from experience, but I do. I was in love once."

"With whom?"

She looked off in the distance, her voice quiet. "Alexander. He was an officer in the Royal Navy. I fell for him the moment I saw him. We exchanged letters for months, and eventually, he asked me to marry him."

Wesley's brow shot up. "You were engaged?"

Rosella gave him a sad smile. "Before I could respond to his letter, I received word that his ship had gone down. He was dead. I was devastated, and I told no one. I thought sharing my grief would make it worse somehow. But I was wrong."

He gently touched her shoulder, his heart heavy with empathy. "I had no idea. I am sorry that I was not there for you."

"I am not telling you this so that you will feel bad for me," Rosella said. "I am telling you because I know what it is like to love fiercely, uncontrollably. And I lost him before I ever had the chance to say it out loud."

Rosella continued. "I know you loved Dinah, but perhaps this is your second chance."

Wesley hesitated for a moment before finally admitting what he had been hiding, even from himself. "I love Melody."

Rosella's smile returned. "Good. Now, go tell her that."

He lowered his hand, uncertainty gnawing at him. "If I tell her, it will change everything between us. Can I afford to do such a thing?"

"Can you afford *not* to do such a thing?" she countered.

Wesley's throat tightened. "And if she doesn't feel the same?"

Rosella's eyes filled with understanding. "To love, you must expose your heart. For you can't truly love without the risk of being wounded."

Wesley had never been so conflicted by anything before. He wanted to run to Melody, to confess his undying love for her, but something was holding him back. The thought of confessing his love terrified him more than any battle or mission ever had. Melody had the power to break him with just a word.

Rosella must have understood his reluctance because she met his gaze. "I can't promise you that it will all work out, but I can tell you that you don't want to live with regrets."

"I already have too many to count," he admitted.

"Then you don't want to make the biggest mistake of your life by not fighting for Melody," Rosella urged.

Wesley hated that his sister was right. He had convinced himself that his feelings for Melody were bound to duty and obligation, but deep down, he knew it was more. He loved every moment he spent with her. She was the person who made his life better just by being in it.

At that moment, he knew that he would do whatever it took to make Melody his. He would even grovel. And he had never groveled before.

Without another word, he strode towards the waiting coach and opened the door. "Shall we?" he asked, his voice filled with newfound determination.

Rosella stepped into the coach. "I take it that this means you are going after Melody?"

Wesley climbed in after her, his heart already racing with the thought of seeing Melody again. "Yes," he said firmly. "I am going after her. Only this time, I am not holding back."

"It is about time," Rosella retorted.

They both retreated to their thoughts as they made their way towards Brockhall Manor. Once they arrived, Wesley exited first, offering his hand to help his sister out. Together, they made their way to the main door.

The door opened and the butler greeted them with a respectful nod. "Lord Emberly. Lady Rosella."

"Please inform Lady Melody that I wish to speak with her in the library," Wesley ordered.

"Of course, my lord," White replied before he walked off to do his bidding.

Rosella turned to Wesley, a knowing smile on her lips. "Good luck, Brother. You will need it."

Wesley offered her a tight smile before making his way to the library on the second level. He started pacing back and forth, the ticking of the long clock in the corner marking his misery. Each tick seemed to stretch into eternity, and his mind raced with thoughts on what he would say. What felt like hours, but was likely only mere moments, passed before the door quietly creaked open.

Melody stepped into the room, her presence like a balm to his restless soul. She wore a pale blue gown and her hair was elegantly piled atop her head. But it was her smile that held him captive. In that smile, he saw something more beautiful than he could ever put into words. It was as if his future were stretched out in front of him—a future with Melody.

She stopped a short distance away, her expression expectant. "White said you wished to speak to me."

"I did… I do," Wesley stammered, his voice betraying the jumble of emotions inside him. Why was it so hard to express his feelings?

In a soft voice, Melody broke the silence. "Thank you for rescuing me," she said. "And I am sorry again for… well, for shooting you."

Wesley instinctively touched his left arm, wincing at the lingering pain. "It hardly hurts," he lied. "But you should never have gone into the gardens alone. That was reckless. Careless. You should have come to me first."

"There was no time," Melody argued.

He dropped his hand, his frustration rising at the thought

he had almost lost her. "Next time, think before you act. You cannot put yourself at risk like that." His tone was much harsher than he had intended.

Melody's brow arched as she crossed her arms. "Was your intention to lecture me?"

"No," Wesley said quickly.

"Then what do you want?"

He ran a hand through his hair, struggling to find the right words. "I want… I want *you!*" he blurted out.

Melody's eyes widened. "Pardon?"

Wesley let out a deep sigh, realizing how clumsy he sounded. "I am not saying this right. I do not know why it is so hard to speak to you about this."

She took a small step closer. "What are you trying to say, Wesley?"

He swallowed, his resolve growing stronger. "All I know is that my life has been better since the day I met you."

Melody opened her mouth to respond, but he cut her off before she could speak. "I love you, Melody. I tried to convince myself that it was just my duty to protect you, but I know better now." His hand went to his chest, over his heart. "It is because I love you."

Melody's eyes remained guarded. "But you loved Dinah. You told me as much—"

"I did," Wesley admitted. "A part of me always will. But from the moment I danced with you, you started to take up space in my heart. And now, there is no room for anyone else."

"Wesley, I don't know—"

He moved to stand in front of her, speaking over her. "Our journey has not been perfect, but it is ours. And I will stick with you until the end. I don't care how complicated this gets because I will always choose you, even on the days we don't understand each other. You are the only person I want to love in the end."

Melody's lips curved into a smile. "May I speak now?"

"Of course," Wesley replied, his heart pounding in anticipation.

"What I have been trying to say, but you keep interrupting me," Melody said, her voice warm and teasing, "is that I love you, too."

Wesley stared at her in disbelief. "You do?"

Melody laughed lightly, shaking her head. "I do not know why you sound so surprised. You are my hero, after all."

"I don't want to be your hero. I want to be your husband," Wesley said.

Her eyes twinkled with amusement. "Was that a proposal?"

Without hesitation, Wesley dropped to one knee, reaching for her hand. "Lady Melody Lockwood, would you do me the grand honor of becoming my wife?"

Melody's smile grew as she looked down at him. "In all my life, I never thought I would see you on a bended knee."

He chuckled. "A man would do practically anything for the woman he loves."

"Yes, I will marry you," Melody said, her voice brimming with joy.

Rising to his feet, Wesley cupped her cheek gently, his thumb brushing over her soft skin. "From here on out, we will be partners in every way."

"I like the sound of that," she murmured, leaning into his hand.

Wesley's gaze dropped to her lips as he leaned closer. "Now, I would very much like to kiss you. May I?"

"Yes," Melody breathed, and before the word had fully left her lips, Wesley pressed his mouth to hers, sealing their love with a tender, passionate kiss. This was not like any other kiss that he had ever experienced. It was the type of kiss he had spent his whole life waiting for. At that moment, he knew without a doubt that he had found the person who completed him, the woman who made him whole.

But their moment was abruptly shattered by a booming voice from the doorway. "Release my sister, Lord Emberly!"

Melody broke the kiss and turned towards the doorway. "Bennett, you are home!" she exclaimed.

Her brother, Lord Dunsby, had a thunderous look on his expression. "What in the blazes is going on here?" he demanded, his gaze flickering between them.

Wesley stepped back, dropping his arms to his sides. "Melody has agreed to marry me."

Lord Dunsby's eyes narrowed, and he turned his full attention to Melody. "Is this true?"

Melody bobbed her head. "It is. He asked, and I accepted."

Lord Dunsby did not look pleased by the news. "First, I hear that you and Elodie were abducted, and now I find the two of you engaged. How, pray tell, did this happen?"

"I suppose it all started when we danced," Wesley replied.

Lord Dunsby shot Wesley a skeptical glance. "I want you to post the banns at once, and I expect you two to behave while you wait to be married."

A mischievous glint sparkled in Melody's eyes. "Oh, we will behave as well as you did when you were betrothed."

"Absolutely not!" Lord Dunsby said as he shook his head vehemently.

Lady Dallington swept into the room. "What is all the commotion in here?" she asked, her eyes darting between her children.

Lord Dunsby gestured towards them. "Wesley and Melody are engaged."

Lady Dallington's face lit up with delight. "Oh, what wonderful news!" she gushed. "It is most fortunate that I have already begun the preparations for the wedding."

"You have?" Melody asked.

With a laugh, Lady Dallington waved her hand. "Yes, it was rather obvious you two would end up together. Why do you think I invited Lord Emberly to join our other guests?" She smiled. "Come along, Dear. We have much to do."

Melody followed her mother towards the door but paused to glance back at Wesley. "I love you," she said.

"I love you, too," he replied with a wink.

Once he was left alone with Lord Dunsby, his friend studied him for a long moment, his expression solemn. "I expect you to be true to my sister."

Wesley held his gaze. "You need not worry. My intentions are entirely honorable."

A small, almost imperceptible smile tugged at the corners of Lord Dunsby's lips. "I never thought you, of all people, would fall into the parson's mousetrap."

"It was the easiest decision I have ever made," Wesley admitted.

Lord Dunsby's smile grew slightly. "Then welcome to the family. You'd better make sure you live up to that promise."

"I will," Wesley replied, his heart light with the knowledge that his future was now intertwined with Melody's—a future he couldn't wait to begin.

Chapter Twenty-One

Melody was deliriously happy as she descended the grand staircase of Brockhall Manor. Every step felt lighter, almost as if she were floating. The reality of her engagement to Wesley still seemed too wonderful to be true. She could hardly believe she would be marrying the man she couldn't imagine living without. He was everything she had ever dreamed of and more.

As she reached the bottom of the stairs, there he was—the object of her affection—waiting for her. Wesley stood dressed in a finely tailored blue jacket and buff trousers, looking devilishly handsome.

Wesley stepped forward as she reached the marble floor, a smile tugging at his lips. "Good evening, Melody."

"Good evening," she replied, her voice soft, though the joy she felt bubbled beneath the surface.

Without hesitation, Wesley reached for her hand and raised it to his lips, gently kissing her knuckles. The simple gesture sent a rush of warmth through her, and she felt her cheeks flush. The memory of their earlier kiss, so full of promise, flickered in her mind. It was a kiss she wouldn't mind repeating—a thousand times over.

In a low voice, Wesley said, "I managed to convince Jasper to join us for dinner this evening. He wasn't exactly keen on the idea."

"I had the same reaction from Aunt Sarah," Melody shared.

As they talked, Melody was aware that Wesley still held her hand. She didn't mind in the least. She rather liked being engaged to him. The mere thought of being near him, of spending her life with him, filled her with a sense of peace she had never known. She couldn't imagine ever tiring of his presence.

From behind them came a booming voice filled with exasperation. "Good gads, please say that we were not this obnoxious."

Melody turned to see Bennett entering the hall with his wife, Delphine, on his arm. Delphine glanced at her husband, her lips curving into a knowing smile. "Oh, we were worse," she revealed.

Melody grinned as she greeted them. "Welcome home, Delphine."

Delphine's eyes roamed the entry hall. "I suppose that Brockhall Manor will do as a home," she quipped.

At that moment, Elodie stepped into the room. "I would be careful with your food, especially your bread. Bennett has a habit of stealing off other people's plates."

"I do not mind," Delphine replied with a loving glance at her husband.

"You will when you have spent loads of time creating the perfect ratio of bread and butter," Elodie said.

Bennett chuckled. "Only you, dear sister, would spend so much time on something as trivial as buttering bread."

Elodie shrugged. "It is a skill."

"A useless one," Bennett retorted.

"Says the man that steals my perfectly buttered bread," Elodie countered.

A Shadowed Charade

A knock came at the main door and White crossed the entry hall to open it, revealing Jasper standing awkwardly on the threshold. Despite his discomfort in formal attire, he looked the height of fashion.

"Good evening," Jasper muttered, stepping inside, his eyes darting around the room as if searching for an escape.

Melody approached Jasper and offered him a private smile. "I never properly thanked you for what you did for Elodie and me. We owe you so much."

Jasper returned her smile. "I am just glad that you both are safe."

Elodie came to stand next to Melody and lowered her voice. "Are you a spy, too?"

Jasper exchanged a look with Melody before replying, "I am not. I am just a Bow Street Runner."

"Pity," Elodie muttered.

Melody shook her head. "You can't just ask everyone if they are a spy."

"Perhaps not, but one might conclude that Jasper would make a good spy," Elodie said.

Just then, their mother entered the room, accompanied by Aunt Sarah. "White just informed me that dinner is ready to be served," she announced. "Shall we all adjourn to the dining room?"

Wesley stepped forward and offered his arm to Melody. "May I escort you to the dining room?"

Melody accepted his arm. "Thank you, kind sir."

"Kind sir?" he repeated with a grin. "I do remember a time when you were not as complimentary of me."

She laughed. "Times have changed. I find you to be quite tolerable."

"Only tolerable?" he teased.

Before she could reply, they entered the dining room and Wesley moved to pull out her chair. He claimed the seat next to her.

Lady Dallington spoke up as the rest of the family settled around the table. "It was a shame that our other guests left when Melody went missing, but I do think it was for the best."

Elodie added, "If I had known all it would take to rid ourselves of Anthony was for me to be abducted, I would have arranged it much sooner."

Wesley met Elodie's gaze with a knowing look. "Lord Belview was far more concerned for you than you give him credit for," he said. "Had we not found you, I suspect he would have sent his men to search every door in the village."

"I doubt that," Elodie said, though her tone faltered slightly. "He was probably more relieved we couldn't finish our argument about pickles."

A soft chuckle rippled through the room, but it was clear to Melody that her sister's usual wit was masking something deeper. Perhaps a hint of uncertainty. She may brush it off as if it did not matter, but Melody knew better.

Jasper, who sat beside Sarah, cleared his throat, breaking the brief silence that followed. "Thank you for inviting me this evening."

"You are always welcome in our home, especially after what you did for my daughters," Lord Dallington said from his seat at the head of the table.

"It was the least I could do," Jasper said, brushing off the praise.

Lord Dallington wasn't finished, however. "My daughters have been rather tight-lipped about the whole ordeal, but I must say, I am most grateful to both you and Lord Emberly for your efforts," he said, raising his glass in a toast.

The footmen stepped forward and placed bowls of soup in front of them. Melody decided it was time to implement her plan.

"Jasper," she began, "what are your plans for when Winston returns from his wedding tour?"

He looked momentarily startled by the question and glanced at Sarah before replying. "I haven't decided yet."

"Well, I think you should remain here," Melody said. "Father is always looking for good men to help run the estate."

Lord Dallington nodded. "That is true. Bennett and I could use your help, especially since you have proved yourself loyal to this family."

Jasper furrowed his brow. "I know nothing of land management."

"Neither does Bennett," Elodie quipped, earning a laugh from around the table, "but that hasn't stopped him."

Bennett shook his head, grinning. "I have missed you, too, Sister."

Elodie pulled out the bent nail from the folds of her gown. "I have a new weapon," she informed her brother.

Bennett glanced at the nail with mild amusement. "It is a nail."

"Yes, but it can scratch you," Elodie declared.

Their mother sighed, waving her hand. "Elodie, put the nail away."

Elodie slipped the nail back into the folds of her gown, her gaze still fixed on Bennett with a playful challenge.

Lord Dallington cleared his throat. "In any case, Jasper, it would be an honor to work alongside you. What say you?"

Jasper opened his mouth to reply but was interrupted by Sarah. "I think it is a wonderful idea."

He looked surprised. "You do?"

"Yes, I do not want you to leave," Sarah admitted in a quiet voice. "But I understand if you need to."

They stared at each other for a long moment, the silence thick with unspoken emotions before Jasper finally spoke. "In that case, I think I will stay."

Melody clapped her hands together, her smile bright. "Wonderful!" she exclaimed. "Now that Jasper is staying, we thought a double wedding might be a brilliant idea."

Aunt Sarah stiffened slightly. "I do not think that is a good idea—"

Jasper cut her off. "I do."

Sarah turned to him, her eyes questioning. "Are you sure?"

Jasper met her gaze with a steady resolve. "Sarah, I have wanted to marry you since the day I first met you. I may not be a rich man, but I would marry you today, tomorrow, or after the banns are posted. It does not matter to me."

Sarah's eyes grew downcast. "I have never cared if you were rich or titled. I left that life behind me a long time ago."

"Then marry me," Jasper urged, his hand reaching for hers.

"It is not that easy," Sarah said, her voice barely above a whisper. "I have a son."

Jasper's grip tightened around her hand. "And I will love him as if he were my own."

Elodie interjected, "Everyone in favor of Aunt Sarah marrying Jasper, raise your hand!"

Laughter ripped through the room as all hands went up in unison. Jasper chuckled. "I do believe your family approves."

Sarah slowly lifted her gaze, her eyes meeting Jasper's. "You need to be sure," she said. "You know my past, the mistakes I have made."

Jasper's eyes crinkled at the corners, his smile warm and reassuring. "Every little detail of your life is what made you into the person you are today. And I happen to love the person you have become."

"But you would have to give up being a Bow Street Runner. How could I ask that of you? How could I take away something so integral to who you are?"

Jasper leaned closer. "You aren't asking anything of me, Sarah. Because being married to you will be my greatest adventure yet. What we build together will be worth more than any case I could ever take on."

Tears welled in Sarah's eyes. "Then, yes. I will marry you."

A collective cheer erupted from the dining hall as Jasper, beaming, leaned forward to press a soft, tender kiss to Sarah's lips.

Wesley leaned in closer to Melody. "Well done, my dear."

"It was obvious that those two belonged together. Just as we do," Melody replied, turning to face him. "They just needed a little push."

Wesley's smile deepened, his gaze never leaving hers. "And you have no objections to sharing your wedding day?"

Melody glanced at Jasper and Sarah, who were still basking in the glow of their newfound joy. They were laughing quietly, their love radiating from every glance and touch. She smiled. "Not at all. It feels right, does it not? Like everything is falling into place."

Wesley kissed her cheek, his lips lingering as if he didn't want the moment to end. "Have I told you how happy I am that you have agreed to marry me?"

"You could stand to do it more often," she teased.

He leaned back slightly. "I love you."

Melody's heart swelled with happiness. She glanced around the room, taking in the joyous scene—her family, Wesley, and the sheer joy that now filled the space. Despite everything that had happened, she realized that life had brought her exactly where she was meant to be.

And it was perfect.

Epilogue

Three weeks later…

The morning sun streamed through the windows as Wesley stood before the mirror, carefully adjusting his cravat. Today was his wedding day. A day he had been anticipating ever since he first asked for Melody's hand. She was everything to him, and soon, she would be his. And he, hers. The thought filled him with a sense of joy he hadn't known was possible.

A knock at the door pulled him from his thoughts, and the door creaked open to reveal Watkins. "Good morning, my lord."

Wesley turned to face him. "Ah, you have finally returned. I was beginning to worry you might miss my wedding."

"Good gads, no," Watkins said. "The journey took longer than expected due to the weather."

Wesley's smile faded slightly, his expression growing more serious. "Are the prisoners secure at Newgate?"

Watkins gave a curt nod. "For now, yes. They are set to be hung in a fortnight. But they didn't give up much information during their interrogation by the spymaster. Which means, for the time being, you will need to be vigilant. Lady Melody's safety remains a priority."

Wesley's jaw tightened. "That won't be an issue. I will hire more guards at my country estate. No one will come near her."

"Pierre admitted to poisoning Mr. Artemis Nelson, but he revealed he had accidentally switched the plates. It was you that was supposed to be poisoned," Watkins revealed. "Marceau had wanted you out of the way. When the poison didn't work, he tried to shoot you."

"Luckily for me, Marceau was a terrible shot."

Watkins stepped closer, making a few minor adjustments to Wesley's cravat. "There, now it is perfect. How did you manage to dress yourself without me?"

"I am not completely incompetent."

"Of course not, my lord," Watkins said with a smile. "But I feel as if I should warn you that Lord Dunsby and Lord Winston are waiting for you on the other side of the door."

Wesley glanced at the door, raising an eyebrow. "And what do they want?"

Watkins shrugged. "I don't rightly know, but it is best if you get it over with."

Wesley walked over to the door and paused. "I am glad you are here, Watkins. I hope you know that I consider you a friend above all else."

"I feel the same way, my lord."

With a tip of his head, Wesley opened the door and stepped out into the hallway, where Lord Dunsby and Lord Winston were waiting with solemn expressions.

"What is this?" Wesley asked.

Lord Dunsby gestured towards the corridor. "Walk with us, Emberly."

Wesley didn't say anything as he walked between the two brothers. Their serious demeanors made him wonder what exactly they had in mind.

Lord Winston spoke first. "We are most grateful for what you did for our sisters, but that doesn't mean we won't be watching you."

"Precisely. If you ever make a misstep with Melody, you will have both of us to answer to," Lord Dunsby said.

Wesley sighed. So that is what this was about. "You need not worry. I love Melody with all my heart."

Just then, the door to a nearby bedchamber opened, and Elodie slipped out, her eyes locking onto Wesley's. "Have you threatened him yet?" she asked with mock seriousness, holding up her bent nail. "Is it my turn now?"

Lord Winston chuckled. "Put that blasted nail away before you hurt yourself."

"I think it is rather effective to get my point across," Elodie responded.

Wesley put his hand up. "There is no need for threats, I promise. I will love Melody above all else, and most importantly, I will keep her safe."

Elodie considered him for a moment, her tone still serious. "I believe you. But if you don't do as you promise, I will ensure you are drawn and quartered."

Lord Dunsby let out a heavy sigh. "You do realize you don't have the authority to draw and quarter anyone? Only the most grievous criminals receive such punishment."

"I will petition Parliament for permission," Elodie said.

"You are just a woman," Lord Winston pointed out. "Parliament will hardly take you seriously."

Undeterred, Elodie shot him a determined look. "Then I shall make signs and protest outside their walls."

With a shake of his head, Lord Winston turned to Wesley. "I love my sister, and her happiness means everything to me. I expect you to be true to her, always."

Wesley met Winston's gaze. "You have my word," he said, his voice unwavering.

As the brothers studied Wesley, the tension in the air

eased slightly. The protectiveness they displayed was no longer something that troubled Wesley. Quite frankly, he understood it completely, for he felt the same way about Melody. He would guard her heart, her happiness, and her life, no matter the cost. Today was the beginning of their future together, and Wesley would ensure that nothing stood in their way.

Melody's voice came from down the corridor, breaking through Wesley's thoughts. "Dear heavens, am I interrupting something?"

Lord Dunsby turned to Melody with a smile on his face. "We just needed a moment to speak to Emberly. That is all."

Melody crossed her arms; her gaze held skepticism. "You mean threaten him, do you not?"

"Some harsh words may have been said," Lord Dunsby admitted with a slight shrug.

"Leave my fiancé alone," Melody insisted. "Besides, shouldn't you be threatening Jasper, as well?"

Elodie held up her rusty nail. "It has already been done."

"I can't imagine Jasper was intimidated by a bent nail," Melody said with a shake of her head. "Regardless, Mother said it is time to leave for the chapel."

Elodie moved to stand next to her. "I heard that Lord Wythburn is officiating your wedding."

Melody's face brightened. "He is, and I am so grateful. He is a man I have always deeply admired," she said as she made her way over to Wesley, standing close enough that he could feel her warmth. "Are you ready to get married?"

Wesley pulled out his pocket watch, pretending to study it seriously. "I suppose I can find the time."

She laughed, just as he had intended. "You'd better be nice to me, considering I wouldn't hesitate to shoot you again."

"Melody shot you?" Lord Winston asked, his eyebrow raised in genuine surprise.

Elodie giggled. "A lot has happened while you were on your wedding tour."

"Apparently so," Lord Winston said. "But I am back now."

"Only until you move into your dilapidated cottage on your sheep farm," Elodie said.

Lord Winston smirked. "Careful, it almost sounds like you will miss me, Sister."

Before Elodie could reply, Lady Dallington's voice came from down the hall. "Why, pray tell, are you all lollygagging in the corridor? We have two weddings today! The coaches are waiting outside, ready to take us to the chapel. Come along, now."

Wesley extended his arm to Melody. "May I have the honor of escorting you to the coach, my love?"

She accepted his arm. "Thank you."

As they walked down the corridor, Wesley took a moment to admire her, his gaze lingering on her beautiful face. "You look lovely today."

"You don't need to flatter me," Melody replied with a playful glint in her eyes. "I have already agreed to marry you, remember?"

"Am I not allowed to speak the truth?"

"Very well. What truth would you like to share with me this morning?"

Wesley came to an abrupt stop and turned to face her. His expression grew serious, and he gently took both of her hands in his. "Life has broken me in so many ways. But when I am with you, every shattered piece falls back into place. And now, we will continue on our journey, together, mended as one."

"I promise that I will always love you, Wesley. For now, I do not feel alone," Melody said.

He leaned in, resting his forehead against hers. "I love you," he whispered. "More than you could ever know."

Lord Dunsby cleared his throat from behind them. "I hate

to interrupt, but if you do not get into one of those coaches soon, I suspect Elodie will threaten you with her rusty nail."

Wesley took a step back and held his hand out. "Are you ready to become my wife?"

"Yes."

A wide smile broke across Wesley's face. "Then let us begin this new adventure together," he said, his voice filled with promise.

As they walked side by side, hand in hand, the future stretched before them, full of possibilities. And in that moment, for the first time in his life, Wesley realized that even forever would not be long enough with her by his side.

The End

Next book in the series...

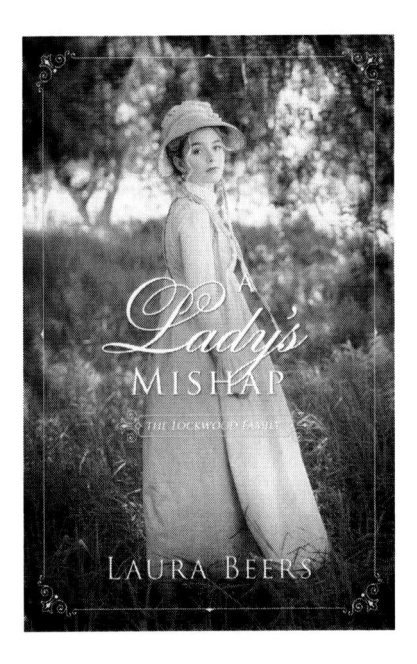

He was the last man she ever wanted to turn to. Now, he's the only one she can't live without.

Lady Elodie Lockwood is content with being a wallflower, but fate has other plans. Declared the diamond of the Season by the queen herself, she finds herself the unwilling focus of Society's relentless gaze—a situation that feels more like a curse than a blessing. When a single misstep leads to scandal, Elodie is forced to seek help from an unlikely source: Lord Belview, her childhood nemesis.

Anthony Sackville, Viscount Belview, has troubles of his own. Tasked with reining in his brother's reckless ways, he's already juggling enough when a young child is left on his doorstep, claiming to be his niece. Determined to shield the innocent girl from the chaos surrounding her father, Anthony turns to the one person he believes has the poise and grace to manage the impossible—Lady Elodie.

Together, Elodie and Anthony form a surprising attachment that runs far deeper than friendship. But before they can explore these new feelings, they must face unexpected opposition tied to their standing in Society. With Elodie under pressure from an eager suitor and Anthony burdened by family obligations, can they defy convention and carve out a path to happiness?

About the Author

Laura Beers is an award-winning author. She attended Brigham Young University, earning a Bachelor of Science degree in Construction Management. She can't sing, doesn't dance and loves naps.

Laura lives in Utah with her husband, three kids and her dysfunctional dog. When not writing regency romance, she loves skiing, hiking and drinking Dr Pepper.

You can connect with Laura on Facebook, Instagram or on her site at www.authorlaurabeers.com.

Made in United States
Cleveland, OH
03 May 2025